Crossing the Line

HEATHER GARVIN

Crossing the Line

Copyright © 2022 by Heather Garvin.

www.heathergarvinbooks.com

ISBN: 9781734908282

For information contact : Heather Garvin
heathergarvinbooks@gmail.com

Editor: See acknowledgments
Cover Design: Sam Palencia, Ink and Laurel
Publisher: Tuskan Publishing LLC

Crossing the Line

TUSKAN PUBLISHING LLC

Dedication

To my mom's friends who are kind enough to buy my books
Please don't tell her about chapter 62

1

Aiden

There are people who love their lives, and then there are people like me.

Don't get me wrong, some have it a lot worse than I do, and I get that, but I still use my job as an escape. Give me all the overtime, weekends, and holidays—I don't give a shit. The last thing I want is a fucking vacation.

Because when you have nothing to do with your paid vacation and no one to spend it with, it makes you think that it's time to reevaluate your life.

And that's the last thing I need.

I would have been happy to work through the next seven days for the extra pay, but the boss wouldn't have it.

You need a break, Aiden.

Don't work yourself so hard.

You've earned some time off.

They're all just code for, *I don't want to pay you overtime because I'm a cheap bastard.*

It is what it is. On the other hand, a break from the construction site might not be so bad. I'd rather have a week off in the peak of summer when I'm sweating my ass off, but so would everyone and their mother. I always forget how hot the summers are here—I think we all do. When you think of New York, you think freezing your ass off in January, not the blazing heat that comes mid-August, but working outside all day will help you remember.

Even my boss, Clint, knows I have no life, though. So when I told him to give me a week off in a couple of months, he asked if I'd take this random-ass week in the middle of May instead.

I said I would.

And here we are.

"You want another?" Jasmine asks, and I give her a nod. I watch as she turns around and fills another draft. "Where's Mike tonight?" she asks over her shoulder.

"Fuck if I know." I lift the glass she sets down in front of me and take a sip.

She shakes her head, but there's a trace of a smile on her lips. She's used to my bullshit. Everyone is used to everyone's bullshit around here, but that's just a product of being from a small town. Most people who are born in Beacon, die in Beacon. I'm not saying that to be morbid, but when you met your best friend in kindergarten, and the girl you're casually hook-ing up with was in your seventh grade English class *and* works at the bar you go to every weekend, you start to understand that you're stuck in a dead-end.

A guy works the bar with her tonight—a new guy. He swaps out one of the kegs as Jasmine finds her way over to me again. She leans across the bar and clasps her hands together, giving me that look that always makes me uncomfortable. I hate when she acts like she has me pegged. We hook up some-times, but she doesn't know me as well as that look warrants.

"His name is Erik." She looks back at the guy before she refocuses on me, staring up at me through those long lashes. "Jealous?" She tops off her question with a wink.

My eyes roll up to one of the TV screens. "Not even a little." I mean it. If she wants to hook up with someone else, she can. I won't waste my breath trying to convince her oth-erwise.

Jasmine's long, blonde hair falls over her shoulder as she lowers her gaze. "God forbid anyone knows you have a heart, right?"

Here she goes again, trying to see something in me that isn't there. When I don't say anything, she shakes her head and turns, leaning her back against the inside of the bar and checking out the new guy. "Relax," she says to me over her shoulder. "He'd be more interested in you than me."

Clearly, she missed the part where I don't give a shit. I

take another sip of my beer and look down at my phone without answering. Seriously, where is Mike? He usually meets me by now, and I don't like the way Jasmine wants me to react to her new, gay boyfriend.

I guess I shouldn't complain. Most nights Mike ends up latching onto a random girl at the bar, and I end up talking to Jasmine anyway. She's still studying me, so when I look up from my phone, I make a point to say, "I'm not jealous," in case she missed it the first time.

She shrugs and steps away to start drying a few glasses. The added space between us makes it easier for me to breathe, so I take another sip and look down at my phone again.

Mike: Hey, man. Can't come tonight.

Fucking Mike.

I'm about to put my phone back in my pocket when another text comes in.

Mike: Well, I can. And I did. And I probably will again. Cindy showed up.

Fucking Cindy.

They've been seeing each other on and off for about a year—more off than on—and every time she pops in for a visit, Mike magically disappears.

"Mike's with Cindy tonight," I tell Jasmine, who's still close enough to make me feel like I'm not drinking alone.

She nods and sets down the glass she's finished drying. "Does that mean I'll see you later?"

I know I'll end up at her apartment, but I hate giving her

a definite answer this early. "Probably."

She's never fazed by my lack of commitment. If anything, I'm sure she's relieved that I don't want more.

I'm not exactly upstanding boyfriend material.

"Well, you know where to find me," she says before walking over to a couple of sad sacks who have been watching her ass for the past ten minutes. I do know where to find her. Honestly, ten years could pass, and I'd still know where to find her because she'd probably still be here.

The door to the bar opens, and I pause mid-sip. It takes me a moment, but I eventually have enough sense to look back at the TV before the bar's newest occupant sees me staring at her like an idiot.

The TV does a shitty job at holding my attention, but I don't dare look back at her.

Why the hell is she here?

I'd rather not have this reunion tonight…or ever. Seeing her makes me think of who I used to be and drags up parts of my past that I'd rather leave behind.

2

Claire

It's official. I've hit rock bottom. After worrying that I'd meet someone better, *he's* been sleeping with Shelly Velasco the entire time.

If stupidity has ranks, dating long distance for over a year—when everyone said you shouldn't—just to find out you've been cheated on for the majority of that year, has to earn some type of medal.

I'm never trusting my judgment again.

Ever.

The floor has been ripped out from under me, and I'm not sure if my feet will ever hit solid ground. I'm free-falling into an endless spiral of thoughts that are too loud. Since when are thoughts *so* loud?

We had talked about getting engaged, getting a dog—a Goldendoodle we'd name Noodle—seeing the world together.

We had made plans—plans for *our* future.

Now, those plans are dead.

Of all the things I'm feeling, anger stands out. I'm assuming most people feel angry when they've been cheated on, but he's such a *hypocrite*. I could never do anything at college because he worried about who would be around me. I had to check in with him constantly, reassure him on more than one occasion, and ultimately, miss out on most of the things my classmates did. All because *he* decided to drop out at the end of freshman year and move back here to live with his dad. I don't think I've ever been this mad, and I kind of want to break something.

Or scream.

Yeah, maybe I'll just scream.

I scan the bar I now find myself in to make sure everyone looks like they can handle the yell that's about to erupt from my throat like a scorching volcano.

It's a Thursday night, but this place is dead even for those standards. A few older women sit at one end of the bar, then a couple of guys, a tall, dark and handsome bartender, and another bartender with a blonde ponytail that makes her look like she could be Rapunzel's sister. At least no one I know is—

You've got to be kidding me.

Aiden Lewis sits at the bar, and I can't scream in front of Aiden Lewis. I was hoping I wouldn't know anyone here. I was hoping the people here would all go home and tell the story of the random girl who stormed into their local establishment and screamed, but if my name gets linked to that story, I'll never hear the end of it.

On second thought, there's a chance Aiden doesn't remember me. It's not like we stayed in touch after high school, and even back then, we were never close. Well, not really. One night in high school Aiden Lewis saw me, but other than that, I might as well have been invisible. There's a good chance he didn't even know my name when I sat next to him in Biology for a year. We didn't run in the same circles or have the same friends. Let's just say, he usually spent his Friday nights at parties, while mine were spent sitting in my bedroom listening to the far-away music of those parties.

Girls noticed Aiden in high school, and by the looks of him now, I'd say they probably still notice him. His shoulders are broader than they were back then, and his dark-brown hair that used to rest at his shoulders is shorter now, a tousled mop of dark waves. But other than the added muscle mass and a half-sleeve tattoo poking out from his black t-shirt, he still looks the same.

I tentatively take a seat, making sure to leave a couple of empty barstools between us and look at the line of bottles that will help me forget that this day ever happened. Pressing my fingers to my temples, I try to get rid of the headache I already feel from the day's events. An occasional glass of wine is usually enough for me, but this day calls for something stronger.

"What'll it be, sweetheart?" The bartender asks as he

walks over to me with a warm smile.

My eyes flicker to Aiden next to me, but he hasn't looked my way. I think it's safe to say he doesn't remember me. "Gin and ginger ale with a lime, but if you're going to call me sweetheart, make it a double." I internally cringe, hating the way that sounded. On a normal day, I would never snap at someone for no reason. That's not me. But *he* calls me sweetheart—or used to—and the words slipped out before I could stop them.

I'm about to apologize to the bartender when I catch a twinge of a smile on Aiden's lips out of the corner of my eye. I don't want to look over at him and risk making eye contact, but I'm curious if he knows who I am. If he does, I can't be a total mess tonight. Word travels fast, and I'd rather not be the talk of the town.

Hunky Bartender grimaces at my remark but recovers quickly enough. "My bad. What's your name then? So I have something to call you." He shoots me a gorgeous smile that, on another day, would have probably made me melt, but tonight, it makes me want to roll my eyes.

"Sophie," I lie.

As soon as the fake name leaves my lips, Aiden's head snaps in my direction, his blue eyes piercing into me.

Well, great.

He definitely remembers me.

3

Aiden

What the hell is Claire Ackerman doing here, and why did she say her name was Sophie? I know I'm staring at her, but I can't help it. Last I checked, Claire was onto bigger and better things—not the type of things that would land her in this shithole on a Thursday night.

She looks over at me with an embarrassed smile, and now that she's facing me, her flushed cheeks and red nose make me think she's been crying. Let's just hope she's over whatever had her upset before. I can't stand it when girls cry. It's messy and loud, and it makes me feel weird.

And seeing her like this reminds me of that night.

I force that thought out of my mind as soon as it enters. I'm not who I was in high school. Hell, she probably doesn't even remember our brief encounter back then. Lord knows I've tried to forget it.

I haven't seen Claire since we graduated—not that we were friends. I don't think she would have liked my friends back then. She was too smart to talk to us. Mike had a crush on her at one point but ended up abandoning his efforts because he didn't think she'd put out.

I sneak a glance at Jasmine to see if she's noticed our newest visitor, but she's still pretending one of the guys at the end of the bar might be lucky enough to take her home tonight.

I doubt Jasmine would remember Claire anyway. The girls who hung out with us back then weren't the type to notice Claire, but I think every guy in that school noticed her—even if they never did anything about it because they knew better.

I look back over at the girl in a sundress. "Sophie, huh?"

She tenses, clearly surprised that I'm speaking to her, but after taking a long sip of her drink, she shrugs. "You can never be too careful."

My eyes fall to the new guy, Erik. "I don't think you're his type."

Her eyes widen, giving me a wounded look, and probably on the brink of tears again. Wow, it only took two sentences to offend her. That has to be a new record. "Apparently, no *girl* is his type," I offer. It's too early for me to be the biggest dick here. Before I can shove my foot further down my throat, I say, "You're Claire Ackerman." This seems to catch her off guard because her lips part in surprise. I take another sip of my beer, and without looking at her, I ask, "What are you doing back here anyway? Aren't you in school?"

11

She blinks a few times, collecting herself. "I am."

"But now you're here."

She takes another sip of her drink. "Very intuitive, Aiden Lewis."

Her comment gets a laugh out of me. I like how she's trying to level the playing field by knowing my name.

"I thought it'd be fun to come home for the weekend, but I was wrong." She says the words as she looks down at the cup between her hands, twirling the small straw around in a circle. They don't even serve drinks in real glasses here. Instead, we get clear plastic that crumples if you grip too hard.

Red flags go up in the back of my mind. I don't know Claire. I didn't really know her in high school, and I sure as hell don't know her now. I'm not trying to listen to this girl vent for the rest of the night.

I'd rather go home and listen to Mike screw Cindy.

"Uh…" I struggle to think of a safe way to respond without opening the floodgates.

Luckily, she gives a casual wave, dismissing the thought. "Forget it. It doesn't matter anyway."

No, it doesn't. I should take the out she just gave me and turn back to the TV, but the way she nervously takes another long sip of her drink tells me she's not okay. I finish off my beer, and like clockwork, Jasmine walks over to me again.

I'm grateful for the break from Claire. She's upset, and even though I should run the other way, I keep feeling the need to look at her. Talking to Jasmine is easy. I don't have to think about what I say to her because, ultimately, I don't give a shit what she thinks of me.

But I shouldn't give a shit what Claire thinks of me either. *And I don't.*

I glance at the two guys Jasmine was just dangling herself in front of. The assholes are clearly still talking about her. They're probably listing off all the things they want to do to her—all the things I probably *will* end up doing to her later. "So, who thinks they're getting some tonight?" I ask with a nod.

She swats my arm with a rag. "Don't be gross." When I keep staring at her, she huffs and rolls her eyes. "The one in the hat."

Looking down, I laugh and shake my head.

"Hey," she says in a warning tone. "I came over here to be nice and get you another beer. Don't make me regret it."

I'm sure I've made her regret worse. My eyes fall on Claire next to me. She's still staring straight down at her drink, so I look back at Jasmine and say, "Yeah, I'll have one more."

She follows my gaze to Claire and lowers her voice. "Do you know her or something?"

I knew she wouldn't remember her newest patron from school, so I shrug and hand her my empty cup. "No."

As soon as Jasmine's back is turned, filling my beer, I glance at Claire to see if she's offended, but she doesn't even look like she's heard me.

"The Boys are Back in Town" plays throughout the bar

louder than it needs to. The music is always too loud in this dump. It's like the manager assumes the place will be packed and wants to make sure people can hear the music over the crowd.

Well, the crowd consists of less than ten people including the staff, and we can fucking hear it.

It's always the same playlist, too. After this, it'll be "Born to be Wild," then "Closing Time", and then "Sweet Caroline."

I come here too much.

I should find relief in the fact that I'm listening to music and not Claire talking my ear off, but there's something unsettling about the way she's just sitting there. It isn't until Jasmine hands me my beer and walks over to her that she seems to even remember where she is. "You doing okay, honey?"

Claire's eyes snap up, her head nodding quickly, and I find it funny that she doesn't bite off Jasmine's head for the pet name.

My phone lights up on the bar top, showing another message from Mike.

Mike: Remind me why I'm not dating Cindy.

I stifle an eye roll as I text him back.

Me: Because you got a text from your sister, and she started throwing your shit out the window thinking you were talking to another girl.

There's always a fatal flaw. Cindy's happens to be unprovoked, borderline insane jealousy.

It doesn't take long for him to answer, but I don't bother looking because I can feel Claire's eyes burning into me.

And for whatever reason, I can't ignore it.

4

Claire

Aiden's phone lights up, and I wonder if he's meeting people here. I'm not sure I want a full high school reunion with Aiden and his friends, so I ask, "Why are you here alone?"

He pockets his phone. "I could ask you the same thing."

That's fair. "Are you meeting someone?"

He shakes his head. "I was supposed to, but things fell through. So now I'm kicking off my vacation solo." He raises his cup to me before taking another sip.

I turn in my chair to face him. "You're on vacation?" His sour expression and stiff posture don't make him look like someone who's about to enjoy some time off.

He looks…angry.

His eyes meet mine, and for the first time tonight, he seems to really *look* at me. Those blue eyes scan every inch of me, pulling my body heat to the surface—or maybe I have the drink to thank for that. Once he completes his scan, he faces forward and mutters, "Yup."

His dismissal makes me think I've failed a test. Glancing down at myself, I don't see anything wrong. That look Aiden gave me went deeper than the surface, though. It felt like his eyes were filing through every piece of my soul.

I stare at the two bartenders for a moment, trying to shake off how Aiden's look left me. They're talking and laughing together—the guy and the girl—and I can't help envying them. I don't know what I'm jealous of exactly, but I feel it. Maybe it's their freedom? Well, the freedom I assume they have. I bet they can do whatever they want, go wherever they want, and be whoever they want. They probably don't have cheating significant others weighing them down.

Cheating.

The word leaves a lump in my throat, so I gulp down more of my drink, noting how the alcohol prickles at my brain. "I want to do something," I blurt out. Ex-Boyfriend-Who-Must-Not-Be-Named has made me realize that I haven't done anything *I've* wanted to do for a long time. I was always thinking about *his* feelings.

Take a girl's trip across the country? Can't because *he* wouldn't like it. *He* didn't even like it when I would try to make friends at NYU. Heaven forbid a guy gets introduced to me at a party. You know what? If he was so worried about me meeting someone at a party, maybe he should have stayed with me. It would have been better than him dropping out to move

17

back here. I can't believe I let him limit my college experience, and for what? So he could slide into Shelly's bed every night that I was away?

I feel physically sick just thinking about it.

Aiden looks at me warily. "Are you talking to me?"

I don't know what I expected from him, but with all these feelings running through my veins, I was hoping for something with a little more oomph. I raise my eyebrows at him expectantly. "Yes, and I want to do something…like go somewhere?"

"You want to go somewhere." Each word rolls off his tongue, slow and deliberate.

"Well, I want to do lots of things, but going somewhere seems like a good place to start." I don't even know why I'm talking about this with him.

Aiden lifts his head in a slow nod. "Okay, so go somewhere?"

Feeling pleased with myself, I nod, "I will." I take another sip of my drink, but I can feel him staring at me, the crease between his dark eyebrows deepening. "What? Do you want to come or something?"

Did I just ask him to come with me?

I eye my drink suspiciously.

How much gin does it take to invite Aiden Lewis on a spontaneous trip with you?

Apparently, not that much.

"*Where?*" he asks, and my eyes snap up to see him facing

me, his elbow resting on the bar as he stares at me.

Now it's my turn to speak slowly. "Anywhere, Aiden. That's kind of the whole point." His eyes narrow like he's trying to decide if he should stop talking to me altogether. I can't blame him. I'm not exactly in my right mind, but I go ahead and ask my next question anyway.

5

Aiden

There's a brightness in her eyes as she says, "If you could go anywhere, right now, where would you go?"

What the hell, Claire? I came here to drink, not to play your little game of what if.

She gives me a small nod of encouragement, and I notice her cheeks are flushed differently now. I think her drink is starting to kick in. It seems Claire is quite the lightweight.

"Uh, I guess I would want to go to Germany."

She frowns at my answer. "Huh."

The hell?

"Did I answer wrong or something?"

Her eyes widen like she's afraid she might have upset me. "No, not at all! I'm sorry. Germany just feels a little unobtainable."

I frown, not sure if I should take offense to that. Does she think because I never got out of this town that I can't afford a trip to Germany? I've got money. Hell, I've got more money than I know what to do with. That's what happens when all you do is work six days a week for over a year. If I wanted to go to Germany, I could. But who would I go with? Mike?

She studies my expression and must gather at least some of what I'm thinking because she adds, "I was hoping your answer would inspire somewhere I could go *tonight.*"

Now it's my turn to raise an eyebrow. "Tonight?"

She tucks her dirty-blonde hair behind her ear and, for a moment, she looks vulnerable—a lot more like what she looked like in high school. "Why not?"

Her answer isn't really an answer, but I'll play along. "So, where do you want to go? If you could go anywhere?"

Her eyebrows pinch together as she stares hard at the cup in front of her, spinning the ice around with the straw. "I think I'd like to go to the beach."

"Okay, go to the beach, then." Easy. I should be a fucking therapist.

She downs the rest of her drink, and I'm starting to think our boy, Erik, might have given her a triple. Her eyes are glassy, but I can't tell if she's buzzed or if it's just leftover proof that she cried before she came in here.

"No, not the beaches here. I want to go to the Carolinas—or Florida!"

Of course, she wants to go to fucking Florida.

"Well, Florida is pretty far. You'd better get going."

21

I was joking, but she nods to herself like my words have convinced her to take the plunge. "Yeah," she says, smiling slightly. "I'm going to do it. I'm going to go."

She can't be serious. "Tonight?"

"Yeah," she says with a smile. "I think I will."

"You're going now?"

She nods.

"Alone?"

She nods again.

"What are you going to do? Ride the train?"

At this, I get a shrug. "That sounds good."

I shake my head, trying to understand her. "You're just going?"

She laughs lightly. "Yeah, I am."

I look her up and down and shake my head. "I'm telling you right now, you can't travel overnight alone."

She rolls her eyes like I don't know what I'm talking about. "Yes. I can."

No, she can't. She's borderline drunk, wearing nothing but a green sundress that clings to her every curve, and the fact that she's giving me the time of day proves that she has terrible judgment when it comes to people.

Leaning toward her, I lower my voice, my eyes never leaving hers. "Claire, I'm a guy. Trust me when I say you look way too fuckable in that dress to travel alone."

She freezes, and her entire body seems to turn red at what I've said. I hadn't thought about it much until I said it, but I'm right. She was pretty in high school, but she's gorgeous now, and that dress—even with her denim jacket—isn't helping to diminish a damn thing.

I think I've rendered her speechless because she's staring at me with those big brown eyes like she's trying to decide if she should slap me. Not that I would blame her if she did. I consider backpedaling my last sentence, but before I can, she hops down from the barstool and rummages through her purse.

"Where are you going?" I ask, thrown off by how abruptly she got up.

"I'm going to Florida," she snaps as she puts money down on the bar. "I'm going to enjoy the beach, and the sun, and I'm not going to let someone like you convince me not to."

I lift an eyebrow. "Someone like me?"

"Yeah," she says as she struggles to close her tiny bag. "You, with your hair, and muscles, and tattoos." She waves an accusatory finger in front of me as the words tumble from her lips.

"My hair?"

"This was great. Really great. I'm glad we could catch up," she says, dismissing me completely.

Then she storms out of the bar as quickly as she came into it.

What the actual fuck just happened? I stare after her, but the girl in the flowery green dress is already gone. The door swings shut behind her, and I'm back to drinking alone with Jasmine.

There's no way Claire is starting a trip to Florida tonight. More importantly, why the hell do I care? She's a grown-ass adult. If she wants to make stupid choices that get her killed, that's her business.

I look at the TV again, but I barely register what's on the screen. My imagination plays out coverage of a homicide involving a local girl who was in the wrong place at the wrong time—like a train to fucking Florida in the middle of the goddamn night.

My foot bounces against the bottom peg of the stool as I try to forget all thoughts of Claire Ackerman. I look back at the door again, hoping she'll realize how crazy she's being and walk back in here any second.

She doesn't.

Don't do it.

Don't you dare chase after that girl.

I grit my teeth, hating the fact that I'm even having to talk myself out of this.

Mind your own damn business, Aiden.

The thoughts are still reeling as I put cash on the counter and head out into the cool night air.

6

Claire

I don't know what just came over me. My head leans against the brick wall outside the bar as I stare up at the night sky. I probably look like I'm on the verge of a breakdown, but I don't have anything left in me to care, and a breakdown doesn't feel far from the truth anyway.

It's strange how quickly your life can change. This morning I was happy. I had an amazing boyfriend—or so I thought. I submitted my paper early and could surprise said boyfriend with a visit. The sundress he always loved happened to be clean. I was even having a good hair day. All the pieces fell perfectly into place.

Until they fell imperfectly apart.

The look on his face when I walked into the apartment still burns in my mind. I didn't even catch them *doing* anything. I think that's the worst part. I would expect him to look that guilty if I walked in on him having sex with her, but all I did was walk in on them watching a movie together, and he *still* looked that guilty.

It would be one thing if it was an unfortunate one-night stand or a fleeting lapse in judgment, but they looked so comfortable together. It was like they were the ones dating, and I was the random girl who didn't belong.

I always thought of Shelly as one of those girls who had peaked in high school. Her cheer uniform used to be her staple, but I guess she's traded it in for an *I'll sleep with your boyfriend* card.

As much as I hate to say it, she's still pretty. And since Garret lived with his mom as a kid, he didn't go to school here and have the pleasure of meeting Shelly back then. She must have looked like a shiny new toy to him.

I wish I had reacted quicker. People in movies always throw things at their cheating boyfriend, but I didn't throw anything at Garret.

Even the thought of his name weighs heavily on my chest, and I instantly regret thinking it.

No, I didn't throw anything at *him.*

Instead, what did I do?

I left.

He chased me down with his car.

And I actually got in to *let him explain.*

I don't think I even heard a word he said. As I sat in the passenger seat, I was completely consumed by thoughts of the two of them together. It didn't take long for me to freak out. I wish there were something else to call it, but it was definitely a freak-out. After screaming at him to let me out of the car at least ten times—not my finest moment—he finally pulled over.

That was how I found myself in the most desolate bar in Beacon. The flickering neon light was right there in front of me, and with nowhere else to go, I decided to go inside to try and collect myself. I thought my day couldn't get any weirder, but of course, the universe wanted to take one last jab. Enter Aiden Lewis.

As if my thoughts have the power to summon him, Aiden bursts out of the bar with enough force to make me jump. He looks left and then right before he spots me leaning against the wall a few feet away, and his posture immediately relaxes.

One hand holds a brown jacket as the other runs through his loose waves. "You're still here."

Thank you, Captain Obvious. "For now." I'm starting to wish I didn't drink everything in that cup because I'm feeling it, and if I'm going to make it to Florida, I need to at least get on the right train.

I'm compelled to collect myself as he walks over to me. He already thinks I can't do this on my own. The least I can do is stand up straight.

As he walks toward me, I can't help noticing how striking he is. His dark hair with those deep blue eyes, his tattoo, his tall, muscular build. They all add up and make it impossible for him not to draw attention. Once he's close enough, he asks, "Change your mind?" with the corner of his mouth quirked and an arrogant glit in his eyes.

"No." I think I'm trying to stand up too tall because I feel my chin jutting out. I collapse a bit and add, "I'm figuring out my next move."

"Your first move."

My eyes narrow, but I don't say anything to that.

He sighs like I'm exhausting him. "Do you even have a car?"

I watch a cute couple walk past us because it's easier to keep my eyes on them than it is to stare back into Aiden's deep, blue, judgmental orbs. "No. I don't exactly need one at NYU." Once the couple weave around the corner and out of sight, I dare to bring my eyes to meet his. "I can get an Uber."

"To the train station?" he asks with a furrowed brow, "It's right around the corner."

Opening the Uber app on my phone, I let out a huff. "I can't get a train to Florida from Beacon. I have to go to the station in Poughkeepsie." Which I only just found out, but he doesn't have to know that.

He blinks. "Poughkeepsie."

"Yup," I say dismissively, still focused on my phone as I debate grabbing a few essentials, but the bag I packed for the weekend is somewhere in Garret's car, and that's not happening.

Aiden shakes his head, pinching the bridge of his nose.

"For Christ's sake," he mutters before looking back at me. "You're going to drive out to Poughkeepsie so you can take the fucking train to Florida?"

My shoulders lift in a shrug as I finally stop looking at my phone long enough to register the incredulous expression on his face. "I like the idea of taking the train," I say, suddenly feeling like I need to justify myself. It's cheaper than flying, and it will give me time to think.

I'm relieved when he leans his back against the wall next to me, breaking our eye contact. The way he looks at me is too intense. It always has been. Even before that night, I could never hold his gaze at school. "So, Florida." He says it like the entire state has offended him by existing. I'm about to ask him what he has against Florida when he kicks off from the wall and says, "Well, I guess we'd better get going."

7

Aiden

She's bluffing. There's no way she'll travel the entire east coast on a random Thursday night. No fucking way—especially since I don't hear her footsteps behind me. Turning to look back at her, I raise an eyebrows impatiently. "Coming?"

That seems to snap her out of it. She hurries after me, but I don't wait for her. As I keep walking, I expect to hear the sound of heels behind me, but her footsteps are clunky. Once she's next to me, I glance down and notice she's wearing boots with her dress and have to bite back a smile. *What the hell did she think she was going to do tonight? Scale the damn mountain?*

"What are you doing?" she pants, still struggling to keep up with my strides. I'm taller than her, but that doesn't make me slow down. If I can wear her out and make her abandon this crazy idea, all the better.

"The train isn't going to pick us up, Claire. I'm driving

us to the station." Maybe, *just maybe*, I can get her to back down by pushing her to go.

It's risky.

But it might work.

And for whatever annoying-ass reason, the thought of her going on this trip makes my stomach twist. Which pisses me off because whether or not Claire Ackerman goes to Florida shouldn't be any of my damn business.

She stops dead in her tracks, and this time, I do turn around to look at her. I guess making her second-guess her plan was easier than I thought. It was so easy that I don't even try to hide my smirk.

"Us?" she asks.

I glance around before looking back at her. "What?"

"You just said the train isn't going to pick *us* up. And I'm not getting in your car."

My smirk fades. "So? And why not?"

Her eyebrows pinch together as she studies me. "Um because I barely know you. Why do you want to come with me anyway?"

For a second, I'm not sure how to answer her. My instinct is to clarify that I don't *want* to go with her at all. It's more like I feel like I have to—like *someone* has to, and I'm the only idiot around to do it. Locking my eyes on hers, I hate how sad she looks. She's like a fucking puppy, and even assholes like me don't want to see a sad puppy. Finally, I settle on, "Because I'm worried about you."

It's the truth. Even if I don't understand it.

Giving me a dubious lift of her brow, she says, "You're worried?" and it's clear she doesn't believe me. "You don't need to worry about me, Aiden. I can do this on my own."

I scoff. "Yeah, maybe when you're sober."

"You can't come with me." She crosses her arms like it's going to make her look more intimidating.

Well, I wasn't expecting this; I'll admit that much. "What?"

"You can't come with me," she says again, and I swear I see her almost stomp her boot.

I can't go with her? She should be *thanking* me. I should get a community service medal for doing this shit.

I try my best not to sound like an asshole as I spit out, "I can't come with you?"

Claire seems to falter slightly, but it doesn't last long. Her arms are still crossed when she answers me with a definitive, "No. I need to do this on my own."

My eyes float past her and land on two guys making eyes at her ass in the alley behind us. Okay, maybe they're just talking to each other, but she doesn't need to know that. I walk up to her, closing the gap between us. Keeping my voice low, I say, "Fine, go alone. But you have no idea what you're doing, and I still stand by what I said about that dress." I make a point to look past her at the two guys and add, "And from the looks of things, they agree with me."

She glances over her shoulder before staring up at me

with the trace of a scowl. "Seriously, Aiden?"

Crossing my arms, I ask, "What would you do? If those two guys cornered you, what's your incredible line of defense?"

Even in the dark, I can see her gears turning. Her head whips around to glance at the guys standing behind her before she turns back to me. She opens her mouth, but I don't give her enough time to get a word out.

"Something you should probably think about." Stepping away from her and heading the other way, I throw a casual hand over my shoulder. "It was nice seeing you, Claire."

I can't believe I almost went to Florida with her. What was I thinking? Well, I know exactly what I was thinking. I was thinking that this half-drunk girl has no business traveling alone.

But what can I do? She didn't listen to reason, reverse psychology didn't seem to do the trick, and scaring her out of it just made me feel like a dick.

Life is so much easier when you don't give a shit.

8

Claire

I'm not sure what just happened, but as Aiden Lewis walks away, something inside me doesn't like it. He's trying to spoil my celebration of independence, and honestly, he's a little rude, but something in the back of my mind screams with every step he takes.

I glance back at the two guys Aiden pointed to and immediately whip my head back around because they *are* looking at me. I try to imagine what I would do if they *did* approach me. What would I use to defend myself if I were in trouble? Throw a boot at them?

They might only look this way because of the argument we just had in front of them, but either way, my gin-infused confidence has been washed away by a sobering force that can only be described as Aiden Lewis.

A sobering but *familiar* force.

And he's basically willing to escort me to Florida.

Biting down on my lip, I stare after him as he walks away with his jacket slung over his shoulder and try to figure out what to do—because he isn't looking back. The hourglass in the back of my mind runs low on sand, and I let out a sharp breath.

Damn it.

"Aiden!"

He stops and turns but doesn't advance toward me. I end up jogging to catch up with him, and I feel pathetic by the time I reach him, my out-of-shape lungs struggling to breathe.

I catch my breath.

But I can't think of anything to say.

And he's staring at me.

Those blue eyes are staring at me, and I'm too busy trying to decipher what's behind them to say something coherent.

Eventually, I manage to speak, but I suddenly feel embarrassed. "So, you said you want to go to Florida?"

He stares at me with an unreadable expression. "I'm pretty sure I've never said those words in my life."

Yup. He's rude. I don't want him to know that I'm affected by his overall demeanor, but my face falls anyway. "But I thought…"

"Shit, Claire, don't give me that look." He practically groans. "What happened to needing to do this on your own?"

I really don't understand him. "What look?" I ask, but then I shake my head and add, "Well, we can ride the train together, but once we get there, I need to go my own way."

"Ouch." He rubs his palm over his chest like I've just punched him.

"I didn't mean—well, I just meant that—"

"I'm fucking with you, Claire." He shoves his hands in his pockets and gives me a casual shrug. "Train ride and nothing more. Got it."

I hold out my hand and can't help beaming because I'm

doing this. Well, I guess *we're* doing this. "It's a deal, then."

He stares down at my outstretched hand for a moment, but then lets out a breath of laughter and wraps his fingers around mine for a single shake.

"I'm still not getting in your car, though." I pull out my phone again but manage to catch the roll of his eyes as I do. After everything is set, I look up and smile. "Our Uber will be here in six minutes."

It all suddenly feels real. I'm going to get on a train with Aiden Lewis. I'm going to Florida. Before I can stop myself, I blurt out, "Why are you doing this?"

He doesn't look at me as he answers, his eyes fixed on the street, watching for our car. "I have no fucking idea."

9

Aiden

Why *am* I doing this? I won't lie, I'm starting to doubt my choices tonight. There's a good chance Claire might have backed out and stayed in New York without my interfering.

Then I wouldn't have to go to fucking Florida.

Right now.

With Claire Ackerman.

She's practically a stranger to me, an enigma of my past. I can't explain why the thought of her, in her hiking boots and flowery dress, sitting on a train alone surrounded by creeps made me do this. It kind of pisses me off. I've gone the past year not caring, and life has been grand.

Okay, maybe that's a lie, but life has been simple. Life has been *easy*.

Nothing about getting on a train with Claire feels easy, yet here I am, opening the door to a damn Uber so we can go to fucking Poughkeepsie.

"Do you even know if a train is running tonight?" I don't look at her while I ask the question because I don't want her to see the glimmer of hope in my eyes. If there's no train, there's no Florida. I'd be able to go home tonight and tell Mike and Cindy about how I *almost* did something stupid. We'd all have a good laugh, and then I'd never have to think of Claire Ackerman again.

"Yeah, I checked the app," she sings happily, "There's an overnight train that goes all the way to Florida, and it hasn't left yet. It leaves in about…" She looks down at her phone and says, "Forty-five minutes."

Well, isn't that fucking convenient?

"Where in Florida?" I ask as I stare down the Uber driver through the rearview mirror. Why anyone would enjoy being driven around by a stranger is beyond me.

Without waiting for Claire to answer, I pull out my phone as the tires start to roll and text Mike.

Me: I'll be out of town for a few days.

I wait for the three dots to appear, but they don't. He's probably preoccupied with Cindy, so I lock my phone and put it back in my pocket.

"Um," Claire murmurs as she stares down at a map on her phone, "the beach?"

A short laugh leaves my nose. "Your options are probably Jacksonville or St. Petersburg."

"St. Petersburg," she mutters slowly as she types it on her

phone. "Yeah, they have a station!" she says, beaming. "I'll go there—or…" She hesitates. "We'll go there?"

"Fine." Leaning my head back against the seat, I try to come to terms with the fact that I'm going back to the place I thought I'd left behind forever.

At least I'll have a place to stay.

Minutes pass of Claire seeming pleased with herself, and me trying not to dive out of this car every time we stop at a red light.

"I can't believe we're doing this!" she practically squeals.

Neither can I.

"By tomorrow, we'll be in Florida. That's so crazy to think about!"

You can say that again.

"I hope the weather is nice there." She claps a hand over her mouth. "What if we go all the way there, and it's raining?"

It probably will be because Florida sucks.

She's still looking at me, and that's when I realize I've only been thinking my answers. Her head tilts so she can scrutinize me with her judging eyes. "You don't talk much."

"You talk *too* much."

Her stare turns into a glare, and I know I've said the wrong thing. "You don't have to come with me, you know."

I look up and see that we've stopped in front of the station. Before I can dig myself into a deeper hole, I open my car door. "Stop doubting me, Claire."

10

Claire

I glare at the back of Aiden's head as he walks toward the station. He's changed since high school. He was always sort of withdrawn—my best friend, Violet, used to call him *cute moody boy* back then, but there was a gentle kindness about him in high school that seems to have disappeared.

My lips are sealed as we purchase our tickets and wait for the train. *I talk too much?* I'll show him how much I *don't* talk. I've been through enough tonight. If Aiden plans on squashing any lingering happiness that spills out of me, I can keep it to myself. I'll bottle it up, savor it, and then set it free on the beaches of Florida where there will be no Aiden in sight.

By the time we take our seats on the train, he's starting to look at me funny, but I don't give in. It feels childish, but I'm committed to my silence at this point. It's challenging, though. I *want* to talk—maybe not to Aiden specifically, but staying quiet kills me.

I take in the other passengers on the train, and even though none of them look any different from the daytime passengers, the fact that there are so few of them does give the train an eerie vibe. When we first walked on, there was a woman who smelled like cat pee sitting alone, and I was relieved when Aiden led us as far away from her as possible. Other than that, there are only a few other people. It seems like I would have fit in just fine if I had traveled solo, but despite his bad attitude, it's mildly comforting having him here with me.

Taking a seat next to the window, I stare at the desolate station outside until I hear his voice close to my ear. "So, what are you running from, Claire?"

I turn to look at him and see that he's following my gaze out the window…at nothing. Now that we're facing each other, I let his accusation break my silence. "I'm not running from anything."

He nods as he leans back in his seat. "Right. I must have misunderstood."

"Misunderstood what?" I don't bother trying to hide my annoyance. Aiden doesn't know me. He doesn't get to make snap judgments about me.

He shrugs and drums his hands on his lap without looking at me. "That you're a runner."

I blink, trying to understand.

His smile grows slightly as he leans toward me in the seat.

"Claire, I've only been with you for…what? An hour?" His eyebrows drift upward to make sure I'm following, so I give a slight dip of my chin and wait for him to continue. "Well, in that one hour you ran away from me in the bar, the two guys in the alley, and now you're running all the way to Florida. So my question is, what are you running from?"

"I didn't—" I don't finish my sentence because he's right, and he just reminded me of the one thing I'd rather not think about. I abandon all thoughts of my breakup and instead think about Aiden's comment that made me leave the bar. No one has ever said anything like that to me. "We should have rules."

He responds with the lift of an eyebrow. "Rules?"

I nod. "No flirting."

He sits back. "Uh, I wasn't—"

I drop my voice to a whisper. "You said I look '*too fuckable*' in this dress." He opens his mouth, but I cut him off. "Which I *hope* is not how you flirt because that's just sad, but either way, I don't want you looking at me that way."

Aiden stretches his back against the seat. "Okay, but fair warning, I've never been good at following rules."

His tone is matter-of-fact, but I still give him a pointed stare. "Aiden," I warn.

"I've never even looked at you that way," he says in defense. Then something shifts in his eyes, and I know he's remembering our brief encounter in high school.

"I just mean," he starts, but I hold up my hand to stop him.

"It's okay. We don't have to talk about it."

He swallows hard and nods, suddenly looking uncomfortable. "Okay."

We're both quiet for a long time. Neither one of us knowing how to navigate the conversation from here.

"Done."

I look up at him. "Done?"

"Yeah, done." He looks me up and down and adds, "Seriously, that dress is hideous. It doesn't do a thing for you. And those boots? Who the hell let you go out looking like that? It's embarrassing."

I bite back a smile, grateful for the lightened mood, and try to refocus. "Okay, next rule."

11

Aiden

More rules? One unnecessary rule is enough. I wasn't even flirting with her when I said that. I was just stating a fact. I've never flirted with Claire—not even back then…not really.

Not even when I wanted to.

I stomp out that thought as soon as it creeps up on me.

"I'm making the second rule." Her eyes widen in surprise, but I don't give her time to protest. "No more running."

She frowns. "I'm not running."

Resting my head on the back of the seat, I close my eyes and let out a sigh. "Keep telling yourself that, Claire."

"Well, we should at least—"

"Nope. Two rules. That's it. You've picked yours, and I've picked mine."

She glares at me. "I'm *not* running." She falls back against the seat next to me with a thud, and the corner of my mouth twitches.

After a few minutes of silence, I can't help glancing at her out of the corner of my eye. She has her hair tucked behind her ear as she stares down at her phone with a furrowed brow. Even with her hardened expression, there's something soft about her. She bites down on her bottom lip, and I can't focus on anything else.

I need to get a grip.

Damn her and her rules for digging up things I shouldn't be feeling.

Sitting up straight, I look at her with newfound resolution, determined not to find her attractive. She's just staring down at her phone, looking miserable, and it's making me uncomfortable.

That's better.

I internally groan before saying, "Christ, if another rule means that much to you, just say it."

Her eyes snap up at me like she'd forgotten I was sitting here. Shaking her head, she mutters, "Oh, no. It's not that."

I watch her, waiting for more of an explanation.

"It's nothing," she says before dropping her gaze again.

I don't believe her, but I should let it go. There's no reason for me to try and figure out what's bothering her. It doesn't concern me, and that's a good thing.

"Claire, look at me." If there weren't so many people around, I'd smack myself for that. *What the hell is wrong with me?*

She lifts her gaze, but it takes a moment. When her

brown eyes meet mine, she looks broken.

Not crying hysterically.

Not sobbing uncontrollably.

She just looks like something inside her has been snuffed out.

"What?" she asks, and for a moment, I'm not sure what to say. I don't know why seeing her this way makes me feel like I need to take some sort of action, but it does. Before I can think of anything, though, she lets out a sigh. "Don't look at me like that."

Her comment makes me falter. "Look at you like what?"

She drops her gaze with a shake of her head, but not before I see her cheeks flush. "Today just hasn't been great," she says quietly.

Nudging her with my elbow, I say, "You're on a train to fucking Florida."

She lets out a breath of laughter before nervously tucking a strand of hair behind her ear. "Well, when you've been cheated on, you've got to do something," she mutters.

Her voice was barely above a whisper, but I heard every word. My eyes widen, and like a reflex, I say, "What?"

She stares at me with those brown eyes that hold so much sadness. Has she looked this sad all night? I know she looked like she had been crying when she walked into the bar, but that went away, didn't it? Or has she looked like she was on the verge of tears all night, and I've just been too distracted by her damn hiking boots to notice?

After a moment, she shakes her head and stares out the window. "It's nothing."

The prick checking tickets picks the worst time to walk over to us. Claire avoids looking at me as she hands him the small paper, and I nearly cram mine into his palm so he can get lost.

"Don't do that. It's not nothing."

She takes a shaky breath, and I hope she's not about to burst into tears.

And I'm not sure why, but I'm pissed.

Finally, she lets out a slow breath. "I found out my boyfriend has been cheating on me." She pauses and then drops her face in her hands. "It's so weird to say that out loud."

"When did you find out?" This trip suddenly makes more sense. There's always a breakup crisis.

Some people change their hair.

Others get tattoos.

And Claire takes the train to Florida.

She glances down at her phone and checks the time. "An hour and forty-seven minutes ago."

"You found out *tonight?*" Most girls I know would have locked themselves in their room with a tub of ice cream for a week. Either Claire didn't care much about this guy, or she's in a way more fragile state than she's letting on.

"Yeah..." She looks down at her hands. "I'm not sure what to make of everything yet. I know I'll have to talk to him eventually, but I couldn't stand the idea of listening to him try to justify what he did."

I can't believe this asshole. "He was trying to make excuses?"

"I mean, I don't really know. He said he wanted to explain, so I got in the car with him, but once he started talking I just couldn't take it. I had to get out, so he finally pulled over in front of the bar tonight."

I turn to face her. "He left you? He let you out of the car, and he drove away?" It's like I can see her visibly shrink when my questions hit her ears. She looks like she thinks I'm going to criticize *her* for something, and the realization only gets me more fired up. Her eyes fall to her hands in her lap again, and seeing her fold in on herself makes me curse under my breath. "Piece of shit."

Her eyes snap up, and she carefully asks, "What are you so mad about?"

Honestly, I don't know. People cheat all the time. Fuck, even I know that, but seeing her reduced to this gets to me more than I want it to.

There are plenty of girls out there who don't mind hooking up. Lots of girls *want* to keep things casual. Why take a girl like Claire and destroy her? One look at her, and it's clear she expects more from people. Why break her? Why put her through all that when you can just find a girl like Jasmine instead?

Shit, Jasmine.

Pulling out my phone, I send a quick text. She won't care,

but the fact that I haven't once thought about our plans to-night still makes me feel like a dick.

Me: Can't come over tonight. Something came up.

Looking up, I realize Claire is still waiting for me to an-swer her. *What did she ask me again?* My phone lights up, and I glance down to read the response.

Jasmine: Still don't know her? ;)

I roll my eyes and flip my phone over. No, I don't know her. Except when I look at her again, and she's still patiently watching me, I'm reminded that I did know her…sort of. See-ing her look at me this way might as well be a recipe for time travel. It's like we're back in high school, and I don't like it. I'm not that guy anymore—the good parts or the bad. I left both behind when I decided all people do in this world is hurt other people, and I don't want to be a part of it.

I let out an exasperated sigh. "I'm mad because we still have over twenty-five hours before we're in Florida, and I'm already going to break rule number one."

12

Claire

Aiden runs a hand through his dark waves, and I brace myself for what he's about to say. *He's going to break my rule?* Now is really not the time.

"Aiden, you really shouldn't—"

He shakes his head. "I told you, I've never been good at following rules anyway. Just let me say this one thing. I'm not trying to flirt with you, but I think it's something you need to hear."

When I don't say anything, he lets out a breath and rests his elbows on his knees before looking over at me. "Listen, when you moved here in the middle of freshman year from Pennsylvania—"

My face must show my shock. I had no idea Aiden noticed me at all back in high school, let alone knew where I was from. My mouth falls open slightly, but he holds up his hand to stop me.

"Yeah, I remember you're from PA. I remember because after I saw you, I wondered if all the girls who lived there were as beautiful as you. For the record—they're not." He shakes his head. "Anyway, when you transferred to our school, every single guy noticed you. Do you know why?" He stares at me expectantly, but I just shake my head. "It's because you were the whole fucking package. And I'm telling you right now, your boyfriend is a dumbass."

I have no idea what to say. That's easily one of the sweetest things anyone has ever said to me—even if the delivery was a little rough. I stare at him with wide eyes, my mind reeling.

Aiden glances around the train, and for the first time, he resembles the Aiden he was in high school—a little less guarded. "That's all I'm going to say."

I blink. Eventually, a small "Thank you" escapes my lips, but I'm not even sure if he's heard me.

"Don't thank me."

I frown, swallowing the lump in my throat. "That was still really sweet."

He leans back in the seat. "Yeah, well, it needed to be said."

The conversation lulls, and I look back at my phone until I hear Aiden mutter, "Huh."

"Huh?"

"Yeah." He says, "I broke a rule. I figured you'd make me go sit next to the cat piss lady or something."

I choke on my laughter and cover my mouth to try and hold it in. "Shh! Don't say that so loud!" Lowering my voice, I add, "You smelled it, too?"

His eyes widen. "How could you think I didn't? I had to hold my fucking breath until we made it over here."

Ducking low, I shake my head, laughter still bubbling in my throat. "She's going to hear you," I hiss as I whack his arm.

"Let's hope she does." He has a straight face as he says it, still not lowering his voice, and it only makes me laugh harder. He looks at me, bewildered. "Shit, Claire. Pull your-self together."

I don't know why I'm laughing so hard. A few minutes ago, I felt like I was on the verge of tears, but now I'm *happy*. Well, not happy with my overall situation, but at this moment, I feel better than I've felt all night.

Finally catching my breath, I say, "I think you're wrong, you know."

He glances at me out of the corner of his eye. "About what?"

"You said guys back then noticed me, but I never had a boyfriend until I went to college." Garret is the only guy I've ever dated, and look how well that turned out. I swallow the bitter taste in my mouth as images of him with Shelly come to mind again.

"I didn't say they wanted to be your boyfriend. I said they noticed you, and trust me, they did."

I frown, not sure what he means. Getting lost in my

thoughts, I look out the window and try to remember those four years. My dad had just gotten his marketing job in New York City, but we couldn't afford to live there, so we moved to Beacon instead. I remember Dad saying it was too far, but there was a quaint charm about Beacon that Mom loved. I had hoped that the move would make things better, but my parents still fought. I'll never understand how two people who hate each other so much can stay married for so long.

Most days, home was the last place I wanted to be, so I spent a lot of time at Violet's house. It's not like my living situation was dangerous or anything; my house was just never a happy home. My parents didn't seem to mind that I was rarely there. They'd set food out for me and leave notes, but I never had to tell them where I was or when I'd be back. They were always more preoccupied with their own problems.

It was hard for me to stay angry with them because, even back then, I knew people who had it worse. There's nothing like someone else's problems to put your own into perspective.

After we moved, I remember feeling so nervous about going to a new school, and once I got there, my anxiety only grew. It was clear everyone had grown up together. Groups of friends were already formed, and I found myself feeling like an outsider regardless of who I tested the waters with.

Growing up in Bucks County, the school dynamic was similar. I had my friends from elementary school, so I never really had to think about how to meet new people. I think that's what made my transition to Beacon so difficult. I was lost until Violet took me under her wing. We did almost eve-rything together for those four years, and considering she's my roommate now, not much has changed.

The thought reminds me that I should text her and tell her about what happened tonight. She never liked Garret. Knowing Violet, she probably saw this coming a mile away. My fingers tap my phone screen, but then I lock it again. I'm not ready to get into this with her.

Plus, she assumes I'm staying with him this weekend, so I won't need to explain anything for at least that long.

As I stare out the window, flashes of my high school ex-perience come to mind. I usually didn't have a date for dances, I never had a boyfriend, and I didn't get invited to parties. And Aiden said people noticed me? He's probably just saying things to make me feel better. If that's the case, I don't mind. It actually goes against what I was starting to think of him: that he's an inconsiderate ass.

13

Aiden

Why the hell did I just say all of that to her? I mean, it's true, but I'm not sure how I feel about her knowing my seventeen-year-old thoughts about her. At least she's not making a big deal out of it. She's been staring out the window for a few minutes now, and I'm trying to figure out if I've somehow offended her.

Again, why do I care?

I'm getting sick of the way she's making me feel tonight. Not that she's done anything wrong. Hell, the only thing she's done is make me feel like I'm second-guessing everything that falls out of my mouth.

My phone vibrates because Mike has finally stopped boning Cindy long enough to text me.

Mike: What the hell? Why? Where are you going?

I answer his text the only way I can:

Me: Fucking Florida.

The three dots pop up right away, and I know he's losing his shit. It doesn't take long for his next message to come in.

Mike: Seriously? Why? Don't let Sam pull you in!

Rolling my eyes, I shove my phone back into my pocket. *Jackass.*

I check on Claire again, but she's still staring out the window. I thought she talked too much, but now I wish she would say something.

"What are you thinking?"

Did I seriously just ask her that? I must have because she's staring at me with those big brown eyes that make me question everything.

"I'm still trying to wrap my head around being on this train with you."

That makes two of us. "Well, you've got plenty of time to let it sink in." Hell, *I've* got plenty of time to let it sink in.

She shakes her head and adjusts herself so that she's facing me. "I'm sorry. It was sweet of you to offer to come with me, you know. Especially considering we don't exactly know each other."

"Claire Ackerman from some small-ass town in Pennsylvania. Honor roll student who went to NYU to major in...English? And..." I take in her outfit again. "enjoys nighttime hikes in dresses. What else do I need to know?"

She smiles, and I'm surprised how much I like the fact that I'm the one who put it there. Narrowing her eyes, she studies me. "For starters, I'm studying education at Stein-hardt." She glances down at her shoes. "And these are *not* hiking boots."

"Uh, those are definitely hiking boots. I've seen them on the yuppies who think it's cool to walk the mountain." There's only one mountain in our town. We used to take the service road up there to drink when we were underage, but now that everyone wants to clean up the town, they're trying to pass it off as a nature trail.

She frowns slightly. "What's wrong with hiking the mountain?"

I run a hand over my face. "Nothing, Claire. Are you a yuppie? No, you're one of us." I glance over at her and can't fight the smile pulling at my lips. "Barely. But you're one of us."

For some reason, this seems to make her feel better. Claire Ackerman is *not* one of us, but if thinking she is means she won't cry, so be it.

She falls quiet again. I don't know why her silence eats at me. I usually can't wait for people to stop talking.

Even Jasmine.

Jasmine isn't even annoying, and every time she opens her mouth to say something, I get the urge to hold my breath until it's over.

When Claire doesn't talk, it's unsettling. My heel bounces against the floor, and I purposefully slam my foot down to make it stop.

What the hell?

It isn't until she turns to me and says "We should play a game," that I feel more like myself and wish she would have kept her mouth shut.

14

Claire

Aiden stares at me with a dubious look. "A game?"

I shrug, suddenly feeling embarrassed. Did suggesting a game make me sound childish? "We've got time, right?"

He seems to think about this for a moment. "I usually only play games that involve alcohol."

I give him a wry smile. "Why does that not surprise me?" Looking around the train, I try to think of something we can do to pass the time. My eyes land on the cat lady again, and I smile to myself. "Have you heard that cat urine is good for cell growth?"

Aiden blinks. "What?"

"It's the game! You've never played it?"

"Have I ever played a game about cat piss?" His dark eyebrows pull together. "Uh, no. I can't say that I have."

I let out a laugh. "No. The game is that you start a sentence with 'Have you heard…' and then you either make something up or say something true. Then the other person has to guess if it's fact or fiction."

He's staring at me with untrusting eyes. "Okay…and it's fun? Because it sounds sort of dumb."

I frown. "Well, what do you suggest then?"

"Can't we just ride the train?"

Leaning back in my seat, I pull out my phone. Without looking at him, I say, "If that's what you want."

It's probably for the best anyway. I have a lot of research I need to do before I get to Florida. I know we're going to St. Petersburg, but I'm not sure how far the beach is once we get there. Not *we, I.* I'm not sure how far the beach is once *I* get there.

I open my Airbnb app and start looking for a place to stay. If I had planned this trip, it probably would have been too expensive to stay close to the beach, but thanks to last-minute timing, prices have dropped. I'm able to find a small two-bedroom bungalow for a price that doesn't break my measly bank account. With it being the end of the semester, I've gotten paid for a lot of extra tutoring sessions these past few weeks, so I at least have a little extra cash to work with.

But how long will I stay?

I know I can stay at least the weekend. Everything past that is unknown at this point.

I've just finished booking the Airbnb when my phone

shows an incoming message from Garret and my heart drops.

Garret: Where are you? I went back to look for you and the bartender said you left with some guy?

Shit.

My hands shake slightly as I stare down at the message. I have no idea how to answer him. Should I even answer him? Part of me feels like I shouldn't, but another, larger part feels compelled to try to explain myself. My stomach ties into a knot as I picture him storming back into the bar and questioning the bartender. He's probably assuming the worst right now. He has to be really angry. My thumbs hover over the keypad, but I can't think of what to say. The blood pounding in my ears won't let me think straight.

"Have you heard that more people die in train accidents than plane crashes every year?"

I jump at the sound of Aiden's voice and look up at him, feeling dazed. "What? That's terrible. Why would you tell me that when we're on a train?"

His lips twitch and as soon as the realization hits, I can't help the small smile that comes to my lips. "You're playing the game."

He laughs. "I think I just won. You should have seen the look on your face."

I drop my phone in my lap and turn to face him. "I have a fear of dying in some type of freak accident."

His face falls. "That's morbid."

With a roll of my eyes, I say, "I'm not saying I think I

61

will. It's just a fear. Like every time I ride the subway, I think about how terrible it would be if something went wrong with the tracks and we collided with another train."

"You think about that *every time* you get on the subway?"

My cheeks burn, and I backpedal. "Well, I don't dwell on it or anything, but it usually crosses my mind at some point." I wave my hand in the air dismissively. "Not the point. The point is that you want to play my game." I don't know why it makes me so happy, but it does.

Shaking his head with a bemused smile, he says, "Yeah, I'll play, but I want to change it."

Of course, he does. "What do you want to change?"

There's a mischievous glint in his eyes as he says, "I only want to hear things about you."

15

Aiden

She's staring at me like I just asked her to get naked and run through the train. "Come on, Claire. We'll be sitting here for a while, might as well get to know each other, right?"

I want to know more about her, and I'm trying not to worry about why that is—probably because I don't have my headphones with me. Sitting here in silence for the last fifteen minutes was driving me crazy; there's no way I could take, however many hours we have left, with her not speaking to me.

"Okay…" she says slowly, still looking more concerned than anything else. This girl needs to relax. "Um…Have you heard that I once ate an entire chocolate cake for a bet?"

This is not what I was expecting, so I let out a laugh. Looking her up and down, I try to figure out where she'd even put an entire cake.

"Well?" she asks, and I realize I've been checking her out.

I sit up straighter and hope she didn't notice. "There's no way you ate an entire cake."

Her smile widens and she shakes her head. "No, that's a fact. I was in middle school, but it definitely happened."

I can't help grinning at her. "Impressive." *Why the hell am I smiling so much?* The gesture feels completely natural and scary as fuck all at the same time.

"Your turn."

"Did you hear drinking tequila increases your IQ?"

She shakes her head. "Nice try. If I have to tell you things about me, you have to tell me things about you."

Shit.

I didn't think this far ahead.

I'm about to tell her something true about me, but at the last minute, I change my mind. "Sometimes I take the tip money from tables at restaurants."

Her face immediately falls.

I knew she thought I was a piece of shit. Making sure not to give anything away, I stare back at her with a blank expression.

She thinks it over for way too long before finally saying, "Fiction?"

The question in her voice makes me roll my eyes. "Yeah, it's fiction. Jesus." I give her a swift nod. "You're up."

She seems to relax now that she knows I'm not a fucking thief. Tucking a strand of hair behind her ear, she fights a smile. "I once got drunk and stripped at a frat party."

"There's no way that's the truth." Even as I say the words, the back of my mind buzzes at the thought. Claire letting loose at a party? It shouldn't, but imagining a wild side of her excites something inside of me.

"How did you know?" She gapes at me. "You didn't even have to think about it!"

I shake my head, clearing my thoughts. "Claire, I hate to be the one to tell you this, but you're a terrible liar."

She bites down on her lip with a smile. "Okay, maybe that one was far-fetched. I'll make the next lie more believable."

I laugh because her last lie would have been more than believable for most of the girls I know. It just wasn't believable coming from her.

I think for a moment. "Have you heard that I've hooked up with a different girl every week for the past year?"

I'm not sure why I say it...or why I care about getting to know her and her opinion of me.

But I do.

I'd rather learn as much as I can about Claire, and not offer a single thing about myself—probably because I shared too much with her a long time ago and ended up regretting it.

She studies me with more conviction this time. It's not true. It was for the first couple of months, but my rebound phase didn't last long.

"True?"

The question in her voice makes my smile widen again. How little Claire thinks of my morale is the only truth that has come out of this game so far—well, that and the cake.

16

Claire

Aiden raises an eyebrow at me. "You think I fuck a different girl every week?"

My cheeks burn. "Um—Well, I don't know." I mean, by the looks of him, I think he *could*. Whether he actually does is a mystery.

"As flattered as I am to know that you find me so desirable—"

My eyes widen. "What? I didn't say—"

He laughs at my flustered response. "Fiction, Claire. It's fiction."

Aiden is nice to look at—okay, *really* nice to look at—but there's nothing going on between us. *So why does his answer fill me with relief?* "Rule number one," I say, pointing an accusatory finger at him.

He's practically grinning at me now, the dimple in his

cheek clearly visible. "That was all you." I open my mouth to say something, but he beats me to it. "Your turn."

Clamping my mouth shut, I exhale through my nose as I try to think of what to ask next. Eager to change to a safer topic, I blurt out, "Have you heard that I have an older brother?"

Aiden rolls his eyes. "I already know you don't. Try again."

"You do?"

Something behind his blue eyes looks apprehensive for a moment, but then he recovers. "We went to the same school. I would have known if you had any siblings." He leans back in his seat. "That one was boring anyway. You can do better."

"Well, excuse me for disappointing you with the facts of my life. You're the one who said you wanted to only hear things about me."

He rolls his head against the back of the seat to look at me. "I was hoping to dig up some dirt on the always perfect Claire Ackerman."

"Right." I scoff.

"I'm serious." He turns toward me, the side of his head still resting against the seat. "Give me a good truth, and if it's a lie, the least you can do is make it interesting."

His comment brings a frown to my lips. My truths are all boring, I know that. I try to think of a lie, but his devilish smirk makes it impossible to think straight. I glance down at my lap to avoid his stare and try to come up with something.

"Okay…have you heard that I once had to scale down the side of my apartment building after getting locked out on the roof in the middle of the night?"

He studies me, and I feel a little bit of pride in the fact that I've finally stumped him. I lean the side of my head against the seat and turn to face him. "Well, what is it? Fact or fiction?"

He narrows his eyes at me playfully. "Fiction." I laugh and his eyes widen. "Fact?"

"Fact," I say, still laughing.

Pulling back to look at me, he shakes his head. "No wonder you wear the boots. Why the hell were you on the roof?"

I sit up straighter. "I like going on the roof to think sometimes, but we're not supposed to have access to it. I'm usually careful about making sure the door doesn't close behind me, but I guess I wasn't careful enough that night. I tried calling my roommate, Violet, but she sleeps through everything."

"Violet," he says the name like it's jogging his memory.

"Um, yeah," I say hesitantly. "She went to our high school." The topic of high school feels like a slippery slope. One missed step and we'll find ourselves reliving the last night we've ever spoken to each other before tonight.

His eyes lock on mine like he might be thinking the same thing. Clearing his throat, he asks, "What did you go up on the roof to think about?"

The way he's looking at me with his full attention is enough to make my entire body hot and cold at the same time.

Like my skin is suddenly overly sensitive to the air circulating around us and my boiling blood beneath its surface.

With a dismissive wave of my hand, I say, "Oh, I don't know. Life, I guess?"

For a moment, I think my answer may disappoint him, but then he says, "Okay, my turn."

I'm relieved by the change of topic. "Shoot."

The side of his mouth quirks. "Have you heard that I almost burned down the school senior year?"

My brain searches for any memory of hearing about this back in the day, but I come up empty. "The school didn't catch fire our senior year."

"Emphasis on *almost*."

"Nope, not true." I shake my head.

Giving me a crooked smile, he says, "You seem sure of yourself."

"Because I am."

Tilting his head, his eyes narrow as he scrutinizes me closer. "And why's that?"

I can't help letting out a laugh. "Because we've been playing this game for a while, and you haven't said a single truth. You've become quite predictable."

He blinks. "Shit, I guess you're right."

I laugh harder, and Aiden eyes me like I'm the funny one.

17

Aiden

Since when am I predictable? Claire should be the predictable one, not me.

She's starting to look at me like Jasmine does, thinking she has me figured out. When Jasmine does it, it just pisses me off, but when Claire looks at me this way, it makes me squirm. I glance around the train but most of the scattered passengers are passed out now—even the cat piss lady.

"I get it," Claire says, pulling my attention back to her. She tilts her chin up, looking pleased with herself. "You don't want me to know the real you."

"I don't give a shit what you know. Ask me anything." I go back to surveying the train as I say it, but there isn't much else to look at. When I reluctantly bring my eyes back to her, she's looking at me like I just gave her a cheat code to bypass all the hardest levels.

Great.

"Anything?"

There's no backing down now. "That's what I said."

"So, we're ditching the game, and I can flat out ask you *anything?*"

I reluctantly nod and try my best not to look as panicked as I feel.

Her fingers tap her chin. "Hmm." She's having way too much fun with this. After thinking for what feels like forever, she says, "What makes you happy?"

I blank. *What the hell?* I expected her to ask me if I ever cheated on a test in school or something—something she could judge me for. I hate the nervous laugh I hear come out of my mouth. "What makes me happy?" When she says nothing and patiently waits for my miraculous answer, I mutter, "Happiness is a delusion."

I guess that disappoints her because the corners of her mouth fall. "No, it's not."

Letting out a sigh, I level with her. "Sure it is. You feel it when you're distracted by something, but when you're left alone with your thoughts, you're just as miserable as everyone else."

Well, she's not looking at me like she has me figured out at least, but now she's staring at me like she's *trying* to figure me out, and it might be worse.

"When's the last time you felt happy?"

This conversation just keeps getting better. "I don't

know, Claire. Why are you asking?"

She shrugs but looks less smug than she did when she asked her first question. "You said I could ask you anything."

Leaning my head back against the seat, I sigh. "Christ." Soft laughter fills my ears, pulling my attention back to her, and I ask, "What the hell is so funny?"

Casually scrolling through her phone, she doesn't even look at me as she answers. "You're clearly such an open book." The corner of her mouth quirks into a half-smile.

Now I feel like a bitch. The last time I was happy? Genuinely happy? My mind surveys the past year. Nothing. I survived this year. It wasn't bad, but it wasn't good.

It was numb.

It was numb because I made it that way, and you can't feel happiness like that.

Not really.

If I'm going to think about the last time I was happy, I'll have to go back further, which I'd rather not do. But as much as I don't want to dive into those memories, Claire is staring at me again, and I know I've already taken too long to answer her question. She doesn't look impatient, though. Her face is calm, her eyes bright as she waits for me to respond. It's getting to the point where I can't hold her gaze without my palms sweating.

Glancing down, I clear my throat and mutter, "It was in Florida."

18

Claire

The last time Aiden was happy was in *Florida?* That's not what I was expecting. Part of me figured he'd say something…well, something less sunny.

Somewhat balking at him, I say, "Um…I know we haven't been on this train together for very long, but from what I've gathered, I thought you *hated* Florida."

He doesn't look at me. "I do."

"Did Mickey Mouse himself kick you out of Disney or something?" I say it in a teasing tone, but the glare I receive shuts me up. Holding my hands up, I backpedal, "Okay, clearly you got burned. I get it." He rolls his eyes so that he's looking straight ahead again, and I realize how my comment sounded. "I just meant—" I groan. "I wasn't trying to make a pun." Aiden finally told me something of substance, and here I am making jokes about getting burned in the Sunshine State.

Kill me now.

When I glance at him again, he's watching me with a subtle hint of amusement. I don't know how he can make me feel completely exposed with just one look, but those eyes pierce into me like nothing I've ever experienced. "Why are you looking at me like that?" I ask.

With a dismissive shake of his head, he mutters, "You're so wound up."

Wound up? I am not.

I'm laid back.

Go with the flow.

Spontaneous.

Did he miss the part where I got on a train and embarked on a trip to Florida?

"I am *not* wound up." I realize I've crossed my arms as I've said it and quickly drop them to look more relaxed.

"Just an observation," is his only response before he casually pulls out his phone.

He doesn't say anything else for a few minutes—neither of us does. It looks like he's texting, and I'm curious to know who he's talking to, but I don't want to come across as nosy. I hate that he thinks I'm uptight—and I hate the fact that I'm dwelling on it even more.

Aiden seems fine with the silence that falls between us, but I don't like it. I want to know more about why he was happy in Florida. What happened on his last trip that was so great? Or not great? I guess if he hates the place now, something must have gone wrong.

But he's not talking to me.

He's texting a mile a minute, and even though I'm extremely casual and laid back, I'm dying to know who he's talking to.

"Who are you texting?" I have no self-control.

He lifts an eyebrow and gives me a sideways glance. "Friends."

I wait for more.

"What?" He leans back slightly. "You said we're going our separate ways once we get there, and I need a place to crash."

I blink. "You have friends in Florida?"

Looking back at his phone, he says, "I used to live there."

Well, I wasn't expecting that. When could he have lived in Florida? It's not like we graduated *that* long ago. If he did live there, it couldn't have been for very long. I assumed that he'd been working since graduation, but I guess I don't know what the past three years have been like for him at all. All I know is that I suddenly want to know a lot more about him.

19

Aiden

"You used to *live* there?"

I knew I shouldn't have said anything.

"When?" She yawns as the word falls from her mouth.

I keep typing my text and ignore her. Ethan is the only one I'm willing to reach out to because he's the only one who isn't annoying. Well, him and Em. Em is too close to what happened, though—she might make it weird.

Out of the corner of my eye, I can see Claire rubbing her hands over her face. I'm not sure if she's frustrated with me or if she's just tired, but let's be real, it's probably both.

"A little over a year ago," I say, still not looking at her. My eyes stay locked on the text I sent to Ethan. I better see those three dots pop up soon.

"What made you move there?"

This is why I shouldn't have said anything. I don't want

to answer these questions, and frankly, I don't owe this girl an explanation. My screen lights up.

Ethan: When will you be here?

I knew he wouldn't ask me why I was coming. I knew he wouldn't make a big deal of it. Thank god for people like Ethan who mind their own business. I need to answer him, but it's hard to do that with her eyes burning into me. Looking up, I say, "Christ, what is it with you and all the questions? Can't I have five minutes to figure out where I'm sleeping tomorrow?"

I look away before I can register more than her eyes widening. She doesn't say anything, and I don't want to think about why she's not calling me an asshole like I deserve, so I take her silence for the blessing it is and keep texting.

My phone lights up again, so I swipe it open.

Chad: Made a group chat since you assholes didn't include me.

I lean my head back and internally groan before answering. I didn't realize Ethan still lived with Chad. Ethan is cool. I like Ethan, and I can't say that about most people. Chad, on the other hand…well, his name is fucking Chad.

Ethan: Sorry. He asked who I was texting.

Chad: Sorry? More like YOU'RE WELCOME. What's this about you coming to town? Time to party????

Taking a deep breath, I let my fingers type a response.

Me: Last minute trip. Didn't plan on it.

Chad: The Natty Shack is back in business!

Ethan: I thought we agreed to stop calling our apartment that.

Chad: Absolutely not.

Chad: How dare you.

Before this turns into an ongoing argument, I get back to the point.

Me: So can I stay with you guys?

Ethan: Yeah. We've got a couch.

Me: I'll take it.

Chad: NATTY SHACK!

Chad: Wait. Does Sam know?

Fucking Chad.

Ethan: Why would you ask that?

Chad: I was just asking!

Ethan: He won't answer, and I'm done texting you when you're in the other room. See you tomorrow, Aiden.

Chad: TOMORROW

Chad: WILL

Chad: BE

Chad: LIT

I suppress a roll of my eyes and turn my phone over. Talking to Chad is like feeding a forest fire. The more you indulge him, the worse he gets.

Something lands on my shoulder, and I look down to find Claire completely passed out, her head leaning into me as her breathing deepens. Another glance at my phone tells me it's just past two. I still can't wrap my head around the fact that I'm sitting next to Claire Ackerman on my way to Florida at two a.m.

I snapped at her.

On the night she got cheated on.

When she's stuck on a train with no one else but the asshole who snapped at her.

I shake the thought from my head. She was annoying, and why does she care anyway? She always has too many questions.

As I look down at her, I can't help noticing how different she is from how I remember. More herself maybe? In high school, she was quiet. This sleeping Claire looks like she could still be that, but there's more to her. The overly determined, uptight, anxious girl she is when she's awake is far from the girl who sat next to me in Bio. This Claire makes me want to stop walking through life numb—and that's fucking terrifying.

20

Claire

Tears stain my cheeks. I keep trying to wipe them away, but based on the way he's looking at me, I know they're still there. He's staring at me with an eyebrow raised like he wants to keep his distance, and it's mortifying. I wish I could disappear. I wish I was anywhere but here. There's yelling in the background. The voices spew hate, and it feels like they're closing in on me.

My hands cover my ears, and I put my head down, trying to drown everything out, but it's no use. I can't take all the shouting. I can't take the noise.

Warm hands cover mine, and my head snaps up to find him staring at me with concern. He doesn't look like he's trying to keep his distance from me at all now, and I can't help wondering if it was all in my head. His blue eyes search mine, worry creasing his brow. "Are you okay?"

I go to answer him, but my voice gets trapped in my throat. Opening my mouth, I try again.

It's no use.

His expression starts to change, his worry shifting back to a face that finds me repulsive. Desperately, I try to talk more. I want to explain so he doesn't think of me this way. My heart races, but the yelling is too loud again, and I can't make it stop. I just want everything to stop. The noise climbs, getting louder until the sound of glass shattering silences everything else.

A jolt of the train wakes me, and for a moment, I'm lost. It's funny how massive events momentarily get wiped away by sleep. My forehead glistens with sweat from my dream, and I wipe it away as I take in my surroundings. First, I'm hit with the realization that it's now bright outside. Then, I take in the fact that I'm on a train. Followed by the feeling of someone next to me—or maybe I'm next to them. I'm the one leaning into their shoulder, after all. A tilt of my head reveals a sleeping Aiden, his face turned toward me as if he had leaned on me just as much as I had on him.

He's peaceful like this.

Less abrasive.

Before I can study his features, memories of the night before flood my mind.

Going home.

Garret.

Shelly.

Mental breakdown.

Bar.

Aiden.

Train.

Florida.

Garret! I never texted him back last night! Dread fills the pit of my stomach like when you forget to submit an assignment on time.

Only worse.

My hands frantically pat the seat around me, scanning for my phone that hopefully hasn't died. Aiden stirs next to me, his eyebrows furrowing before he squints an eye open.

"Seriously? You even wake up like a fucking spaz?"

I narrow my eyes at him but don't have time to comment on his insult. Lifting his arm, I mutter, "I can't find my phone. I had it last night, but I'm not sure where——" Wedged between us, my phone lies in all its glory. I snatch it up and let Aiden's arm fall back against the seat with a thud.

"Jesus, Claire. Where's the fire?" He groans as he rubs a hand over his face.

Please don't be dead. Please don't be dead.

The screen lights up.

Thank you!

My relief nose-dives when I see six unread messages from Garret.

"Shit!" I hiss as my thumb frantically punches in the passcode. "Garret texted me last night, but I never answered. He's probably freaking out." Remembering that his last message accused me of leaving the bar with *some guy* sends another wave of dread over me.

Aiden nonchalantly lifts a brow. "Garret?" My cheeks flush, suddenly embarrassed. I don't like the sound of that name coming out of Aiden's mouth. Aiden and Florida are great distractions because neither of them has anything to do with the guy who broke my heart less than 24 hours ago. "Your ex?"

I manage to look up from my phone long enough to register his face.

He's judging me.

Or pitying me?

It's hard to read his somber expression, but I don't bother wasting time trying to figure it out. Garret is probably worried after I didn't answer him all night. Things may not have ended well between us, but we were still together for over two years. A brief haphazard nod is the best I can offer Aiden before my eyes are glued to the small screen in my hand again.

The messages pick up about an hour after his first text.

Garret: Hello?

Garret: What the actual fuck? You're just going to ignore me now?

Garret: We've been together for over two years! You won't even let me explain? Who are you with??

Garret: You're overreacting. We were watching a fucking movie!

Garret: I watch a movie with a FRIEND and you go home with some guy? We're fucking done.

Garret: I bet you've been spreading your legs for guys at NYU all along. I'll make sure to have a great time with Shelly tonight. Fuck you.

The sides of my temples prickle with sweat, and I'm suddenly aware of the lack of fresh air on this train.

He's mad.

He's *really* mad.

And his comment about Shelly…I'm going to be sick.

Even though I've read through the messages twice, I can't stop staring down at my phone. *How could he say those things to me? Why do I feel like this is all my fault?* Maybe jumping out of the car before he could explain was a little premature?

No.

I can let myself think plenty of things about this, but I won't regret leaving when I did. I'm not the one who cheated. I'm not the one who broke us.

Even if his texts make me feel like I am.

"What's wrong?" Aiden's voice feels far away, and somehow these messages are so much louder.

"Claire?"

Garret wasn't worried—at all. How could someone who's done everything he's done be the same person who said they loved and missed me a few days ago?

"Jesus, Claire." I don't even realize my hands are shaking until Aiden wraps his warm fingers around mine to tilt my phone toward him.

I can't bring myself to look at him, so instead, I keep staring at the now glaring screen tilted away from me. I can't make out the words from here, but it doesn't matter. My memory has no problem displaying the six messages in the front of my mind like a damn PowerPoint. Blinking away the image and the burning threat of tears, I fixate on Aiden's hand around the back of mine, steadying it as he reads. My fingers—and my phone—look small in the frame of his palm, and even though his hands are rough, there's a gentleness to them. The way he cradles my hand in his so carefully almost makes the fact that he's reading my private messages a little less rude.

Almost.

Lifting my gaze, I jolt when I realize he's watching me.

Great.

Here it comes. I don't know what *it* is exactly, but I know it can't be good. He'll say terrible things about Garret, or maybe he'll tell me how stupid I am for dating someone like him. Bracing myself for whatever words are about to fly out of his mouth, I grit my teeth and blink back hot tears, burying them as deep as I can.

"Are you okay?"

His voice is so low that it takes me a second to register that he's not berating me. I don't know if it's Aiden, or if it's the fact that I genuinely expected Garret to be worried about my well-being, but something inside me flips. My emotions fall flat, and I'm surprised that I no longer wish Garret hadn't cheated on me. I don't wish we were still together. I don't even feel like I miss him at this moment. Right now, all I can focus on is how *wrong* I was about him, and if this is the real him, I'm glad to be over a thousand miles away.

Finally looking up at Aiden, I'm met with deep, blue eyes that seem to comfort me and make me restless all at once.

21

Aiden

Those messages have me fuming. If Claire didn't look like a flowerpot half an inch away from falling off a windowsill, I'd probably take her phone and throw it out the window. But I don't want to be the thing that smashes her into a million pieces.

"Um," she hedges as she takes her phone back. She stares down at her asshole ex's texts again before muttering, "I think so."

She's studying the messages. I can tell by her slight frown and furrowed brow that if she wasn't able to recite those texts by heart a minute ago, she can now.

"Claire." I'm not even sure what I'm going to say, but I can't let her drown in those words.

She doesn't look up from her phone when she answers, "Yeah?" She's just scrolling up and down through their text messages like she's trying to find the pivotal point where it all went wrong.

"Claire," I say again.

This time she looks up at me. She's not crying. In fact, she doesn't even look like she's on the verge of tears. Now, her face shows no emotion—which might be worse. My hands are sweating, so I rub them against my jeans and start, "Listen, you shouldn't—"

"I'm not."

My eyebrow lifts.

"I'm not doing whatever you think I am." She sounds so calm; I start to second guess myself.

"Then what are you doing?"

She stares down at the phone for another long moment before turning it over in her lap and looking at me. "I don't know, but I can tell you what I'm not doing." She takes a steadying breath. "I'm not texting him back. I'm not believing him. I'm not wishing we were still together because, clearly, he's not the person I thought he was." Another glance at her phone, and she closes her eyes. "And I'm trying not to picture what he was doing last night."

I wince at her last sentence. "Yeah, that's probably for the best." When she opens her eyes, they've dimmed like I just confirmed all of her deepest fears, but I won't lie to her. The guy is a dick, and the fact that he already had this other girl in his apartment is a pretty clear sign that he wasn't talking out of his ass. "Hey," I say to get her to look at me. "You're better off without him, right?"

She nods and then stares down at her locked phone in her lap. "I know I am."

I can't help analyzing the shit out of her as she sits there, stone-faced. I know that look. That's the look of someone who just overdosed on reality, and now they're going to keep moving the only way they know how: by being numb.

△　△　△

Well, we're in fucking Florida.

She didn't say another word for the last four hours of the trip, and I let the silence swallow her whole. A quiet Claire might be my new least favorite thing, but I couldn't bring myself to do anything about it. She was digesting everything that's happened, and any attempt to distract her from that felt like I was invading something oddly intimate.

As soon as we step off the train, we're met with the warm night air that makes it impossible to know if you're the one sweating, or if everything else is just sweating around you.

One of the many things about Florida I thought I'd never have to relive.

It's after 11 pm, and Ethan and Chad know I'll be at their place soon.

I have to admit, as much as I hated the fact that I got on the damn train, it wasn't as bad as I thought it would be. Considering her ex is a complete jackass, it's probably a good thing that she wasn't sitting alone for twenty-plus hours. The thought of her reaching out to him pisses me off, and a small part of me is glad that I was here to distract her from doing exactly that.

"Well, I guess this is it."

It's the first thing I've heard her say in a few hours, and even though I don't want it to, it disappoints me.

"Yeah," I mutter. I thought I'd be itching to get rid of her, but I'm not. "You've got a place to stay?"

She nods. "I booked an Airbnb, and my Uber is on its way." She doesn't meet my eyes as she says it, and I hate it. I want her to look at me.

As much as I don't want to admit it, we were having fun together—for part of the ride anyway, and I want to see her smile again. I want to be the one to make her smile again.

On second thought, maybe I need some distance from Claire. She's making me feel things that I don't want to feel.

"My car is here," she says quietly as she looks from her phone to the busy street.

That was fast. What are these drivers doing? Waiting around the damn corner? "You sure?" Looking out at the street, I try to follow her gaze to make sure her driver isn't some sketchy bastard.

"Right here." Claire walks to the curb, but I stay where I am. Turning to face me, she already has her hand on the door handle as she says, "Well, it's certainly been interesting."

The driver is a middle-aged woman who looks like she's

made a lifetime of shitty choices that landed her here. I'll take it, though. Better her than some prick college kid who might try to get Claire to go to a party.

I hate this. I hate how awkward this is. Scratching the side of my head, I manage to get out, "It's been something."

This brings a small smile to her lips. "Hey, have you heard that after every soul-crushing breakup comes your next great adventure?"

I force a short laugh. "I have no idea if that's fact or fiction."

Opening the car door, she shrugs. "Neither do I."

And just like that, she's getting into the back of a fucking Ford Focus.

22

Claire

"Claire, wait!"

I'm about to step into the Uber but turn back to find Aiden walking toward me.

"Hey," he says when he reaches me, suddenly looking less sure of himself.

Tilting my head at him, I try to fight my smile as I say, "Hey."

"Give me your phone."

Looks like we're back to being rude again. "Um, why?"

He waves his hand impatiently. "Just give it to me."

Slowly, I reach into the pocket of my dress and hand my phone over to him.

Rolling his eyes, he pushes it back into my hand. "Claire, you have to unlock it."

"Oh, right." I punch in the code and hand it back to him.

"What are you doing?"

He doesn't look up from the phone as he answers. "Giving you my number."

My mouth opens in protest, but he cuts me off before I can say anything.

"Relax, will you? I'm not breaking your precious rule. I know you're on this trip alone, but if you need anything, you should be able to reach at least one person in this garbage state." He finishes saving his number and locks the screen before handing it back to me.

Pocketing my phone, I mutter, "Oh, um, thanks." I'm not even sure why my first reaction was to tell him not to give me his number. It can't hurt to have it saved on my phone.

Aiden steps away from the curb and gives me a casual wave. "Have fun finding your next great adventure, Claire Ackerman."

I go to wave back to him, but he's already turned and started walking the other way. Slowly lowering myself into the car, I can't help staring at my phone screen with mixed feelings. The first thought my phone brings to mind is still Garret and his slew of messages. He hasn't sent me anything since—which I'm grateful for—but my phone was starting to act as a constant reminder of the things he said. All it takes is one swipe to reread and relive one of my lowest moments, and considering I've been doing it all day, I must be a glutton for punishment.

Now, however, as I stare down at the dark screen, I'm

not thinking of Garret. I'm picturing the dark-haired guy who just gave me his number, and instead of feeling pain, I'm struck with a small sense of comfort knowing that he's still within reach.

△ △ △

I love my Airbnb.

The adorable two-bedroom space has tons of windows that I'm sure will flood with natural light in the morning. For now, though, I close the curtains feeling a little paranoid that someone walking the beach might see me. The space overflows with bohemian décor throughout, and I'm definitely taking mental notes for my own apartment. A large circular rug takes up the center of the living space, and I let my bare feet glide against its many tassels as I sit on the couch and take it all in.

I did it.

I'm in Florida!

Well, I guess you can say Aiden and I did it.

I glance at my phone on the rattan end table next to me, half expecting it to light up with Aiden's name until I remember he doesn't have my number. I can't help wondering what he's doing right now. Hopefully, he's having a great time with his friends, but knowing Aiden, he's probably sulking on their couch, determined to hate every minute of it.

The thought makes me laugh a little to myself.

Getting up from the couch, I stretch my arms overhead and pad across the oak floors to the bathroom. I had to stop at the convenience store on the way here to grab a few essentials, so the brand new toothbrush and toothpaste are still in a plastic bag on the bathroom counter. Fishing out everything I need, I change into my new oversized FLORIDA t-shirt. The store didn't have much, and I wanted something comfortable to sleep in, but this shirt is hideous. The cartoon alligator wearing sunglasses on it takes tacky-tourist attire to a whole new level.

Grateful for a chance to brush my teeth after sleeping on a train last night, I spend a little extra time on my oral hygiene before plopping back down on the couch and streaming Across the Universe. It's one of my favorite movies, and tonight is all about comfort. There's something about Jim Sturgess singing Strawberry Fields Forever that makes my relationship problems fade away.

23

Aiden

They threw a fucking party.

Well, to be unmistakably clear, Chad was the one with the bright idea, and the cherry on top is that he wanted it to be a damn surprise. Now I'm exhausted, in fucking Florida, and the couch I'm supposed to sleep on has seven people I've never met sitting on it.

Ethan knows I'm pissed, but Chad is too dense to see how much I want to kill his ass right now.

I'll just stand here and drink my beer until this shit is over.

"Who wants another shot!" Chad calls out to the party where he's answered by a chorus of enthusiastic whoops and hollers. The thing about Chad is as much as he annoys the shit out of me, everyone else *loves* him. He's the one every girl wants attention from, every guy wants to be bros with, the life of the party, and I'll never understand it.

He doesn't annoy me because he's good-looking, or because he has a lot of friends. He annoys me because he's an idiot and no one seems to notice. They're too busy getting caught up in whatever bullshit good time he's showing them.

"Aiden, you better take a shot!" Chad calls out to me from the kitchen.

Raising my beer, I give him a nod and say, "Why don't you do one for me?"

"Oh, man," Chad drawls out the words like I'm twisting his arm. Looking down at the two pretty girls next to him, he grins. "Two shots? I don't want to get myself into trouble."

I shake my head because that's exactly what he wants. Luckily, he's already forgotten that I'm here, and he's laughing as the two girls urge him to take a double.

With both hands up in the air, he says, "Okay, okay. How am I supposed to say no to those gorgeous faces?"

The girls look at each other and beam like they couldn't be more thrilled to share his attention.

I'm still watching him somehow manage to flirt with both of them at the same time when Ethan comes up to me. I can tell just by looking at him that he's still dating Em. He hasn't talked to another girl all night, his clothes are nicer than anything he could have picked out himself, and his once wild afro is now trimmed with a flawless fade. Ink covers most of his arms, and knowing Em, she probably did most of the work herself. She's always put a lot of effort into appearances, but as an artist, I can't fault her for it. Hell, she tried to dress me up a few times until she realized I wouldn't play along.

"Yeah, he hasn't changed much," Ethan says as he joins me in watching Chad.

I force a laugh. "He hasn't changed at all. Aren't we getting too old for parties like this?"

"It's usually not like this. I think he was just excited you were coming. Usually, we just hang with Em. She's tattooing tonight, but she'll be home later."

The fact that Chad was *that* excited to see me makes me feel like shit. I probably could have gone my whole life never seeing him again and not thought twice about it. "She lives here now?"

"Yeah, it's new, but it's been great having her here," Ethan says with a nod.

The two started dating around the time I moved here, and Em is one hell of a tattoo artist. They're one of those couples you know will last with just one look. It's crazy how solid they are. "It'll be good to see her again," I say without thinking.

"Yeah." Ethan shifts his weight slightly. "So, um, have you reached out to—"

"No."

"Oh."

"Yeah."

He takes another sip of his beer. "Okay."

An all too familiar weight flops down on my shoulder. Before I even have time to look, Chad's voice rings through my ears singing, "Natty Shaaaaaack is fucking baaaaacckk!" I would shrug him off, but there's no point. He looks down at my beer and practically jumps back anyway. Gaping at the glass bottle in my hand, he points and utters, "You're not drinking Natty?"

"You do know Natty Lite is disgusting, right?" Ethan chimes in.

"It's fermented rice water," I add.

Chad's committed, though. Shaking his head, he says, "No, no, no, no, no. We *always* drank Natty in the Natty Shack. Come on, man!"

A quick sideways glance makes me point out, "Ethan isn't drinking it."

Chad's head whips around to his roommate. "Not you, too!"

Ethan just shrugs and takes another sip of his IPA. "We're not as broke as we once were. We've got options now."

"Weren't you just doing shots in the kitchen anyway?" I ask.

Clapping me on the shoulder again, he says, "Oh! That reminds me! Aiden, this is Daniella." Gesturing to one of the girls I saw him talking to earlier, he waves her over and adds, "Daniella! Meet Aiden!" In a strangely smooth move, he manages to let go of Ethan and put his other arm around the girl so that he's standing between us. "You two would make a *beautiful* couple. I'm just saying." Then he breaks away from us and slithers back into the party like the snake he is.

As soon as he looks over his shoulder, grinning, I flip him the bird, but it only makes his mischievous grin widen as he gives me a reassuring thumbs up. I look for Ethan, but he seems to have found something better to do because he's suddenly nowhere to be found.

Fucking Chad.

With no other distractions, I'm forced to look at the girl in front of me—Daniella. Her long blond hair could probably rival Jasmine's, and so could her body if I'm being honest. But that doesn't change the fact that Chad is a dick for making this fucking awkward.

Letting out a sigh, I surrender and say, "So, how do you know Chad?"

She blushes and tucks her hair behind her ear before smiling up at me through her thick lashes and saying, "I mean…we've known each other for a while."

Of course, they have.

And by the way she's biting back a smile, I'm pretty sure they've *known* each other in a variety of places and positions.

I somehow manage to hide my real opinion and say, "Nice," as I finish off the last of my beer.

This is going to be a long night.

24

Claire

My phone vibrates on the wood coffee table, waking me up. I started to fall asleep about halfway through the movie and turned it off, making the room nearly pitch black. I have no idea what time it is, but it feels like I've been out for a while.

Too tired to sit up, I reach for my phone and tilt it toward me. The glow of the display screen burns my eyes, making me squint to see who could be calling this late.

Garret

You'd think the name itself just bit me the way I snatch my hand back, leaving my phone to buzz and glow in the otherwise dark room. With unblinking eyes, I watch until the screen eventually goes black, leaving me in complete darkness.

Until he starts calling again.

25

Aiden

Daniella tastes like cigarettes and Smirnoff Ice.

I don't even know why I let her lead me out onto this balcony. We're the only two people out here, and as soon as we were out of sight from the rest of the party, this girl fucking pounced. Now she has me up against the wall, and her tongue is in my mouth.

There may have been a time when this shit turned me on, but those days are behind me. I'm not in the business of random hookups anymore, and there's no going back. A year ago, this was how I coped. The less I knew about the girl, the better, but eventually, it gets old. Eventually, it doesn't matter how hot she looks or what she's willing to do because, to a point, they're all the same.

I wonder if Daniella needs to cope, and that's why she led

me out here. Maybe there's something she's using me to forget.

Maybe she's like Claire.

My mind pictures Claire acting like Daniella—throwing herself at some piece of shit Floridian. Her fingers knotted in his shirt as he feels every part of her through the thin material of that sundress.

As soon as the image comes to mind, I'm turned off even more. I gently put a hand up, creating space between us.

"I can't do this."

She pulls back, her brows furrowed in confusion. I'm sure she rarely gets turned down—if ever. "Why? Do you have a girlfriend or something?" I open my mouth to answer, but she cuts me off. "Because it's okay if you do. I have a boyfriend, but he lives in another city, so it doesn't count."

For fuck's sake.

Daniella is definitely not like Claire.

26

Claire

I'm frozen in place, his name taunting me in huge letters on the screen as the answer bar dances below it.

It's hard for me to understand what I'm feeling. On the train, I had such a sense of resolve…but that was before he called. Anxiety fills the pit of my stomach, but there's a smaller, much quieter part of me that's a little bit glad he's calling.

Not in a, *I'm so glad you called, I've been wanting to talk to you* sort of way, but maybe in a, *I'm glad you're thinking about me* way. Garret should be thinking about me—he should feel some sort of remorse for what he did.

The phone goes dark again, and my lungs remember how to breathe. My shoulders drop as my body releases some of its tension, but I still can't take my eyes off my phone.

It stays dark.

My breathing gets easier, and I wipe my now sweating palms on my oversized t-shirt. Reaching for my phone, I look down at it in still trembling hands to see the 2 Missed Calls from Garret notification.

I wonder what he wanted.

I wonder what he's doing right now.

I wonder why he would call me so late.

There's no time to wonder more because his name pops up for the third time, and it takes more effort not to drop my phone than I'm proud to admit. Squeezing it tightly in my still damp hand, I hold my breath as my thumb swipes across the bottom of the screen.

27

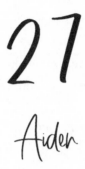

Aiden

Daniella stares at me expectantly, and I finally remember I'm supposed to answer her.

"Uh, no. I don't have a girlfriend." She hasn't given me enough space to get away from her, so I'm still just standing awkwardly up against the wall. Backed into a fucking corner.

Apparently, this was the wrong answer to give. She pops a hand on her hip and looks me up and down. "Are you gay?"

For a moment, I consider saying yes for the sake of getting her away from me, but not before my lips twitch. It takes a lot of confidence to assume the *only* reason a guy doesn't want to be with you, is that he'd rather be with another guy. With a light laugh, I shake my head. "No."

Her eyes narrow like she's trying to decide if I'm lying. I have a feeling that regardless of how this conversation goes, she'll go back to her friends and tell them I'm in the closet.

"So, what is it then?"

The way she sways as she asks tells me she's drunk, and I'm way too sober for this shit. I hate this part. The part where I have to be an asshole because I'm too honest for my own good. "I'm just not interested."

Her eyes widen, and I know I've insulted her. "Seriously?"

With tight lips, I give an uncomfortable nod of my head.

Luckily, she rolls her eyes and leaves, and I'm left alone for the first time tonight.

Alone and thinking about Claire.

It annoys me that she's still on my mind, but I can't help wondering what she's doing right now. I keep picturing her making out with some guy in one of these shitty dive bars, and the thought alone is almost enough to send me looking for her.

I won't.

But that doesn't mean I don't think about it.

28

Claire

"Claire?"

Garret's voice is soft.

Calm.

Familiar.

And I hate the mixture of feelings that wash over me at the sound of it.

"Uh, hi." I hate how small my voice sounds.

"Are you okay?" I hate how that question makes me long for his comfort.

"Yeah." I'm not sure how I can hate that one word, but I do.

"I'm worried about you." That sentence alone makes my eyes burn.

Staring up at the ceiling, I take a steadying breath and try to clear my thoughts. "You didn't sound worried in your texts."

There's a pause before he answers, but that pause feels like an eternity. "I was mad."

His response makes me roll my eyes, and I suddenly feel like I have my bearings again. His voice was barely above a whisper and my suspicions get the best of me. "Why are you being so quiet?"

"What do you mean?"

My brows furrow and I'm suddenly not sure if he's actually calm or if he's trying to avoid being overheard. "Where's Shelly?"

He scoffs on the other end of the phone. "Seriously, Claire? I love *you*. Shelly is just a friend. *Was* just a friend. I told her we can't hang out anymore because it obviously upset you."

I hate that I want to believe him.

"Garret, please don't lie to me." I want to sound stronger, but I sound like I'm begging him.

"Baby, I'm not lying. This is all in your head. You're making yourself go crazy over something that doesn't even matter." His voice is so smooth on the other end of the phone.

Too smooth.

"Something that doesn't even matter? You had a girl in your apartment. You had your arm around her—"

"No, I didn't."

I try to think back and picture what I saw when I opened the door to his apartment. I could have sworn the two of them were snuggled up close and that he had his arm around her.

Before I can think of a response, he goes on to say, "You're so obsessed with this idea of me cheating on you that you're remembering things wrong. We weren't even sitting close enough for me to reach her."

Were they sitting that far apart? My head throbs, unable to keep up with my swarming thoughts.

"Plus, you left the bar with some guy anyway. What do you care?"

His accusation feels like a punch to the gut. "I didn't leave the bar with anyone." It's not a lie. I left the bar on my own, and Aiden followed.

I hadn't really thought about Aiden since we split ways, but I can't help wondering what he would think of me sitting here, talking to Garret on the phone.

He'd probably keep his mouth shut.

But those damn eyes would tell all.

Garret's soft voice brings me back to our conversation. "That's not what I heard."

"Why are you talking so quietly?" I ask again.

Intuition is a funny thing. You can want to believe everything a person says, cling to their every word and want to see the best in them, but there are some things that your gut just knows—even when your head pulls out all the stops to convince you otherwise.

And even though I can't see Garret, I somehow know that he's at his apartment with Shelly sleeping in the next room. I know he's talking to me in the furthest corner from her and looking over his shoulder every few seconds to make sure he doesn't wake her. I can see it like a movie in my head, playing out in real-time as he continues to whisper all the things I want to hear.

Garret sighs into the other end of the phone. "What do you want me to do? Yell?"

"Yeah."

"What?" He practically laughs out the word.

"I want you to yell," I say flatly.

He scoffs. "I'm not going to yell at you over the phone. I'm not that kind of guy."

That statement gets to me because there have been multiple times throughout our relationship when he was exactly that kind of guy. "Garret, yell."

His voice changes into a harsh whisper, but he keeps his volume low. "I don't have to prove anything to you, okay? Get over yourself, Claire."

A tear escapes the corner of my eye, and I quickly wipe it away like I can erase that it ever happened. I don't want to cry over him. I don't want to cry over anyone who acts like this, but he just confirmed what I was suspecting, and it's more painful than I want to admit.

"I have to go, Garret."

His fast talking starts on the other end of the phone, but I hang up before he gets the chance to spin more lies. Glancing around the small Airbnb, I'm reminded of how alone I am again. Only this time, my solitude doesn't feel like something to celebrate.

29

Aiden

"Hey, man, what the hell did you say to Daniella?"

Well, there goes my solitude. Chad pokes his head out from the sliding glass door, his sandy blonde hair falling to one side. He looks like he spends most of his time at the beach. I wouldn't say Florida suits most people, but for whatever reason, it seems to suit Chad just fine.

Leaning my head against the outside wall, I mutter, "What did she say?"

He steps out onto the balcony with me and shakes his head. "She didn't tell me. She just said, 'What's wrong with your friend?' on her way out." Chad laughs to himself before looking over at me. "So, what the hell is wrong with you, man?"

I can't fight my smile. Chad's charm even gets to me sometimes. I shrug. "I wasn't feeling it."

His eyes widen. "Have you *seen* her? She's well above the Natty Shack standard." He leans against the wall next to me and crosses his arms. "You messed up."

Staring out over the balcony, I take in the view before answering. You can't see the beach from here, but when the town is quiet, you can hear it in the distance. There's a strip of shops, bars, and restaurants within walking distance, and once you get past that, you'll find the ocean. "Maybe."

I don't look at him, but I can feel him scrutinizing me. "Who is she?"

"Who is who?" I ask, finally giving him my attention.

"Who's the reason you didn't get with Daniella?"

I look away from him again because this is the type of shit that annoys me. "There is no who."

He's still staring at me, the tiny lightbulb in his brain flickering.

"Wait a minute…" he says like he's a damn detective on SVU, but I already know where he's going with this, so I cut him off.

"No."

"You don't even know what I was going to say!" He steps in front of my view, ruining the last good thing about this balcony.

"Yes, I do, and the answer is no." I want to go inside to get away from him, but there are just more people in there I'd rather not talk to.

"Alright, man. If you say so…" He takes a step back, and

I hope he's about to go inside.

"I do."

Holding his hand up to his ear in the shape of a phone, he says, "We could call her up, you know. Have a little reunion sesh."

I give him the finger. "Go inside."

He laughs but does as I say. Before closing the sliding door, he can't help getting the last word in. In a rushed voice, he spits out, "I always thought you guys were cute together!" before slamming the door and disappearing into the party.

Fucking Chad.

I pull out my phone but there are still no messages from Claire. I should have figured as much. She made it clear that she wanted to do this on her own—whatever *this* is. I'm not sure how a shitty trip to Florida is expected to get you over a breakup, but then again, I did worse things after mine. She is uptight…maybe Florida will help her let loose a little. Maybe she's already having fun and moving on, and maybe I should just shut up and be happy for her.

30

Claire

It's taking everything in me not to cry.

Garret hasn't called again, which I know is a good thing, but it doesn't necessarily feel good. I think it's safe to say our relationship is officially over. I wouldn't call that last phone call closure, but it's probably the closest thing I'll get to it.

My Airbnb has two bedrooms, so I got to take my pick of where I would sleep, but both beds have light bedding on them. The blankets here are so thin.

Probably because this is Florida.

And Florida is hot.

But when you're lonely and sad, sometimes it's nice to wrap yourself in a thick blanket. Sometimes it's nice to let a heavy quilt hug you and swallow up all your worries. I miss my bed at home. I miss Violet.

There's no way she'd let me wallow. She's not the wallowing type. She'd have had me up, dressed, and out on the town before I would have been able to protest. Then Garret would have called me while we were out at a club, and I would have tried to hide my phone from Violet because *she* would have wanted to talk to him.

Pulling the blanket up around me a little tighter, I smile at the thought.

As much as I miss her, I'm glad that I'm here. I'm not exactly the nightclub type, and going to one when I'm on the verge of tears sounds terrible. There will be plenty of time to go clubbing once I get back to New York. For now, I'll just stay wrapped in this wispy blanket and try to get some sleep.

Opening my phone, I click on my contacts and see Aiden's name. Knowing he's here gives me a sense of comfort, and I can't help wondering what he's doing. I'm tempted to message him, but I'm not sure if it's because I actually want to talk to him or because he's my closest ally right now.

He's the only person who knows what happened.

He's the only person who knows I'm even here.

31

Aiden

The blinding morning sun makes me squint, and I have a brief moment of forgetting where I am, but there's only one place that would have the audacity to be this bright so early.

Fucking Florida.

I ended up falling asleep in the hammock on the balcony because the party wouldn't end. Luckily, it was cool out, so I didn't spend all night sweating my ass off. I need a shower, though, and I know it's only a matter of minutes before it gets to be hotter than hell out here.

My phone nearly slips out of the hammock as I try to sit upright, but I manage to catch it.

Still no text from Claire.

I wish that wasn't the first thing I noticed. There's a text from Mike and one from Jasmine, both making sure I'm alive.

Well, Jasmine wants to make sure I'm alive. Mike just

wants to make sure the state of Florida is still intact and that I haven't Godzilla-ed the place yet—his words.

I shoot them both a quick response and groan as I get out of the hammock. There's no graceful way to get out of a fucking hammock. I feel like a damn turtle stuck on its back, and I'm glad no one is awake this early to witness it. Once my feet are on solid ground, I stretch my arms overhead and stare out at the balcony view. Soft orange and yellow hues make everything look warmer. The only movement on the streets below comes from the early risers walking their dogs, riding bikes, and doing whatever else mentally stable people do this early. A few men walk toward the beach with buckets and fishing gear in hand, and I sort of envy them. Not the fishing part. I don't give a fuck about fishing, but waking up early on a Saturday morning to go sit by the water with a fishing pole seems like something only happy people do. I can't picture someone who hates the world packing up a tackle box and a cooler as they start their day.

Leaning my arms on the railing, I stay a little longer. Nothing is waiting for me in the Natty Shack. Chances are the guys aren't even awake yet, and this view isn't something to rush.

I wonder what view Claire is waking up to this morning.

Hopefully, it's one like mine.

I think she'd enjoy it.

32

Claire

My toes sink into the sand with each step, and I love it. I've been out and about all day, alternating from enjoying the beach with a good book, to weaving in and out of all the little shops near the pier. The only negative to this trip so far has been having to buy *everything*. Coming to Florida empty-handed probably wasn't the best idea. Today alone I've purchased sandals, a bathing suit, shorts and a t-shirt, a beach bag, sunglasses, sunblock, Maybe Someday by Colleen Hoover, coffee, a disappointing bagel and egg sandwich, and now I'm waiting at a food truck on the beach for a shrimp wrap.

That's all I can think of right now. Point being, traveling unprepared is expensive.

But worth every penny.

"Claire!"

My head snaps up to see the man in the food truck smiling at me. Slipping on my sandals for the sake of having one less thing to hold, I pick up my order from the truck window and find a seat on a shaded bench. The sun shines through the tree branches overhead creating a dancing light show on my legs. I think it's the little things like this that make Florida feel kind of magical. Could this happen to me in Central Park? Absolutely. But there's something serene about the slower pace of a Florida beach.

Florida living is leisure living, and there's nothing leisurely about New York City.

I've been leisure-living all day, though, and I'm starting to look for something more. Being alone can be a great way to recharge…but it can start to feel like you're the only person in the world.

I'm getting to that point.

This morning I dreamt of loud party music, piercing blue eyes, and shouting again. Even when I'm awake, that night has crept into my thoughts more frequently lately. Seeing Aiden seems to have opened pandora's box, and the memories I've tried hard to forget now demand my attention.

Speaking of Aiden, my phone still showed his contact info when I woke up. I guess I fell asleep staring at his name last night…which is weird. Something I'm glad he'll never know.

Taking a bite of my wrap—which is delicious—I pull out my phone again and open my contacts. Scrolling down to the bottom of the alphabet, I pause at Violet's name.

I *should* call her, and part of me wants to, but another part of me isn't ready to divulge everything that's happened. The thought of saying some of it out loud again is enough to make my stomach drop.

I quickly abandon the thought of calling her and scroll to the beginning of the alphabet instead. Aiden's name sits at the top of the list, and my thumb hovers over it. I don't know why I feel nervous to reach out to him. He's the one who gave me his number in the first place, but my hands start to clam up as I type out a message.

33

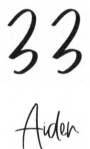

Aiden

Claire: Have you heard that Florida is responsible for 60% of the nation's shark attacks?

Of all the things for Claire to text me, this wasn't what I was expecting. I'm considering how to respond when another text from her comes in.

Claire: It's true. I looked it up before getting in the water.

My lips twitch with a smile as I text her back.

Me: Of course, you did.

I wait for those three dots to appear, but there's nothing. After a few seconds, I send another text.

Me: How was your first night? As liberating as you thought it would be?

"Who's that?"

My head snaps up to find Ethan casually looking at me. Em and Chad are both staring, too. We decided to come to their favorite Tex-Mex place for lunch, so now we're sitting out on the front patio of the restaurant.

"Yeah, who is that?" Chad echoes.

"No one," I say as I set down my phone and go back to eating.

Em and Ethan seem satisfied enough with that response, but of course, Chad can't keep his mouth shut.

"Whoever it is, you put down your burrito for them. You don't put down your burrito to answer a text unless it's from *somebody.*"

Swallowing my bite, I mutter, "Maybe I just needed a break from my burrito."

Chad's eyes widen. "Bruh, no way. Burritos are what I live for."

"Chad, you're just jealous because he wouldn't have put down his burrito to answer a text from *you.*" Em winks at me before taking another bite, ignoring the dramatic look of offense on Chad's face. She's dyed her hair since the last time I saw her. It used to be blonde, but now it's a vibrant red. Like Ethan, she's covered in more tattoos. I guess that's to be expected with her line of work.

Chad snaps his fingers. "Ethan, control your woman."

"She calls the shots," Ethan says with a shrug of his shoulders.

Em playfully sticks her tongue out at Chad. I like Em. She's always been cool. She's one of those girls who can easily hang with the guys without making it feel like you're no longer hanging with the guys.

Claire: It was good. How are your friends?

I stare at her text for a moment. There's nothing wrong with it, but at the same time, there's something I don't like about it. *It was good* doesn't tell me much, and Claire usually doesn't have a problem sharing. So either something happened that she's embarrassed about, it was a bad night, or it was a great night, but she doesn't want me to know about it.

Or maybe it was just good.

Christ, she's got me over-analyzing a fucking text message.

"What do you guys think, tiki tonight?" Em asks as she stands up from the table to throw her trash away.

"I'm down," Ethan says.

Chad claps his hands together. "Hell yeah!"

They all look at me, so I nod and say, "Sounds good," before texting Claire.

Me: They're good. Want to meet us at the tiki bar tonight?

Why did I just do that?

I'm practically on the edge of my seat as I wait for her to answer.

The three dots appear, so I know she's typing, but then they go away and my heart sinks.

Then there's nothing.

The dots finally appear again, and I get her response.

Claire: Sure.

34

Claire

My nerves start to get to me as I get ready to go out with Aiden and his friends. I know what would have happened if I had said no, though. I would have ended up staying in tonight and watching another one of my favorite movies to try and distract myself from my new reality.

Going out with Aiden and his friends is probably a better idea.

My Airbnb has a washer and dryer, so my sundress from yesterday is clean. I know it's the last thing he saw me in, but I'm not buying another outfit for the sake of Aiden Lewis. I pair my dress with my new sandals, leave my hair down, and head out the door.

35

Aiden

We're sitting at a picnic-style table with a straw umbrella over-head, but I haven't told them Claire is coming. They'd only grill me with questions about who she is to me and how I know her—neither of which I want to answer. Plus, Chad is a nosy asshole, and I know he'd make a big deal out of something that is definitely not a big deal.

"What are you looking at?"

Speaking of the nosy asshole, I didn't realize I was staring at the front entrance and quickly take another sip of beer before looking at him. "What do you want me to do? Stare at your ugly mug?"

Chad gives me a taunting smile that makes me wish I would have sat across from Ethan instead. Practically grinning, he says, "Don't hate me because I'm beautiful."

"Hey, guys. This is Lauren," Em says as she brings over

a pretty brunette. "I just met her at the bar, and she's new to town! She's here with her roommate, but she sounds like a bitch." Em shrugs it off and takes a seat, leaving Lauren to stand there awkwardly.

Ethan looks up at his girlfriend's new friend. "Is that true, Lauren? Is your roommate a bitch?"

The poor girl immediately turns pink. "Oh, um. We just don't really know each other yet. I'm here for the summer term, and she doesn't seem interested in doing anything with me. I don't even know where she went." She looks around the bar before turning back to us with an apologetic smile.

While she's not looking, Chad stares at me with wide eyes and mouths, *"Mine."*

I give him a thumbs up with as much enthusiasm as I can muster and get up for another beer from the bar. "Nice meeting you, Lauren," are my only parting words.

The tiki bar isn't packed, but the place will get busier as the night goes on. For now, though, it's easily noticeable when someone chooses to stand right next to me among the empty barstools.

"Can I have a sangria?"

I know that voice.

Turning to her gives me deja vu because she's wearing the same dress, and for some reason, that makes me happier than I've been all day. Seeing *her* makes me happier than I've been all day. Looking down, my face falls. "No boots?"

Extending one of her feet to show off her new shoes, she

shrugs. "I thought these might be more appropriate."

I nod. "Save the boots for your night hikes."

She presses her lips together, trying to fight her smile. "I was not hiking that night."

"Could have fooled me," I say casually.

She looks different.

Holy hell does she look different.

I don't even know how, but damn. If Florida has ever done anything right, it's whatever it did to Claire Ackerman.

Her hair looks lighter like it's been naturally brightened by the sun, and her entire body is covered in a warm, glowing tan. The straps of her sundress don't line up with where her bathing suit straps were, putting a couple of tan lines on display, and I don't think I've ever been more thankful for anything in my life.

Taking a sip of her drink, she tucks a strand of hair behind her ear. "So, uh, where are your friends?"

Of course. She probably thinks I tricked her into coming here alone or some shit. Gesturing behind me, I say, "Our table is over there."

I can't stop staring at her.

The sun even brought out a few freckles on her nose.

"Shouldn't we go over there, then?" She's staring at me like I'm an idiot.

Probably because I am an idiot. Why am I drooling over her? What the hell is wrong with me? Collecting myself, I say, "Right this way," and extend my hand out in front of me so she can take the lead.

36

Claire

Each step toward the table makes me wonder if I should have stayed home. It's been a long time since I've been introduced to new people. At school, I never went out much because it always ended up causing a fight between Garret and me. At a certain point, it just wasn't worth it. So, most of my college experience has been movie nights with Violet or staying in while she goes out with her friends from the Art program.

"Everyone, this is Claire." Aiden quickly introduces me before taking a seat, and I follow his lead. He gestures to the rest of the group. "Claire, everyone."

Forcing a smile, I try my best to hide how out of place I'm feeling because they're all looking at me like they had no idea I'd be joining them. There are two girls and two guys, and their eyes keep jumping between Aiden and me.

Just as I'm about to squirm, a pretty redhead covered in

tattoos reaches across the table to extend her hand. "I'm Emily." After shaking my hand, she sits back and gestures to the guy who sits next to her. "And this is my boyfriend, Ethan."

Ethan gives me a small wave. The frames of his large glasses are clear, and there's a quiet calmness about him that makes me immediately take a liking to him.

Emily gestures to the other girl with long, brunette hair and says, "This is Lauren. We just met her, but apparently, her roommate is a bitch."

Feeling a little more at ease now that I know I'm not the only new person here, I say, "Nice to meet you," to all of them. I look over at the last guy who hasn't introduced himself yet, but he seems to be having a hushed conversation with Aiden. It only lasts a second once they both feel the rest of the table staring at them.

Clearing his throat, the tall, muscular guy extends his hand to me. "Chad, and I'm sorry for gawking at you when you walked up. I just didn't realize Aiden had any friends other than us."

I can't help laughing as I say, "That's okay."

Without missing a beat, Aiden looks at Chad and says, "Oh, you thought I was your friend?" He looks down at his beer before raising his eyebrows and adding, "That's embarrassing."

We all laugh, but Chad doesn't seem to mind being the brunt of the joke.

"Don't listen to him," Chad says as he puts his arm around Aiden. "We're thick as thieves. In fact, he loves me so much he's about to buy me a beer."

"Absolutely not." There's no emotion on Aiden's face, but I can't tell if he's trying to be funny or if he really doesn't like Chad.

"Oh, you absolutely are! Come on, grump-ass." Chad gets up from the table and shakes Aiden's shoulder to follow.

I have to admit, I'm impressed with Chad's confidence. Aiden doesn't look like he's about to get up and follow him, but that doesn't stop him from turning and walking toward the bar like he expects Aiden to do as he says.

All eyes are on Aiden.

He seems to have a silent conversation with Ethan because, after a long look, he sighs and gets up from the table to head to the bar.

"What was that about?" I ask the rest of the group.

Emily pops a fry into her mouth. "When it comes to Chad, none of us really know."

37

Aiden

Chad's waiting for me when I get to the bar, so I start by saying, "I'm not buying you shit."

Waving his hand in the air, he mutters impatiently, "I know. I know." He goes on to say, "But how do you know Claire? Do you know her? Or do you *know* her?"

I wish I could pretend that I didn't know what he was talking about, but instead, I sigh and say, "I just know her." He does a small fist-pump in the air that makes me somehow like him less than I already did. "I thought you were into Lauren."

He nods his head too many times as he thinks over his new dilemma. "Lauren's hot, for sure. But like...have you *seen* Claire? What's her story? Single? Fair game? You want dibs?"

I hate that he just used Claire and *dibs* in the same thought, so my immediate reaction is to shake my head no.

He furrows his brow. "What are you saying no to? She's not single? Not fair game? Don't want dibs?"

He said it again. Feeling defensive, I mutter, "I don't want dibs."

Clapping me on the shoulder, he practically yells, "I love that you came to visit!"

Without so much as a second glance, Chad saunters back to our table, looking like he's a foot taller.

What the fuck just happened?

When Chad sits at the table again, he immediately strikes up a conversation with Claire. She looks over her shoulder and scans the bar until she finds me. Tilting her head, she gives me a questioning look like she wants to know why I'm still standing here.

I don't know why I'm still standing here.

All I know is that, after talking to Chad, I think I have chest pain. I don't want to care. Claire needs a Chad. She needs a meaningless distraction that's going to get her through a hard breakup. She needs someone to hit on her and tell her she's pretty, to momentarily excite her so that she isn't feeling so down, to want to kiss her with no expectations.

I force my mind to stop there because I know that's not all Chad wants to do.

Ignoring the sudden pit in my stomach, I head back to the table and take a seat next to Lauren. The last thing I want is to listen to Chad hit on Claire for the rest of the night, but even though I'm at the opposite end of the table now, my ears strain to listen to their conversation.

"So, do you live with Chad and Ethan?" Lauren asks as she stares at me all bright-eyed.

I *should* want to talk to her.

Trying to refocus, I say, "No, I'm visiting from New York."

I didn't think it would be possible, but her eyes seem to shine brighter. "The Big Apple! Oh, I've *always* wanted to go. What's your favorite part of The City?"

She says *the city* like it's a movie title or some shit, and I don't want to be the one to crush her dreams. The city is a fucking dump, but instead of saying that, I just shrug and say, "I'm more upstate."

She sits back a little, and I know I've lost some of her interest. She's polite about it, though. "Oh, I'm sure it's beautiful."

"It is." I mean it, too. I'd much rather be surrounded by winding roads and mountains than concrete blocks and overflowing trashcans. I feel obligated to ask her about her life now, so I say, "Are you liking college here so far?" She tilts her head back and forth like she doesn't want to say what's really on her mind. After a moment, I add, "I hate Florida, and your roommate sounds like a piece of work, so don't worry about offending my opinion of this shithole."

She laughs and then grabs my arm. "Okay, well in that case, yeah, Florida sucks. Like really sucks."

I find myself smiling. Maybe Lauren won't be such bad

company after all.

38

Claire

I've just finished telling Chad how I know Aiden and why we're both in Florida.

He might be in shock.

He's staring at me with his mouth open.

"So, yeah…" I say in an attempt to make things less uncomfortable. "Now we're both here, but I'm not sure how long either of us will stay. I'll probably have to get back after this weekend."

Blinking, he shakes his head. "You rode a train with him for almost *thirty hours,* and you somehow made it out alive?"

I laugh and sneak a glance at Aiden. He's talking to Lauren at the end of the table, and he's *smiling.* The dimple in his cheek is showing, and I can't seem to tear my eyes away. Even if he wasn't nice to look at, the sight of him happy still catches me off guard, and I'd probably find myself staring regardless.

Looking back at Chad, I just laugh and say, "Oh, come on. He's not so bad."

Chad looks over at Aiden, too. "Yeah." He studies him for a moment before looking back at me and playfully whispering, "He's worse." Before I have time to respond, he puts a hand on my leg. "Hey! You should stay with us! There's plenty of room at the Natty Shack."

"Oh," I say, looking down at my knee where his hand rests. The gesture took me by surprise, and I instinctively shift away from it. "That's okay. I already have a place not too far from here."

"Are you sure?" Chad leans in and drags out the question like he's trying to entice me. "It's always a party at Natty."

"Why do you call it that?" I ask. Partying is the furthest thing from my mind right now. My quiet Airbnb gets better and better the longer I talk to this guy.

"Because, for a while, all we could afford to drink was Natty Light, and we drank *a lot* of it. There were always a ton of empty cardboards from the 24 packs lying around, so when I accidently kicked a hole in the wall, we just stuck a flattened case over it."

"You accidentally kicked a hole in the wall? How?" I can't fight the smile in my voice.

"I can't tell you that," he says, turning serious.

I gape at him. "You can't preface the entire story with you kicking a wall and not tell me why you kicked a wall." I think the sangria is doing a great job of soothing some of my social anxiety. It's either that, or Aiden's friends are easier to talk to than I thought they'd be.

"Is he telling you how the Natty Shack was born?" Ethan asks, cutting into our conversation.

"He is," I confirm. "But he's telling it terribly."

"Claire!" Chad exclaims. Then in a harsh whisper, he says, "I trusted you."

Playfully shaking my head, I turn to Ethan. "Can you tell me how he kicked a hole in the wall?"

"Oh, I can tell you that," Emily says with a raise of her hand. "There's not much to the story. Chad was drunk and thought he could do parkour."

My bubbling laughter threatens to spray the table with sangria. Swallowing hard, I manage to ask, "And I take it he can't?"

"There are a lot of things Chad can't do," Aiden says from the far end of the table. I hadn't realized that he was paying attention until now.

Chad holds up both hands. "Hey, I still think I could have done it if the wall would have held."

"Not likely," Ethan mutters with a shake of his head. "Anyway, we covered the hole with a Natty case and ended up using that repair method more than a few times. People started calling it the Natty Shack, so Em made us a Natty backsplash for our kitchen, and the name stuck."

I glance at Emily, surprised that someone with her style would entertain a beer case backsplash.

She seems to read my mind. "It fit the rest of the house, and at the time, I didn't live there, so what did I care?"

"But you live there now?" I ask.

"Yeah." She laughs. "I didn't think things through."

"See how much fun it is at the Natty Shack, Claire?" Chad says in his enticing voice again. "Are you sure you don't want to stay with us?"

"That's okay," I say, but he's still staring at me, so I add, "really," to hopefully drive the point home.

He leans back and playfully points at me. "Alright, but let me know if you change your mind. I'd make sure you get the best hospitality." He winks. "You'd be a VIP guest."

I'm not sure if it was his hand on my leg, but as soon as he gives me that wink, I come to the conclusion that Chad is extremely good-looking.

The realization almost shocks me.

But now that I've noticed it, I don't know how I didn't notice it before. Tan, athletic, has great hair, and just the right amount of scruff.

Violet would lose her mind if she saw him. After hearing him talk, he's not her type at all, but based on physical looks alone, she'd lose it.

I realize I'm staring at him, so I laugh a little and try to hide my embarrassment. "Thanks. I'll let you know if I change my mind."

He goes to take a sip of his drink but pauses with the cup raised to his lips. "You better."

I'm not sure if it's him or my drink, but my cheeks start to warm.

I may be in trouble.

39

Aiden

Claire is more than buzzed.

I've been talking to Lauren for most of the night, but every once in a while, I catch Claire out of the corner of my eye. In my experience, girls who drink too much usually get loud or overly emotional—or both, but Claire isn't either of those things as she takes another sip of her third sangria. When Claire drinks, she's....open. I'm not sure how else to describe it. She laughs more, says what's on her mind, and ultimately, blossoms into the Claire she's been hiding all along.

"Ah! There you are!" Lauren yells out excitedly to someone behind me. She's on the verge of being loud and annoying, but she's still pretty cool. Glancing over my shoulder, I see a girl with dark curly hair, a couple of guys, and another girl with short blonde hair.

"Hey!" The girl with dark hair calls back to her before

turning to her group of friends. "You guys! This is my new roommate I was telling you about!"

The group of friends plaster on some of the fakest smiles I've ever seen and all mutter things like, "Oh, my god. So crazy," and "Wow, so nice to meet you," while Lauren gets to her feet to join them.

It's amazing how alcohol can make two girls who don't like each other feel like they're best friends. Lauren doesn't rush to introduce me, and I'm more than okay with that. I welcome the break and head to the bar for another beer.

The sun steadily dips lower beyond the horizon, casting a deep orange glow over everything in sight. We used to come here all the time when I still lived here. It's weird being back. When you leave a place, you don't really think about how everything stays in motion while you're gone. I feel like a different person now. Last time I was here, I was happy, in love, and excited about the future.

What a fucking joke.

As the bartender fills my glass, someone bumps against my elbow. Claire's already tanned cheeks are rosy as she looks up at me and grins. "We have to stop meeting like this."

A short laugh escapes me. "Maybe it's a sign that you should stop hitting the bars so hard."

Her mouth pulls into a tight-lipped smile. "And miss all the fun?" After a moment, she adds, "Hey," and places her hand on my arm. "Your friends are *fun*. Why don't you have fun like them?"

I can't help glancing down at her hand on me, liking how it feels.

She follows my gaze, and quickly pulls her hand back, making me wish I would have ignored it.

Turning to face her, I take a sip of my fresh beer. "Trust me, I'm plenty fun."

She squints like she's scrutinizing me. "Are you, Aiden? Are you?"

Leaning my elbows on the bar, I look down and shake my head before looking over at her. "Claire Ackerman, you have no fucking idea."

Our eyes lock, and for a moment, I think she'll accuse me of breaking her rule. Finally, she swallows whatever she was about to say next and fidgets with the straw in her cup.

But she doesn't call me out.

Which only makes me want to break her rule more.

"Where's your buddy Chad?" I ask as I scan the crowd of people around us.

She bounces back at the sound of his name, and I both hate and love that for her. As much as I wish things were different with Claire, they're not. I have no interest in being what gets her over her ex, and she's only looking for a distraction. She doesn't want me to be the one to distract her anyway.

She wants Chad.

"I think he went to the bathroom." Glancing over her shoulder, she doesn't look so sure about that.

Chad better not play games with her. If he's going to be

her rebound and help her get over this breakup, he needs to be a fucking good one. The last thing she needs is for him to give her attention until he turns around and acts like a playboy to the rest of the girls here. "You like him?" I hear myself asking before I can shut my damn mouth.

Fidgeting with her straw again, she slowly shakes her head. "Oh, I don't know." After a moment, she adds, "He's very flirty, though."

Of course, he is.

Snapping her head up with a sense of urgency, she says, "Do you think I should let him kiss me?"

My first instinct is to tell her, *fuck no*, but I get myself under control and ask, "Do you want him to kiss you?"

"Maybe." She bites her lip as she thinks about it, and I can't stop staring at her mouth. "Maybe this is what I need, you know? Maybe I just need to stop overthinking and have some fun."

My eyes jump back to hers, and I try to shake what just came over me. Chad is the one who will bite that lip later, not me. She's made it clear she doesn't want anything like that from me—so clear that she made a fucking rule about it.

Which I know is for the best.

But that doesn't mean I have to like it.

She needs to have fun. I just wish she wanted to do that with just about anyone but Chad. "Doesn't hurt to let loose a little, Claire."

Excited that I'm agreeing with her, she smiles. "Right?"

Her shoulders relax a bit. "I feel like I've never done that."

"Are you sure about Chad, though?" I scrunch up my face a little, and she laughs.

"Be nice! He's been a perfect gentleman." She lifts her chin like she has something to prove to the world.

"Oh, I'm sure he has been." With a shrug, I add, "As much as I hate to admit it, he's the perfect rebound for you. If you want to have meaningless fun, Chad's your guy," and I try to ignore the feeling that hits me in the gut as I say it.

40

Claire

I don't like the word *rebound*. It makes my interaction with Chad feel cheap and dirty even though nothing has happened between us. However, if something *does* happen between us, I know that'll be what it is. He'd be a rebound, and based on how quickly he hit on me, I don't think he's looking for anything serious either. Chad is fun and *hot*, but I don't think we connect on much.

"What's wrong?"

Aiden's question catches me off guard, and I realize I've spaced out. "Oh, sorry. I just don't like the idea of having a rebound."

The corner of Aiden's mouth twitches into a smile like he finds me funny. "There's nothing wrong with the occasional hookup." He shrugs before taking a sip of his drink and adding, "I know I've enjoyed them."

Before I can question him on these *occasional hookups*, Lauren is at his side and slips her arm through his. "I was looking for you!" She stumbles a little, and Aiden dips to steady her. "I was going to introduce you to my bitchy roommate, but you disappeared!"

Aiden nods slowly before unapologetically saying, "I'm right here."

Using her fingertips to crawl up his tattooed arm, my eyes lock on her touching him. The ink poking out from his shirt sleeve looks like the bottom of a forest, and it makes me want to see the rest of his tattoo. Lauren brings her face close to his and my attention snaps back to her. Resting her hand on his shoulder, she says, "Have I told you how cute you are? Because you are, and I was thinking we could…" She whispers the rest of that sentence in his ear.

But I think I have a good idea of what she's suggesting.

My eyes widen, but Aiden doesn't seem phased as he gently pushes the girl away from him so he can turn to face her. "Why don't we go sit down?" he asks her as he guides her away from the bar. He briefly looks at me before stepping away, but, as usual, those blue eyes reveal nothing.

As they walk away, Lauren's comment about Aiden being cute lingers in the back of my mind. I know Aiden is good looking—I've always known that. I haven't wanted to let myself see him that way, though. In high school, I gave up thinking about Aiden Lewis in any sort of way that might get me hurt.

If someone had asked me to describe Aiden and his over-all demeanor five minutes ago, I would have said he can be sort of intimidating, but, as Lauren so kindly pointed out, he's definitely not unattractive.

Quite the opposite, actually.

What's wrong with me?

First Chad, now Aiden? I stare at my drink suspiciously since it seems to make me attracted to everyone in the room. My thoughts are interrupted as a now-familiar arm lands around my shoulder.

Chad's voice is low in my ear. "Hey there, beautiful."

I beam at him and try to hide the fact that I was just checking out Aiden—sort of.

Is that what I was doing?

Lord, help me.

"Hey! I was wondering where you ran off to."

"I bumped into some old friends and saw you were talk-ing to Aiden." Squeezing my shoulder, he says, "I knew you were in good hands."

"You know Aiden well, then?"

Chad seems to consider his answer before speaking. "I mean, I guess so? He lived with us for a while before he went back to New York. He's a pretty private guy, though."

"Why did he move back?" Maybe Chad can give me in-sight into why Aiden hates Florida so much.

Unfortunately, he just shrugs. "Not really sure. He and Sam split, and he left right after that."

"Sam?"

"Yeah." He takes another swig of his beer before adding, "His ex. They were crazy about each other for a while."

"He just dumped her and left?"

Chad thinks for a moment before saying, "I don't know who broke up with who. It was weird because he had talked about wanting to move in with her and stuff. Then he just up and leaves, and if anyone asks him about her, he looks like he wants to bite their head off."

"Sounds like a serious relationship," I mutter as I try to picture Aiden and Sam—whoever she is. In my head, she's a beautiful blonde like the girl working at the bar where I found Aiden on Thursday night.

"Oh, it was," Chad confirms with a nod. "It was the only time I've seen Aiden *almost* look happy. It was amazing."

A laugh escapes me, and I can't help taking a quick glance around the bar to see if I can spot Aiden and Lauren, but they're nowhere to be found. If anything, I have more questions now, but I know I can't stand here and ask Chad about Aiden all night, so when he changes the subject, I drop my lingering thoughts.

"Now," Chad says as he gives my shoulders another squeeze, "What do you say? Another drink?"

I'm already buzzed, but thinking about Aiden has so-bered me up a little. I don't know why I'm so interested in his past, but I want to know what happened between him and Sam. I want to know where he went with Lauren. I want to know what they're doing and if he likes her.

I shouldn't be thinking about Aiden, though. I should be thinking about Chad because I have fun with Chad.

Right?

Yes, I *like* Chad.

"Thanks, I'd love that," I say and try to convince us both that I mean it.

41

Aiden

Turns out Lauren did shots with her shitty roommate, and now she's wasted.

Oh, and her roommate? Nowhere to be fucking found.

Now I'm stuck sitting with her on the patio of the tiki bar. There's an outdoor couch in the corner, and I'm practically force-feeding her water and trying to keep her hands off me. How did I end up getting stuck as this random girl's babysitter? It's bullshit.

"Just take me back to your place," she slurs, and I fight the urge to roll my eyes.

"I told you, I don't have a place," I mutter as I move her hand off my thigh. I scan the bar for someone I know. Where the hell did Ethan and Em go? They'd know what to do.

Leaning her drunken, heavy head on my shoulder, Lauren mumbles, "We could find a place."

I let out a sigh. "Yeah, but we're not going to do that."

Looking up at me, she frowns. "You don't think I'm pretty?"

For fuck's sake.

"You're pretty, but it's not happening." I wouldn't let it happen with any girl who's drunk off her ass. I'm still looking for Ethan and Em with no luck, and I'm starting to get pissed.

"Is it because you'd rather be with that other girl? The one in the dress?"

"No," I deadpan, borderline ignoring her.

"Yes, it is." She's practically pouting. "You can hardly take your eyes off her."

This makes me look at her. "That's not true."

"It is," she says almost defiantly, which only pisses me off more.

I scoff. "You know that guy she's with? I'm the one who thinks it would be a good idea for them to hook up, so trust me, I'm not interested in her."

Lauren points to the other end of the bar. "You mean the guy she's making out with?"

"What?" My head whips around fast enough to give me whiplash, and sure as shit, Chad has Claire up against the bar. One hand rests on her hip while the other stays on the bar top like he's barricading her only exit as he crams his tongue down her throat.

And it physically hurts.

I may have known them getting together was a good idea,

but that doesn't mean I want to fucking watch it happen. Can't they go somewhere else until I can get over my annoying-ass feelings for her?

I know Lauren is watching for my reaction, but I don't give a shit. I scan the place again, and, this time, Ethan and Em finally decide to show up, so I push the girl off me and get up from the couch. Looking at Em, I say, "Your new friend is wasted. Help her," and start walking.

"Wait. Where are you going?" Ethan asks.

"I need some fucking air."

I'm still close enough to hear Lauren call after me, "We're already outside, asshole!" but I ignore her and keep walking.

42

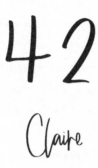

Claire

I'm letting loose.

I'm supposed to be having fun.

I'm buzzed on a beach in Florida with a hot guy kissing my neck.

But I don't like it.

This feels wrong.

I don't know if it feels wrong because, for the past two years, I've only kissed one person? Maybe that's it. Maybe this is just different, and it will take a little more time—and a little more alcohol—to feel the excitement of hooking up with a gorgeous stranger.

Maybe I'm not trying hard enough.

Squeezing my eyes shut, I try to clear my head. Chad has one hand in my hair and the other on the small of my back as it slowly creeps lower. His mouth is warm and eager on mine, and I can still taste the whiskey on his tongue. He's a good kisser, but it isn't enough to get me out of my head.

Because instead of thinking about Chad, or kissing, I'm still thinking about how wrong it all feels.

And I'm thinking about Aiden.

I'm wondering what it would feel like to have him kiss me like this, his hands fisted in my hair as he pushes me up against a wall. The thought alone is enough to make me gasp and press my hands against Chad's chest, creating some much needed space between us. This is too much. My mind is playing games with me. I haven't thought about Aiden in that way for a long time, and it's really inconvenient for my brain to start throwing these thoughts at me right now.

I'm trying to have *fun*, and of all the words I'd use to describe Aiden Lewis, I can't say *fun* is one of them.

Chad's staring at me with mild concern. "Everything okay?"

Trying my best to avoid his gaze, I mutter, "Yeah, of course. I'm sorry, I just need a minute." Smoothing down my dress and doing my best to collect myself, I head toward the nearest exit. "I'm sorry," I say again over my shoulder. "I won't be long."

My balance is off from drinking too much, and I'm starting to wish I had stopped at two sangrias. The people around me are a loud blur, and I try my best to weave through the crowd with as much grace as my current state will allow.

Finally, I get to the exit and place both hands on the

metal push bar. The door flies open, and even though the tiki bar is essentially outside, I welcome the cool night air as it hits my face. Straight ahead of me stands a railing facing the ocean, and I don't stop walking until my stomach hits the edge of it, giving me something to lean on. Taking a deep breath, I stare down at the dark water below and let the salt air bring some life back into me.

I'm not sure if my stomach feels uneasy from the alcohol, making out with Chad, or thinking of Aiden in ways that I shouldn't—or maybe a combination of all three—but I hurry to get away from everyone and have some space.

Breathe, Claire.

"Looked like you were having fun in there."

Closing my eyes, I internally groan as I brace myself for what's about to come because I already don't like his tone. Taking a final, steadying breath, I look up from the ocean to find Aiden with his elbows propped on the same railing a few feet away.

I let out a breathy laugh and sarcastically say, "Yeah," as I turn around. My back rests against the barrier now as I stare back at the bar. My shoulders relax a little when I don't see Chad anywhere. I was worried he might have tried to follow me.

Aiden scoffs and gently kicks the wood post by his feet. "Yeah."

"Where's Lauren?"

Staring out over the water, he mutters, "Don't know.

Don't care."

Well, I guess that answers whether or not he likes her. My eyebrows furrow as I study him. "Is something wrong?"

"Nope."

He's lying. "What's the problem?"

"No problem," he says coolly with a shake of his head.

I analyze him further. He has to feel me staring at him, but he continues to gaze at the ocean like I'm not even here. "You're being weird," I finally say, giving up.

He looks down and laughs, shaking his head as if I've just said something far-fetched. I didn't, though. He's acting strange, and I want to know why.

"Where's Chad?" he finally asks, still not looking at me.

I can't believe him. Glancing at the sky, I try to compose myself before answering. Not that it matters. When I go to answer him, he's still staring at the damn ocean. "Is that what this is about?"

No answer.

Taking a step toward him, I say, "Why would you care about what I do with Chad?"

"I don't."

I wait for more of an answer, but it doesn't come. "In case you forgot, you *told* me I needed to let loose. You said Chad would be a great way to…to—"

"Forget?"

"No," I say, feeling defensive. This isn't about Garret, but then I find myself adding, "I don't know." Because if I

hadn't been dumped two nights ago, would I still want attention from Chad?

Probably not.

"I meant what I said, but I didn't think you'd let him be
all over you in the middle of the fucking bar." He's standing
up straight now, gesturing toward the place to show me all the
people I've clearly embarrassed myself in front of. Dropping
his arm, his stare burns into me with more intensity than I've
ever seen. The only illuminating light comes from a few
torches scattered outside the bar, and watching the flickering
flames ricochet against him only makes him that much more
intimidating.

I kind of wish he would look back at the water.

"Classy," he says as one final jab.

The word leaves me heated, and all caution goes to the
wind. Marching up to him, I point my finger at his chest. "You
don't get to do that. You don't get to tell me to do something
and then make me feel like shit for the way I do it." Pushing
my finger against him again, I spit, "Fuck you, Aiden."

His blue eyes blaze, making me stagger back a step, but I
don't wait for his response. Turning on the spot, I head
straight toward my home away from home and as far away
from Aiden Lewis as possible.

43

Aiden

Oh, no she doesn't. I never thought Claire could have me feeling as pissed as I am right now. I call out, "What about your precious rules?"

She turns, her dress flaring around her knees, and glares at me. "What about them?"

My heart pounds in my chest. The last thing I need is for Claire to think I've wanted to flirt with her. "So, what, I have to follow yours, but you don't have to follow mine?"

Those big brown eyes stay narrowed into slits as she stares at me. Finally, she mutters, "It's not the same." She doesn't wait for me to answer. Instead, she starts walking.

"Like hell it isn't." I start after her. I'm not letting her get away with this.

She's already gotten a head start on me, but I know I can easily catch up with her. My legs are longer than hers, so that alone will close the gap between us. I have no idea where the hell she's staying, but I take the fact that she isn't getting into an Uber as a good sign that it's close.

Glancing over her shoulder, her body tenses when she sees me behind her. Facing forward, she practically growls, "Go back to the bar, Aiden."

I know she's only this angry because she's been drinking. Sober Claire would have bottled this shit up and put a bow on it.

I don't answer.

We're walking along the side of a busy street, and I don't feel like yelling over the noise. She has a decent lead on me until she gets to a crosswalk, and I know I have her. There's no way Claire will walk before the sign tells her she can. I'd bet money on it.

Her thumb presses against the button like it's a damn pinball machine, but the red hand doesn't budge.

At least something's working in my favor tonight.

Giving up on the silver button, she crosses her arms and looks over her shoulder at me. Rolling her eyes, she says, "Stop following me."

Finally, catching up to her, I say, "It's dark, and you're drunk, and as fucking infuriating as you're being right now, you shouldn't walk back alone."

Before she can answer me, the sign shows the walk symbol, and she wastes no time. Quickly looking both ways, she fucking speed walks to the other side of the street.

"I said stop running, Claire!"

"Ugh!" She cuts across a smaller side street, and I have to pick up my pace to keep up with her. Going straight for a set of wooden steps that lead to a matching wood front door, she calls back, "I'm not running! I just don't like you right now!"

By the time she punches in the key code, I'm standing behind her. "Look who's breaking the rules now," I say as I watch her struggle to get the number right.

When the door finally opens, she slides in and spins, ready to shut the door in my face. "Please, just go."

I catch the door before she can shut it, and that's when I finally get a good look at her. She looks like she's about to cry, and the sight of it throws me off. "Wait, did something happen?"

If Chad did something to her, I'll kill him.

She lets out a frustrated sigh. "No."

I study her before saying slowly, "If Chad did something—"

"Oh, my god," she says as she abandons the front door and heads further into the house.

I take the still open door as a sign that I can come in. I'm only a few steps behind her, but she doesn't slow down.

What does she think she's going to do? Outrun me in this tiny ass house?

"For fuck's sake, Claire, stop."

She turns around to face me, and runs a frazzled hand

through her hair, tucking a loose strand behind her ear. "What do you want me to say, Aiden? I'm sorry I let your friend kiss me. I thought it didn't matter. Maybe I'll go back later tonight and find someone you don't know *at all* and let them take me back to their place? Would that be better for you? Or should I bring them back here instead? I'd hate to do something you might not like. Haven't you heard, you can be a real jerk about stuff like this?"

"Haven't I heard——" I'm about to ask her if Chad is the one who told her that, but then I realize she's playing a new version of her damn game. My heart pounds in my chest as I try to erase the image of her bringing some random asshole back here later.

This isn't me.

But this is what she does to me, and I'm over it. I'm over her fucking rules and her fucking games. Walking toward her, I say, "You want to play games, Claire?" She takes a step back without looking behind her, and I move closer. "Okay, let's play." She backs into the kitchen island and those brown eyes are locked on me because she knows she has nowhere to go. Closing the space between us, I say, "You let Chad put his hands all over you, but I heard you didn't like it." The threat of tears is gone from her eyes. Her lips part like she's going to say something, but she can't seem to find a response. I can't help narrowing my eyes at her as I say, "I heard you left because you couldn't *stand* it."

She swallows, and my gaze momentarily dips to the base

of her neck. A small hickey is starting to show, and the fact that he left a mark on her sparks new anger.

Lowering my voice, I lean in like I'm telling her a secret. The smell of her shampoo might be more intoxicating than anything I've had to drink tonight, but I make sure not to touch her when I say, "I heard it's because you want someone else, right?" When her breath catches, I know I have her. She's thought about me—maybe not as much as I've thought about her, but it's there. I pull back and study her reaction. Her wide eyes jump back and forth between mine, but she still says nothing. I prompt her again. "Fact or fiction, Claire?" She wets her bottom lip, and I can't tear my eyes away from her mouth. She has a perfect mouth. I remember having the same thought in high school. Even back then, there was something about her lips that got my attention. I force my eyes back to hers. She's watching me like the answer to my question lies within me, not her. "Well, wha—"

She pushes up on the tips of her toes and gently brushes her lips against mine. The shock of it steals the air from my lungs, those perfect lips exceeding all of my expectations. She pulls back just enough to break the kiss, and we both freeze.

I don't know what the fuck just happened.

But I need more of it.

Breathlessly, I somehow manage to say, "Claire," but her mouth cuts me off again, and I've never been so fucking happy to have been interrupted.

44

Claire

Kissing him was inevitable. I had to know if it would feel just as wrong.

It doesn't.

Aiden's hands gently hold either side of my face as he takes control of the kiss, and I let myself melt into him.

I wasn't sure if he'd kiss me back.

But he is *definitely* kissing me back.

Holy shit is he kissing me back.

When he does pull away, it's only for a moment. His lips find my neck as his hands push up the bottom of my dress to hook under my thighs, and in one swift movement, he lifts me onto the countertop. I let my legs fall to either side of him, the flowy material of my dress bunching up between us. His lips aren't rushed and eager the way Chad's were. Aiden's kiss is slow and deliberate like he's savoring every second, and I'd do just about anything to make it last forever. His hands grip my hips, and I hook my legs around him, pulling him closer. Hesitantly, I put my arms around his neck, my fingers moving up into his hair. My breath catches as his tongue sweeps over my bottom lip, and he doesn't hesitate to part my lips further. I can't get enough of the taste of him, the feel of him—I can't get enough of *him*. My hands tighten in his hair, and a groan escapes him. The sound alone makes me rake my hands down his back to try to pull him in even closer.

I wish I hadn't.

Because that's when he pulls back to look at me, and I was nowhere near ready to be done kissing him. There are a million things I could say right now, but my mouth and brain don't seem to be communicating. If they were, I'd tell him that I want this...but that I'm scared...but that I'm also not scared...that's as far as I get because those blue eyes are locked on me, and all I can focus on is what thoughts might lie behind them.

Leaning his forehead against mine, Aiden says my name again, and this time I don't cut him off. Our mouths are so close to touching, though, and it's killing me. After a long pause, he says, "Why did you walk out on Chad?"

I don't dare pull away from him, so keeping my forehead against his, I say, "It felt wrong." When he doesn't say anything for a moment, I add, "I was stuck in my head…I couldn't…it just felt wrong."

He lets out what sounds like a breath of relief but then pulls away from me. The sudden space between us feels like a void. "I should go."

"What? Why?" My head snaps up to look at him. "I thought we…" I let my words trail off.

"You thought we what?" he asks, and I wish I could read his expression better.

I can't answer him. Forcing out a laugh, I just say, "Don't make me say it."

He takes a step toward me, closing the space between us again, and my entire body reacts. It's like my nerves are all standing at attention, just waiting to be touched by him again. His voice is barely above a whisper when he says, "Don't make you say what?"

I give him a pleading stare.

"Don't make you say that you want me to carry you to that bed in there and fuck you until you forget about everything that's happened?" He's waiting for me to answer, but my mouth has gone dry, and I don't have any words to give him. He tucks a strand of hair behind my ear and lets his fingers trail down my neck, giving me goosebumps. "Because I could," he finally says. "I could make you forget. I could make you call out my name over and over again until it's the only name you know."

I can't breathe. His words alone make my legs fall open a little more, inviting him closer. Somehow I manage to get out, "But you don't want to?"

He lets out a short laugh, running his hand under my dress and up my leg, his thumb skimming my inner thigh. "Oh, no. I've thought about it, and I *definitely* want to."

Bracing myself for the worst, I utter, "But?"

Just when his thumb threatens to graze over the thin, wet cotton of my underwear, he pulls his hand back and gently hooks his finger under my chin, forcing me to look at him. My heart pounds relentlessly in my chest and my entire body aches for him as I wait for what he has to say.

He stares at me for a long moment, his pupils swallowing the blue of his eyes. Caressing the side of my cheek with his thumb as he holds me in place, his gaze dips to my mouth again.

I need him to kiss me.

But instead, he locks eyes with me and simply says, "But I'm not your rebound." He steps away and runs a hand through his hair.

"But—"

He doesn't let me speak before saying, "Goodnight, Claire. I'll see you tomorrow." And just like that, Aiden turns and walks out of the kitchen, lightly pounding his fist against the countertop on his way out.

The door opens, then closes.

That's it. He's gone.

And I'm left sitting on the kitchen island straddling nothing.

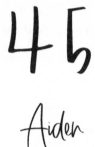

45

Aiden

Walking back to the tiki bar is the last thing I want to do right now, but I can't stay with Claire. I don't trust us not to do something we'd both regret. Ethan's place isn't far from here, but I don't have a key, so I head back to the bar without much of a choice.

My body buzzes with the thought of kissing her. Her tongue was still sweet with sangria, and it's taking all my self-control not to go back for another taste.

Fuck me.

My imagination runs wild with what might have happened if I stayed, and none of it makes this walk any easier. Claire Ackerman is a great kisser, and being that close to her made me feel more alive than I've felt in over a year.

But she's drunk, and she's only been single for a grand total of 48 hours—neither of which is a green light for me.

Maybe if she hadn't downed four sangrias, I would have let it go further...or maybe if she didn't just go through a life-altering breakup, the fact that she was drunk wouldn't have been as big of a deal.

But the combination?

It had red flags all over it, and as selfish as I am, I'm not stupid. Doing anything with Claire is a bad idea. Chances are she's still hung up on her ex, and as much as I hate to admit it, I like her too much to just be the guy that helps her get over him.

So, here I am. Walking alone, back to a bar I don't want to go to, to see the guy who just had his hands all over the same girl I wish I still had my hands all over.

This is bullshit.

Part of me was hoping they wouldn't still be here, but they are. They're sitting on the same couch where I was babysitting Lauren. She's nowhere to be seen, though. Thank god.

They're all staring at me when I take a seat.

After enough awkward silence, I mutter, "The fuck are you all looking at?"

Em grimaces. "I'm *so* sorry I left that girl with you."

"It's fine," I say, even though it isn't.

Chad is staring at Em like he wants her to do his bidding. She gives in too easily. "So," she says, shifting in her seat. "Where's Claire?"

"Her Airbnb," I answer without adding anything more.

It's none of their business where she is—especially Chad.

"Is she okay?" Ethan looks like he doesn't want to pry, but it doesn't stop him from asking the question.

"She's fine." Can't they see how much I don't want to talk about this?

Chad finally breaks his silence. "You sure? She seemed kind of upset."

No shit, Sherlock. I don't say what's on my mind, though. I don't know how much Claire told Chad about what happened between her and her ex, and it's not my business to tell. "She wasn't feeling well. I walked her to her Airbnb, and now I'm back. Anything else you guys need to know?"

They all shake their heads, but I can see the questions brewing in Chad's otherwise empty fucking head.

They're all quiet, and it's pissing me off, so I say, "I'm going to the bar," even though I don't want to drink more tonight. All I want to do is go back to Claire's and bury myself in her.

But if I can't do that, I'd rather just call it a night.

It's impossible not to stand right on top of people with how busy the bar is now. When I finally get through the crowd, I order water, and the girl next to me looks over her shoulder when she hears me.

"Water?" She asks in surprise. "Come on, that's no fun!"

I have no interest in talking to anyone else tonight—especially not this random girl. "Maybe some people just want to drink fucking water," I say flatly.

Her face falls, and she turns back to her friend.

Smart girl.

A gentle hand brushes my arm, and I groan. *Are Florida girls really this forward?* But when I turn around, I'm surprised to find Em standing behind me. Her petite frame probably had no problem weaving through the masses.

She peeks around me to check out my drink on the bar. "Water. Good choice."

"Yeah, well." Instead of finishing my sentence, I take a sip. Em has always weirdly understood me in a way that most people don't.

Standing on the tips of her toes, she leans over the bar and signals to the bartender. "I'll have what he's having."

"You too?" I ask.

She shrugs. "I've had enough to drink tonight. Plus, I don't want you to write off what I'm about to tell you because you think I'm too inebriated."

"Oh, boy." I look straight ahead at the display of liquor bottles behind the bar. "Here it comes."

She smiles a little before turning to face me. "So, Claire."

"What about her?" I ask, giving her a sideways glance.

She gapes at me. "Oh, *come on.*" Rolling her eyes, she says, "You're no ray of sunshine, but earlier you were *pissed*— way more pissed than Lauren could have made you."

I knew fucking Lauren opened her big mouth. "She gave you an earful didn't she?"

Em shrugs. "Not really. She was all over the place, but I

did make out that you couldn't take your eyes off Claire all day."

"It's nothing," I say dismissively.

"Clearly, it's not."

My jaw tightens, and I'm starting to wish there was something stronger in this cup. "It needs to be nothing."

"*Why?*"

Shaking my head, I say, "It's not the right time."

When I don't say anything more, she asks, "Because she just broke up with her boyfriend?"

This makes me take her a little more seriously. "How do you know that?"

"My mind-reading powers," she says with her fingers pressed to her temples, and I'm reminded of how much of a weirdo she can be. When I roll my eyes, she slaps my arm and says, "She told me!" She laughs then because she always laughs at her own jokes. "It was earlier. We both went to the bar together to order another round and ended up talking."

"People tell you too much." It's true. Em has a way of getting people to open up. It's one of the many reasons conversations like this put me on edge. I always end up telling her more than I should.

"They do." She nods seriously. "But it's a good thing because now I can tell you with complete confidence that you shouldn't worry about the timing."

"And Chad?"

She waves the words away as soon as I say them. "Don't

worry about Chad. They kissed, so what? You know he's not heartbroken."

She's right. I'm tempted to make a smart-ass comment about Chad having the attention span of a goldfish, but instead, I hear myself say, "You don't think she needs more time?"

Em leans her head to the side as she considers my question. "That, I don't know." Resting a hand on my arm, she adds, "But I will tell you this, I don't think she still has feelings for her ex. I don't think she needs closure either. She's got a good head on her shoulders, and I think what he did to her was enough to make her cut ties for good."

The flame in my chest that I've been working hard to extinguish all night flickers back to life. "You don't think she needs to be single for a while?"

Her eyes widen slightly. "Aiden, are you saying you'd want a *relationship* with her? Like a *committed* relationship?"

"No—I don't know. No." I wave her away from me, shaking my head.

She nods slowly with a stupid smile on her face that lets me know she's not buying my answer. "Okay," she says finally. "Well, I don't know Claire, but not everyone needs a ton of time before they move on. Some people hate dating around and would rather let things happen organically. And if that's her case, it sounds like you showed up at the perfect time."

46

Claire

My parents are fighting again. I hate when they yell. I've learned that I can't escape it anywhere in the house, so now I go outside when they fight like this. The fall air is cool against my skin, and I wish I had grabbed a jacket on my way out, but I didn't, and there's no way I'm going back in there. I don't even know what they're fighting about this time, but it doesn't matter. It's usually the same argument. It's always about money. Who makes it, where it's going, who deserves to use it more.

I hate money.

That being said, I wish I had some right now. Not a lot, but just enough to get me somewhere. I could walk to the ice cream parlor, but walking there when you have no money feels sort of pointless. Plus, I'm already cold, and there's a good chance they're closed by now.

But the alternative is sitting here, and I don't want to do that either. Our front porch is so rickety that I'm surprised the old wood floorboards are strong enough to hold my weight as I walk across them and take a seat on the top step. *Rubbing my hands over my arms, I try to get the goose-bumps to go away.*

That's when I hear them start to call each other names. It doesn't happen every time, but it's one of my least favorite things to hear. I hate the name-calling, and I hate when they throw things.

They haven't thrown anything tonight.

Not yet anyway.

My father is still yelling obscenities at my mother when I start to cry. I wish I could say it didn't get to me, or that I was tough enough to brush it off, but I'm not. It doesn't matter who the insults are directed at, as soon as they start attacking each other, I always cry.

There's music playing in the distance, and it feels weird to cry to party music. It happens a lot, though. Kelly Prescott has parties almost every weekend.

I only know that because I live here, not because I've ever been to one.

"*Are you okay?*"

His sudden presence scares me, and it feels like my heart stops at the sound of his voice. At first, I don't recognize him, but then he takes his hood down, and I relax a little. It's just this boy, Aiden, from school. I quickly wipe my eyes. It's dark outside, but I really don't want him to see that I've been crying.

"*I'm fine,*" *I answer, hating how thick my voice sounds.*

He glances at the house. "*Do they do this a lot?*"

A nod is my only response. This is so embarrassing. I wish he would just go away. It would be one thing if he were just some random person, but he's one of the cutest boys in school—at least I think so. We were lab partners in biology last year, but I could barely speak to him, and he wasn't exactly trying to strike up a conversation with me, so most of the year we just quietly asked each other to pass things. He barely even looked at me.

The new school year started a few weeks ago, and this is the first time we've said anything to each other this year.

"Does it ever get worse?" He's still standing at the end of our walkway. It's probably smart of him to keep his distance—I wish I could.

"What do you mean?" I ask.

Shifting his weight, he shrugs in the darkness. "They don't hit each other or anything, do they?"

I shake my head.

He nods as he takes in my response, but doesn't say anything else.

And he doesn't leave.

He just stands there.

I don't know how long we stare at each other in silence, but it feels like a really long time. Finally, I ask, "What are you doing?"

"Just making sure you're okay." His eyes pass over the house again before looking back at me.

"I'm used to it." I lie.

He nods again. After a pause, he says, "Can I sit?"

"Okay," I say as I wipe my eyes one more time for good measure.

Aiden takes a seat next to me on the step, and it feels a lot like Biology class. Not in the sense of measuring stuff in beakers, but in the sense of both of us sitting side by side, staring straight ahead, and not talking.

We sit like that until I hear a loud shriek of laughter from Kelly's house. "Don't you want to go back to the party?" I ask.

He shakes his head. "Not really. It wasn't that fun. That's why I went for a walk." His words are accompanied by a glass shattering inside, and I wince at the sound.

Aiden glances over his shoulder but doesn't seem phased by it. He stares at the house for a long time like he's debating something, and when he finally looks back at me, he says, "Do they ever take it out on you?"

Hugging my knees to my chest, I shake my head. "No."

I can feel him watching me, so I hug my knees a little tighter. It's a long time before he says anything, but when he does, his voice is barely above a whisper. "You can tell me if they take it out on you." I turn my head to look at him, and he adds, "My dad takes stuff out on me sometimes."

My eyes widen. "He does?"

Aiden stares down at his hands for a long time. "He gets mad."

"But he hits you?" I ask, looking at him a little more closely. He's wearing jeans and a black hoodie, so there's not much of him I can see.

He shrugs off my question. "Do they hit you?"

Shaking my head, I quietly answer, "No."

"Good," he says.

I feel like I should ask him more about his dad, but I don't want to scare him away, so instead, I ask more about the party, and he tells me that I'm not missing anything, but I'm not sure if I believe him. It sounds like everyone over there is having a lot of really loud fun.

Then we talk about the kids at school.

Then he notices I'm cold, so he gives me his hoodie.

Then we talk about Mr. Ricci and his probably glass eye.

Then we both start to get tired, but neither of us leaves the step.

And then I ask him about his dad again, and this time, he tells me about how his dad hits him. He doesn't go into detail about it, but when I don't know what to say, I hug him, and he holds me for a long time. It doesn't feel as weird as I thought it might feel to hug someone you barely know. It actually feels nice. After a moment, I start to think that the reason he holds me there for so long is that he's upset but doesn't want me to see.

Eventually, we let go of each other and talk about movies. He likes Vince Vaughn.

My parents stop yelling. The lights in the house go dark, and neither of them comes out to check on me or tell me to go inside.

The party gets quieter and quieter until there's no sound coming from Kelly's house.

That's when it feels like the whole world has gone to sleep, and it's just Aiden and me. That's when we just look at each other, his hands holding mine. I want him to kiss me. I've never been kissed before.

When he shifts the way he's sitting and faces me, my heart pounds in my chest so loud I'm afraid he can hear it. I start to panic because Aiden Lewis is the kind of boy who has definitely kissed girls before, and I'm afraid I'll do it wrong.

He smooths my hair away from my face, and I like the way it makes me feel.

Safe.

Cared for.

Seen.

No one has ever made me feel like that. No one has ever looked at me the way he does.

But he doesn't kiss me.

He says, "I should probably go home."

And then I say, "Okay," and offer to give his hoodie back, but he tells me he'll get it from me later.

So I say "Okay," again.

He stands from my front step, and says, "Goodnight, Claire. I'll see you Monday," and I watch him walk away until I can't see him anymore. Then, I stand up, go inside, and sleep in the hoodie that still smells like him.

I wake up feeling emotionally drained by my dream. That night has been on my mind a lot since seeing Aiden again, but that was the first time my dream made me feel like I was reliving it. Aiden never talked to me after that night. He never even asked for his hoodie back. I had it in my closet for years before I finally donated it. I would wear it around the house sometimes when I was younger, but I never wanted to wear it to school because I thought he would think I was weird for wearing his clothes.

I could never understand why he acted like that night never happened. It always made me wonder if something was wrong with me. Was it my parents' fighting that scared him away? Or was it me? That night left me embarrassed and made facing Aiden in the hallways at school even more difficult than before. It felt like we had connected on a level that I had never connected on with anyone, but he didn't seem to care.

I wonder if that will happen again.

Yesterday was a whirlwind that turned everything upside down and left me with little to no answers.

But so many questions.

Does he regret the kiss?

Did he tell Chad what happened?

Am I a terrible person for kissing two people on the same day?

That last one lingers. I've never done anything like that. If three days ago, someone told me I'd kiss two different guys in a matter of hours, I'd think they were being ridiculous. If they then told me that one of those guys would be Aiden Lewis, I would have tried to get away from them as quickly as possible because I'd think they were insane.

But here I am, and I'm not sure how I feel about it. I don't regret kissing Aiden, but I regret kissing Chad—which is strange because kissing Aiden was the furthest thing from my mind yesterday morning, but now it's all I can think about.

As I throw open the covers and walk to the bathroom to brush my teeth, there's a pit in my stomach. This all feels too familiar—especially after reliving that night in my dream. I know how Aiden Lewis operates, and there's a good chance that I won't hear from him again.

Which is okay, I guess.

Well, not okay, but I know I'll live through it.

My phone lights up while I'm brushing my teeth, and my heart skips a beat when I see Aiden's name. I practically stab my phone with my finger to see what he has to say.

Aiden: Come outside.

47

Aiden

I expect to see Claire open the door, but instead, my phone vibrates.

Claire: Seriously?

I'm not sure how to take her response.

Me: Yes?

The three dots appear right away.

Claire: I just woke up. Are you really standing outside my door right now?

Me: You just woke up?

Claire: The bed is still warm.

I try not to think about her bed.

Me: It's after 10. You should be awake by now.

Claire: I should be no such thing.

Me: I thought you'd be an overly punctual 'early bird gets the worm' type of person.

Claire: You thought wrong.

Me: I'm done texting you through a door, Claire. Come outside.

It only takes a few seconds for her to get to the door and open it. Her hair is up in a messy bun, and she's wearing a giant ass t-shirt with an alligator on it. It's probably the most obnoxious piece of clothing I've ever seen, but the way it stops mid-thigh on her makes me extremely thankful for it.

I'm still on the bottom step, staring at her like an idiot, so I try to collect myself. "You woke up like that?"

Claire wrinkles her nose like she thinks my question might be insulting. "Yeah? Why?"

"Jesus Christ," I say, walking past her and into the Airbnb. Maybe it is too early for this. I thought I'd be ready to see her, but I wasn't expecting her to look this good in the morning—and considering the fact that her shirt is basically a neon sign for this garbage state, that's saying something.

"Why don't you come in?" she mutters sarcastically behind me before closing the door.

I'm barely inside when I turn around and run a hand through my hair. I've been antsy all fucking night, and I need answers. "Why did you kiss me?"

Her eyes go wide at my question. She didn't think I'd bring it up so quickly. I might be bringing it up too quickly, but right now I'm too sleep-deprived to care. She crosses her arms over herself like she's trying to hide. "I don't know…I guess I wanted to see if it would be different."

186

I don't know what she was comparing me to. Chad? Her ex? I want to ask, but all that comes out of my mouth is, "And was it?"

Glancing down, she nods.

"So, what does that mean?" I notice my arms are crossed now, too.

"I don't know," she says again.

I fucking hate those three words. "That's bullshit."

Her eyes narrow. "Why did you kiss me back, Aiden?"

Part of me wants to shrug and give her the same shitty answer, but I promised Em I'd put my cards on the table. "Because when I'm with you, I'm not numb." When she doesn't say anything, I add, "I know that sounds fucking stupid, but I feel more with you than I've felt with anyone in a long time." She's still staring at me, and it's making my heart pound in my chest like a caged animal. "I've only ever loved two people, okay? My mom left when I was two, so I don't even count her. I only had my dad—and I loved him. Because that's what kids do; they love their parents even when their parents don't deserve it. The only people I've ever loved hurt me in ways that they shouldn't have, so I stopped trying. I stopped trying to feel—but I feel things with you." Her eyes are unblinking as she watches me, and it's making me sweat. "It's not always a good feeling," I blurt out. "Sometimes, when I'm around you, I just feel bad about the shit that comes out of my mouth. I don't want to hurt your feelings." She frowns, her eyebrows

furrowing, and I feel like I've said the wrong thing. "But sometimes it is a good feeling, like you being in the same room
makes me feel less alone." I'm putting my foot in my mouth.
Letting out a sigh, I give up and say, "Seeing you happy makes
me happy."

Claire chews on her bottom lip as she studies me, and I
wish she would just say what's on her mind.

And I wish I could bite that bottom lip.

Fucking focus, Aiden.

Finally, she says, "Who was the other person?"

I lift my gaze, unsure of what she means at first.

"You said you've only loved two people, but you don't
count your mom, so who's the other person?"

Shaking my head, I shrug it off like it didn't bring my
world crashing down. "Just an ex."

Her mouth presses into a thin line as she thinks about
what I've said. I hope she doesn't ask more questions. I don't
want this conversation to turn into one about Sam.

"Why didn't you ever talk to me after that night?"

I blank. "What?"

"In high school," she prompts.

My guard immediately goes up. "I thought we weren't
talking about that night." That night was the first night I told
anyone what was going on. I was so ashamed when I got home
that night, and every time I looked at Claire after that, the
shame would creep back in.

She bites her thumbnail and paces into the kitchen. "I

had a dream about it last night. I just don't understand why you never spoke to me after that."

Now I'm in another moment where she's unintentionally making me feel like shit. Following her into the kitchen, I say, "I told you something no one knew that night. I guess I didn't like that you had so much power over me. You knew too much."

Her back rests against the counter as she studies me with those big, brown eyes. "I didn't feel like I had any sort of power over you. If anything, it felt the other way around."

The kitchen reminds me of yesterday, and I'm getting distracted, so I pick a spot a safe distance from her before answering. "Claire, I told you about my dad. I didn't know what you'd do with that information. If you had told anyone about that, my life would have changed completely."

"I thought about it," she says quietly. After a pause, she adds, "But I would have talked to you first." When I don't say anything, she adds, "How are things with your dad now?" and her voice is barely above a whisper.

Her question strikes a nerve. I don't talk about this. With anyone.

But this is Claire.

Taking a steadying breath, I shrug. "We don't talk. I moved out senior year when I was seventeen."

"Where did you go?"

This isn't exactly the conversation I thought we'd be hav-

ing. "My girlfriend's parents let me stay with them until graduation."

She nods slowly like she's remembering something. "Julie
Moretti."

She's right, but she seems to know that already, so I keep
my mouth shut.

"I wanted you to kiss me that night, you know. There was
a second that I thought you might have."

Her confession might as well transport me back to that
moment. I remember her looking up at me. I remember feeling like she was waiting for me to do something, and I remember leaning in until I chickened out at the last minute. I glance
down before daring to bring my eyes back to hers. "There was
a second that I thought I might, too."

48

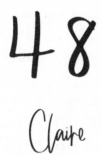

Claire

Hearing Aiden say he thought about kissing me that night soothes an old wound. That night, I felt truly seen by him, and when he didn't speak to me again, the rejection cut deep. It's one thing if someone who barely knows you brushes you off, but after our talk, it felt like we knew each other better than we knew most people. He probably knew more about me than most of my friends at school, and the fact that he wanted nothing to do with me messed with my head more than I'm proud to admit.

"I'm sorry." Aiden's voice brings me back to the present.

Shaking my head, I say, "Don't be. You had a lot going on." It was selfish and immature of me to want him to kiss me after revealing what he went through with this dad. That should have been the last thing on my mind, but I was sixteen.

Leaning back against the kitchen cabinet, he says, "And

you have a lot going on now." His voice is low as he says it, and I have a feeling we're both thinking the same thing.

Timing sucks.

"Yeah." I practically sigh out the word. I haven't even told my best friend about what happened with Garret. She'll expect me home tomorrow, so I know I'll need to call her at some point today.

Because I'm not ready to go home.

"Claire," Aiden says, pushing off from the cabinet. Once he's in front of me, the closeness makes it harder for me to think straight. "I should have kissed you that night."

"Really, it doesn't matter. That was so long ago," I say with a shake of my head, but even as the words leave my lips I can feel my cheeks warming. "It's not a big deal."

He scratches the side of his head, looking unsure of himself. It amazes me how much younger he seems when he's less guarded. "I never knew how to act around you. I could barely talk to you when we sat next to each other in class because I thought you were so pretty."

I can't contain my laugh of disbelief. "That's why you didn't talk to me?"

Aiden's eyebrows furrow. "Why else would I have not been able to talk to you?"

"I just thought you didn't like me." My back leans against the kitchen counter, and I hope I look more casual than I feel. It's hard being in this room with him. All I can think about is yesterday and what it felt like to have him lift me onto the countertop.

And what it felt like to have his hand grazing up my leg.

And how much further I wish we would have taken things.

Shifting my weight, I clench my thighs at the thought and hope he doesn't notice.

With a breath of laughter, Aiden shakes his head. Catching me off guard, he asks, "Who was your first kiss?"

Trying to get my bearings, I blurt out, "Gabe Evanston," I answered too quickly. It's easy to remember your first kiss when you haven't kissed many people. My total is up to five—and two of them happened yesterday.

Aiden grimaces. "The guy from *Montana?*"

Sliding away from the counter and away from him, I start putting away some clean dishes to clear my head. Everything he said about how I make him feel makes me want to kiss him way more than I did yesterday. "What?" I can't fight my smile. "He was a perfect gentleman."

He scoffs. "I'm sure he was." After a second, Aiden looks at me more closely. "Wait, didn't he only go to our school senior year?"

I try to stay busy, but I'm running out of dishes to put away. This is the part that gets embarrassing. I was hoping he wouldn't do the math.

Aiden gapes at me, and I brace myself for him to start cracking jokes about how I didn't kiss anyone until my senior year of high school.

"So, I could have been your first kiss that night?"

I'm still reaching up to put a dish in the cabinet when I look over my shoulder at him. Not the direction I thought this would go, but still sort of embarrassing. "Uh, yeah. I guess you could have." Keeping myself busy, I grab a couple of spoons I had washed and put them back in the drawer, but I can feel his eyes on me.

"Is it weird that I want to give you that kiss?"

"What?" I ask with a laugh. He's being absurd, but when I look up at him, his face is serious.

His blue eyes pin me in place as he says, "I want to give you the first kiss I should have given you back then."

Just the thought of kissing him again gets my heart pounding. Somehow I manage to say, "Didn't you do that yesterday?"

The corner of his mouth twitches as he walks up and places a hand on the kitchen counter to either side of me. My chest rises and falls with my quick breathing as he holds me in place. Leaning in, he points out, "Yesterday, you kissed me."

"Oh, right." I give a weak laugh and drop my gaze. The way he's looking at me makes me feel like he can read everything I'm thinking, and right now I'm having a few thoughts I'd rather keep to myself.

"Claire?"

Swallowing hard, I only manage a, "Hm?" as I dare to lift my eyes to meet his again.

He looks at me like he finds me amusing, and it only

makes my cheeks flush hotter. "I'm going to kiss you now. Okay?"

I can't help wetting my bottom lip with my tongue, and Aiden's focus immediately shifts to my mouth. "Okay," I say, but my voice is barely above a whisper.

"Just one kiss." His eyes stay fixed on my mouth, and I'm not sure if he's telling me or himself.

Before I can nod in acknowledgment, Aiden presses his lips against mine. He has this way of being gentle but solid, and I don't know how he balances this perfect combination. Yesterday, he pulled away when I became too eager, so today I try to just enjoy the kiss. His lips slowly move over mine, but I can feel him holding back, and all it does is make me want to see what he's like when he lets himself go. Pulling away softly, he kisses my cheek, the side of my mouth, and eventually my nose before stepping back.

The kiss on my nose brings a smile to my lips, but I'm still out of breath.

Now it's his turn to drop his gaze. "I can't be your rebound," he says in a low voice.

"What makes you think you would be?" After yesterday with Chad, I can at least say with confidence that Aiden doesn't feel like a rebound.

He smiles, but there's a sadness to it. "Because it's too soon."

As much as I want to keep kissing him, deep down I know he's right. "You mean to start a relationship?"

Aiden forces a laugh. "No." His eyes meet mine and he adds, "Fuck, I don't know." He shakes his head. "All I know is if we try this, I don't want to share you with anybody."

I can't help laughing. "So, like a relationship."

He groans and rubs the back of his neck. "That word stresses me out."

If I'm being honest with myself, that word stresses me out right now, too.

He steps toward me, and for a moment, I think he might kiss me again.

He doesn't.

Instead, he holds out his hand, and a rush of disappointment washes over me even though I know it shouldn't.

"Friends," he says.

Doing my best to hide the sinking feeling in my gut, I let a faint smile pull at the corners of my mouth. "Friends who just kissed."

He grins, making his dimple show, and it's incredible. "Friends who just kissed and may or may not date later."

His words leave an ache in my chest because it doesn't feel like enough. I want more, but my head keeps telling me it's too soon to want more.

And my stupid head is usually right.

Aiden seems to sense what I'm thinking, and an awkward silence falls between us. I'm still thinking about how easily he picked me up and put me on the kitchen counter yesterday and how badly I want him to do it again.

I need to eat something and get my head on straight.

As if reading my mind, he clears his throat and says, "I told everyone that I'd meet up with them if you want to come. Em wants us all to go to brunch."

At the thought of seeing Chad again, a wave of hot embarrassment washes over me. "Um...are you sure that's the best idea?"

Aiden's face hardens, so he must know what I'm thinking. "Don't worry about Chad."

"Did you tell him about—"

With a firm shake of his head, he says, "No."

"Then why shouldn't I worry about him?" Making out with Chad in a bar while I was drunk is definitely on my list of mistakes, and I'd rather not have to explain that to him.

Aiden stands up straight, lacing his fingers behind his neck. "Because I can guarantee that he's already hit on at least three girls since you left him last night."

I'm not sure if I should feel offended or relieved, but I go with relieved. "Oh, okay. Well, in that case, I guess I can go. I just need to shower, but I'll be quick."

49

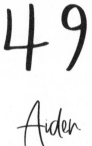

Aiden

Fucking hell.

Claire Ackerman will be naked in this tiny two-bedroom beach house, and I'm just supposed to sit here and wait for her without making a move.

Kissing her was a bad idea. I knew it was a bad idea before I did it, but apparently, I have no self-control when it comes to this girl. We already kissed yesterday anyway, so no harm no foul, right?

I don't fucking know.

The reason I came over here was to make sure things stopped between us, not to kiss her, but I wasn't prepared to talk about that night.

I wasn't prepared to think of her as the sad girl sitting on her front porch who made me reveal things about myself that I had never revealed to anyone. I knew she wanted me to kiss her that night, but I was too much of a coward to make it happen. I was too much of a coward to even talk to her again.

So I kissed her.

And now it's taking everything in me not to do it again.

Jesus Christ.

She's still staring at me, waiting for some type of response, so I say, "Yeah, sure. Take your time," before walking away from her and sitting on the sofa in the living room. I don't have a reason for sitting over here other than it being the furthest point from her right now—which, in this tiny-ass house, still isn't enough.

50

Claire

I can barely function as I gather my other outfit and head toward the bathroom. Aiden has his board shorts on with a t-shirt, so I grab my bathing suit to wear under my clothes. All I can think about is Aiden sitting in the living room and how badly I don't want to be his friend.

But I don't want to be his girlfriend either.

Yet.

Maybe one day.

But definitely not today.

I sneak a glance at him as I walk to the bathroom, and it's infuriating how casual he looks as he stares down at his phone. He doesn't even look at me. Doesn't he feel what I'm feeling? I can't be the only one feeling this charged.

I'm tempted to see if he's feeling this too, or if he's really so content with nothing happening between us. I already made the first move on him yesterday, though, and I had a little liquid courage to help me do it.

Once I'm in the bathroom, I take a good, long look at myself in the mirror. I completely forgot how crazy this shirt looks when it's the only thing I'm wearing. Actually, I think it would look crazy regardless. No wonder he's more interested in his phone than me.

He said he wants us to be friends.

The more I think about that word leaving his lips, the more desperate I feel to make him need me as something more.

51

Aiden

She didn't close the damn door. It's not completely open, but it's not fucking shut. I was trying to stay busy on my phone because I could barely keep myself in check while she was walking around here in her giant-ass t-shirt. When she went into the bathroom, I thought it would be safe to look up.

But I wasn't expecting the door to be cracked.

And I certainly wasn't expecting to have a clear view of her standing in there.

She needs more time.

She needs more time.

She needs more goddamn time.

I shouldn't look. I should go back to staring down at my phone.

But I can't.

She isn't even naked. She's still dressed, and I can't take

my eyes off her. There's something about the way that she carefully sets the clothes she plans to change into near the bathroom sink. Honestly, everything she does is captivating. It always has been. Even when we were in high school, she had a way about her. I felt like a dick the night I found her crying on her front porch because, even though she was sad, in my mind I had hit the jackpot. I was finally going to talk to her without my friends making stupid jokes in the background. In high school, talking to anyone different draws too much attention, and Claire and I were about as different as they come.

I'm so wrapped up in my thoughts that I almost don't even notice that she's caught me.

In the reflection of the mirror, Claire's eyes are locked on mine, and it takes everything in me not to let my heel anxiously bounce against the floor.

I expect her to realize her mistake and scramble to close the door, looking flustered and cute.

But she doesn't.

She looks back at the mirror and slowly takes the bottom hem of her shirt, calmly pulling it up and over her head.

Knowing that I'm watching.

She's only wearing white cotton underwear and a matching bra now, and I don't think I've ever felt more turned on. My mind races with all the things I'd like to do to her and her fucking tan lines, and it's getting to be too much. There's a drum in my chest, and it's the only thing I can hear. It drowns out everything, all my reason, and all my fucking restraint.

203

52

Claire

I'm about to turn on the shower when, out of the corner of my eye, I see a figure leaning against the bathroom doorframe. My head snaps in his direction, and as usual, he's impossible to read.

We both stare at each other for a long moment, and I'm suddenly overly aware of the fact that I'm wearing only my underwear in front of him. My instinct is to try to hide behind something, but I force myself to stay put.

Those blue eyes take me in from head to toe before he says, "Come here," in a way that makes me obey without thinking.

I carefully pad across the bathroom floor until I'm standing in front of him. My entire body feels like there's an electrical current going through it, but I do my best not to reveal it.

His gaze momentarily dips to my mouth before he says

in a low voice, "Are you playing games with me, Claire?"

Breathless, I manage to say, "Maybe."

His expression looks torn, but only for a second before I hear him mutter, "Okay, let's play then," and his mouth is on mine.

And he isn't holding back.

Picking me up so that my legs wrap around his waist, he kisses me deeper, forcing a moan to escape me. My arms are around his neck, and I knot my fingers in his hair, tightening my grip on him.

Rounding the corner, Aiden effortlessly brings us into the closest bedroom, never breaking our kiss until he lays me on the bed. Holding his body over mine, he kisses my neck in a way that makes my entire body arch in response. I tug at his shirt, and he lets me pull it off him.

Good lord.

The lines of his muscles are clearly visible. I had no idea *that's* what was hiding underneath his clothes all this time. My eyes trace over each of those lines until I arrive at his half-sleeve tattoo. Finally getting a good look at it, the black and grey ink goes from a dense forest to the head of an owl, and the detail is captivating. Pulling him closer, I try to guide his mouth back to mine, but he starts leaving a trail of kisses from the top of my stomach to right above my underwear. Skipping over the cotton, he kisses the top of my thigh, letting his lips linger. Slowly, he works his way down until he's on his knees and kissing my ankle that now rests on his shoulder.

Lowering my leg, he climbs on top of me again, this time pressing himself into me. Moving my hips, I rub myself against him and he groans. Aiden's lips finally find mine again, and they're back with a vengeance. They move to my neck, my chest—he's all over me.

Holy shit.

I've never felt anything like this.

This is more than just wanting someone.

My body *needs* him.

Now.

I grind my hips against him again, trying to soothe the building ache, but it only makes me want him more.

Aiden pushes himself up so that our bodies are no longer touching, and I practically whimper in protest. Breathing hard, his blue eyes turn to ice as he stares down at me. Slowly, he brings his mouth to my ear, and my chest rapidly rises and falls in anticipation. His lips barely brush my ear as he says, "Don't tease me, Claire. I promise you'll lose that game." He drags his teeth over my earlobe before moving himself off of me. Pulling his shirt over his head, he says, "Meet us at The Patch. It's on the far end of the pier, you can't miss it."

Scrambling to sit up, I gape at him. "You're leaving? Right now?"

He turns to grab his phone from the end table, putting it in his pocket. "Yeah. We're not doing this."

I should feel uncomfortable having this conversation with him in my underwear, but my growing anger makes that the least of my concerns. Sitting cross-legged on the bed, I say, "So you don't even know if you want to be with me, but it has to be all or nothing?"

Letting out a sigh, he says, "No. It just has to be more." He runs a hand through his hair. "Listen, I meant all that shit I said before about you making me finally feel something. The last time I let myself want something with a girl, it fucked me up. I'm not going back there again if I can help it. I can't set myself up for failure with you." His eyes rake over my body before he adds, "And that's exactly what this would do."

Hearing him talk about his ex spurs new questions in the back of my mind, but I have a feeling he wouldn't want to give me answers. Narrowing my eyes at him, I say, "In case you forgot, my ex isn't the greatest either, but I'm not going to let it affect what I do and who I do it with."

Aiden's jaw tenses and I know I've said the wrong thing. His voice is deadly when he says, "And in case you forgot, you didn't want anything from me. You were so worried about me even *flirting* with you that you made a fucking rule about it, Claire."

Pressing my lips into a hard line, I hate that he's right. I roll my eyes at the ceiling, refusing to look at him, but I hear him gather his things.

"Be at The Patch in thirty," he says.

Then, he leaves.

And I'm done having Aiden Lewis walk out on me.

53

Aiden

Jesus, this girl is going to be the death of me. I'm sure I'll pay for that later, but I think I made my point.

And she might be pissed.

Tearing myself away from her was probably one of the most difficult things I've ever done. As soon as I decided to give her a taste of her own medicine, I knew it would be, but I wasn't prepared for those damn hips to move the way they did. Just thinking about it makes me want to turn around and go right back through that door, but I grit my teeth and keep walking.

And keep thinking about how good she felt.

And tasted.

And looked.

Damn it.

By the time I reach The Patch, I'm so wound up I don't

even want to be here. Then I see Chad and remember that he's tasted Claire too, and now I *really* don't want to be here.

Em tilts her head at me when I sit down. "Where's Claire?"

"She'll be here." Actually, I'm not so sure about that. It depends on how pissed she is.

"Does she miss me?" Chad asks, thinking he's funny.

"No."

Ethan and Em exchange a quick glance that says a whole lot more than the nothing that's coming out of their mouths.

"What?" I ask as I glance down at the menu.

When no one says anything right away, I look back up to find them all staring at me like I'm a puppy that's about to get kicked.

"What?" I demand.

"So, don't freak out," Em says cautiously, "but Sam is here."

Her words nearly knock the air out of my lungs, but I don't dare show it. Instead, I look back down at the menu.

Em slowly continues, and I know she's treading carefully. "She came over to our table and said hi before you got here. I told her you were in town and she seemed really interested in talking to you." In a small voice, she adds. "We didn't know she'd be here."

"It's fine," I say, and I mean it. I know they're all still friends with her. They have no reason not to be. It's fine that she's here. My rapid heart rate might suggest otherwise, but I have no issues with Sam. It's been over a fucking year.

Regardless of any of this, I catch myself straining to hear her voice. We're outside on the patio of The Patch, so there's a lot of background noise and overlapping voices, but a few times I wonder if I hear her laugh.

The thing that really throws me off is that she wants to talk to me.

"No, but really. Does Claire miss me?" Chad grins at me like he's already had enough endless mimosas to make him annoying.

Well, more annoying.

I glare at him, and Em puts a gentle hand on his arm. "I think you're going to have to let this one go."

"No way! Have you *seen* her?"

Neither of us says anything, but Em and I exchange a glance, and it seems to miraculously be enough for Chad to put the pieces together.

Glancing back and forth between us, he says, "Wait. Seriously?" After a few more glances, Chad's wide eyes lock on me. "No way!" He's looking at me like he just found out I'm secretly a millionaire. "Aiden, you filthy dog!" He goes in for a high five, but I just stare at his hand for a moment before looking back down at the menu.

"I need a drink."

Em gives me a look of pity that I pretend not to see. Luckily, the server notices another person at the table and comes over to see if I'd like anything.

Yes, I fucking would.

54

Claire

It's been more than thirty minutes, so I texted Aiden to see if they're still there, but he hasn't answered me yet. I don't know why he assumed I'd be there in thirty minutes. It's at least a fifteen minute walk from the Airbnb and I still had to shower and get ready. I'm wearing the denim shorts and white cotton shirt that I bought to wear over my bathing suit on my first day.

I can't help wondering what Aiden's friends must think of me after the Chad fiasco. They probably think I'll make out with anyone—especially if Aiden's filled them in on our kiss.

I bite my lip just thinking about it.

What it felt like to have his mouth all over me plays on repeat in the back of my mind. It's gotten to the point where even when I'm not thinking about it, I'm still thinking about it—like white noise in the background that keeps getting persistently louder.

My phone vibrates in my back pocket, letting me know Aiden has finally texted me back.

Except he hasn't.

Violet: What time will you be home today?

My phone buzzes again.

Violet: Also, we need more duct tape. Don't ask why.

I wish I could say her second text was unusual, but for Violet, it really isn't.

Instead of texting her back, I decide to call her as I start walking toward The Patch. If Aiden won't text me back, I might as well just go see if they're still there. It's not like I have anything else to do.

Violet picks up on the first ring. "Why are you calling me? Was it the duct tape?"

"Of course not," I say back. "I'm fine with you taking hostages as long as they deserve it."

"Oh, they definitely do."

She sounds like she's preoccupied, so I ask, "New medium?"

"Yup." The sound of tape tearing in the background accompanies the word. "I'm not sure how I feel about it, though. Right now, it just looks like a lot of fucking tape."

If there's one thing I've learned about living with an art major, it's to expect the unexpected. Our apartment constantly shifts to accommodate her latest project. I can already picture her with every different color duct tape everywhere.

"I'm sure it will turn out great. What do you always say? You have to give the art time to reveal itself?"

"Yeah…" she says slowly, and I know she's analyzing her latest piece. "But this looks like garbage."

Taking a deep breath, I try to get the conversation on track. Letting out a sigh, I say, "So I called you because I'm not coming home today."

She doesn't bother trying to hide the suspicion in her voice when she says, "Why…?"

Slowing my pace, I look down at the sidewalk cracks as I say, "Garret and I sort of broke up."

Silence.

"Vi? Did you hear me?"

When she speaks again, she sounds out of breath. "I'm sorry. I put the phone down to do a happy dance."

"Are you serious?" I'm not offended. Violet's been telling me to dump Garret for the greater part of our two-year relationship, and she's been upfront about it from the start.

"You know I am." After a brief pause, she adds, "But also, are you okay? What happened?"

"I'm okay," I say, and I'm surprised how easy it is for those two words to come out of my mouth.

And how much I mean them.

"He cheated on me," I continue, and those four words are a lot harder to say for some reason.

She gasps. "He did not!"

"Yeah." I'm at the pier now and can read a sign that says The Patch in the distance.

"Well, good riddance. When you said you weren't coming home, I got scared he might have proposed to you or something."

This makes me laugh. "Yeah, not exactly."

"So, wait. When did this happen? Why *aren't* you coming home?"

Pressing my lips together, I try to think of the best way to word what I want to say. "It's kind of a long story, but I'm in Florida…with Aiden Lewis."

She bursts out laughing, and I realize there are probably a million better ways I could have worded that.

When I don't say anything, she goes, "Wait. Why aren't you laughing?"

Looking up at the perfectly blue Florida sky, I say, "Because I'm actually in Florida with Aiden Lewis."

"What in the world, Claire. How does that make sense?"

I shrug even though she can't see me. "It doesn't."

She lets out another laugh. "You can say that again." We're both quiet for a moment until she says, "Did you hook up with Aiden Lewis?" Her voice is packed with excitement, but her question still makes my face turn red, and I'm glad she can't see me.

"No…I don't know. Not really."

"Claire!" Her voice is practically a squeal now, and I no longer hear duct tape in the background, letting me know I have her full attention. "You hooked up with *cute moody boy?* This is amazing."

"I didn't hook up with him," I say, trying to sound convincing.

"But you want to?"

I let out a huff. "Isn't it too soon?"

"To what? Hook up with him, or like, date him? Do you like him or something?"

"I don't know." The words come out sounding more like a groan.

Another squeal. "You do!"

"But it's too soon, right?" I try again.

She seems to consider my question for a moment before saying, "Well, that depends. Are you worried it's too soon because of how you're feeling, or because you're worried about what other people will think? I'm going to go out on a limb here and say it's the second."

She knows me too well. "Probably."

"In that case, no. If you're over Garret—which there isn't much to get over—and if you like Aiden—which it sounds like you do—I say go for it."

For some reason, hearing Violet tell me there's nothing wrong with exploring my feelings for Aiden makes them that much more real.

"This is the greatest phone call of my life," she adds before I can say anything else.

"I'm glad I could entertain you." I've reached The Patch,

216

so I say, "Hey, I've got to run, but I'll keep you posted on my travel plans."

"Please keep me updated on a lot more than that."

I let out a small laugh. "Okay." Before she can hang up, I add, "Hey Vi?"

"Yeah?"

"Thank you."

Softening her voice, she says, "You deserve to be happy, Claire."

We hang up, and I'm about to enter the front patio of the restaurant when my phone rings again. Pulling it out of my bag, I say, "Do you really miss me that much?"

"Uh, what?"

I freeze.

That's not Violet's voice.

Did I seriously just ask Garret if he misses me? Pulling the phone away from my ear, I look at the name at the top of the call.

Garret

Oh, no, no, no, no, no.

Immediately, my forehead starts to sweat, and my drumming heart in my chest is relentless.

"Oh!" My voice practically squeaks as I step away from the restaurant and stand on the side of the pier.

The other end of the phone is quiet.

"I was just talking to Violet. I figured she forgot to tell me something." I know I don't owe him an explanation, but my embarrassment makes me word vomit. Looking over my

217

shoulder, I desperately want to get off this call and back to my plans. "What is it, Garret? I'm kind of in a hurry."

There's a pause on the other end of the phone. I think he may have hung up on me, but before I can pull the phone away from my ear to check if we're still connected, he says, "We need to talk. When's a good time for you?"

Frustrated, I say, "I don't think there's much for us to talk about. Can we figure this out later? I really have to go."

"This won't take long, just hear me out."

"Uh-huh," I say, barely listening. I'm already late, and all I want to do is find Aiden and his friends.

55

Aiden

"Want to do a pitcher of 'mosas?" Chad asks the table like he's a ringleader full of bright ideas.

Ethan and Em say, "Sure," as I say, "Hell no."

They get a pitcher, and I get a beer. I only like beer and bourbon. That fruity shit gives me a headache.

I still haven't seen Sam, and honestly, I'm hoping it stays that way. It would have been better if I could have come to Florida and left without her ever knowing I was here, but I guess that would have been asking too much.

I should have known better.

Em is still good friends with Sam, so I'm sure Ethan sees her all the time. Chad has probably hooked up with her by now for all I know. I don't blame them for being friends with her. If I were in their shoes, I'd still be friends with her, too.

I'm not in their shoes, though. I'm in mine, and they're

uncomfortable as hell. I left an ex-girlfriend, and my closest group of friends, and their world kept turning. It was only my world that felt like it came crashing to a screeching halt. Moving back to New York was a desperate attempt to keep my sanity. I think they were all pissed at me when I first left, but there's no way I could have stayed here after everything that happened. I would have been torturing myself.

To be fair, it still feels like the past year has been its own form of torture, but at least I didn't have to see her. Sam was out of sight, out of mind, and eventually, I stopped caring.

Whoever said that thing about the opposite of love being indifference was right.

The server brings our drinks, and I take off the orange slice they put on my beer because garnish is stupid.

Bringing the glass to my lips, I'm tempted to chug it. My heel bounces against the patio, and I find myself glancing at every person who walks by our table to see if it's Sam. I don't understand my fucking head sometimes. I want to see Claire, and I don't want to see Sam, yet every time I look up, my first thought is that it might be Sam.

I haven't even finished my beer yet, but as our server walks by, I flag him down and ask for another. After what happened with Claire this morning, and knowing that Sam is here now, my nerves are jacked.

△ △ △

I'm on my fourth beer in a fairly short amount of time when it happens. Sam slides into our table like it's old times, and seeing her leaves me stunned. I know I'm not the first person to feel awkward around an ex, but since Sam is pretty much the only real ex I've had, this is new territory for me. She manages to nestle herself between Em and Chad, and I do my best to give her an uninterested nod as I try to hide the fact that my hands are probably shaking.

Em smiles at her friend before looking at me and mouthing *be nice.*

This is the shit that pisses me off. I shouldn't have to be nice.

I will.

But I shouldn't have to.

"Long time no see!" Sam says as she beams at me with her perfect fucking teeth. She's wearing her hair in a ponytail with a ballcap, and I bet she wants to make it look like the whole thing was effortless.

I know better, though.

I know she probably stood in front of the mirror for a half hour making sure her damn ponytail was at the perfect angle. Every loose strand pinned into place, all so she can look like she grabbed the hat on her way out the door.

"Yeah," I say, taking a sip. "It's been a while." If she thinks I'm going to act like I'm happy to see her, she's lost her goddamn mind.

She doesn't let my response phase her. She's too much of

a pro to be thrown off by my game. "How have you been?" she asks, still fucking smiling.

Keeping my voice low, I say, "Well, I'm in this hell hole, so I've been better." I feel the need to look at the other three people at the table and add, "No offense."

Ethan shrugs. "None taken, man."

Em just laughs.

And I don't care what Chad does, so I don't bother checking.

"As charming as ever, I see." Sam playfully scrutinizes me, and I'm starting to think I should have drank faster. I could have maybe gotten another one down before she decided to walk over here and shit on my day.

"I try," I say dryly as I take another sip.

She shakes her head at me knowingly before leaning forward and saying, "Do you think we can go somewhere and talk?"

Part of me wants to flat out answer *no*, but another, more curious part takes control. "Yeah, I guess."

And this is how curiosity killed the fucking cat.

She seems to wait for me to take the lead, so I get up and walk us over to the far corner of the patio. My arms rest on the railing as I take in the view. Now that no one else is around, I let out a sigh. "What do you want, Sam?"

Her mouth quirks into a sad smile as she says, "I was afraid you might hate me."

"I don't. I just have nothing to say to you."

"Ouch." She grimaces before turning to look at the water as well. "Well, I have something to say to you."

The beer may have done something to take the edge off of this conversation, but it doesn't stop my mind from reeling. Picking at the label, I say, "Let's hear it, then."

She turns to face me. "I'm sorry, okay? I made a mistake. A really big mistake, and it's one that I'll always regret. I know that now." She puts a hand on my arm, and it takes everything in me not to flinch at her touch. "You're a good guy, Aiden, and I shouldn't have done that to you."

Lifting an eyebrow and looking at her out of the corner of my eye, I ask, "Is that all?"

She lets out a huff and gently pulls my arm to make me face her, so I give in. I stop looking at the beautiful ocean and look at who I once thought was the most beautiful girl in the world. "Seriously, Aiden? Don't you ever miss me?"

"Not anymore." It's true. In the beginning, I missed her every fucking day, but over time the feeling faded.

I wish I could say the same about the damage she caused.

"Well, I miss things sometimes," she says with that sly smile. "Like when you used to always put those stupid ducks in my car."

My mouth twitches at the memory. One of my favorite breweries had a claw machine full of different rubber ducks. I'm talking ducks of every color and every fucking occupation. When Ethan and I would go—which was a lot—I'd always get a new duck to put in Sam's car. She'd wake up to go to

223

class or work the next day, and there'd be a new duck staring her in the face on her dashboard.

Catching my smile, she points at me. "See! You remember. I used to always take them out, but eventually, I just gave up and ducks were everywhere."

"Of course, I remember." Trying to forget something is a lot different than actually forgetting.

"Or how we'd cover Chad in shredded cheese whenever he'd pass out drunk."

Okay, this one makes me laugh. "And sour cream."

"That's right!" she exclaims, her eyes widening. "I forgot about that, but you're right. The cheese always stuck."

"I miss pissing Chad off on a regular basis."

"I miss how much fun we had," she says, and even though there's a sadness in her voice, her eyes are practically sparkling as she says it.

"Yeah," I say with a shrug. "I know what you mean."

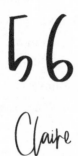

56

Claire

Ending the call with Garret unscathed, I take in my surroundings again. The front patio of The Patch is packed, but it doesn't take long for me to spot a very loud Chad sitting at a nearby table. He's open-mouth laughing at who knows what when he spots me, too.

"Claire!" He waves his hands eagerly to get my attention even though I was already looking at him.

Well, at least he still looks happy to see me. Putting on my best smile, I head over to the table where he sits with Em and Ethan who both wave as I walk up.

"Well, look who finally decided to show," Ethan says.

"I'm sorry." I take a seat and set my bag down on the bench next to me. "I didn't know if you guys would still be here. Where's Aiden?"

Em and Ethan exchange a glance that makes me think

they're having a silent conversation. Then Ethan stands up from the table and says, "Hey Chad, let's get a drink."

Staring down at his still full mimosa, Chad says, "But I have a dri—" Before he can finish the last word, it's obvious Em kicks him under the table. He glares at her before getting to his feet. "Yeah, okay. Let's go get *another* drink."

The two guys leave Em and me sitting across from each other. "What was that about?" I ask, eyeing her curiously.

Waving her hand dismissively, she says, "Chad's just been getting on my nerves all morning. I need a break."

Sure.

Nodding, I shift in my seat and try again. "So, uh…is Aiden here?"

Lowering her voice, she says, "Yeah, he's talking to Sam over in the corner. They dated for a while when he lived here, and she wanted to talk to him when she found out he was in town."

Oh.

Looking over to the corner she referenced, I immediately spot Aiden with a beautiful tan brunette. Sam is nothing like I pictured. Her long ponytail sticks out of her baseball cap, and as gorgeous as she is, she still manages to make it look like she woke up that way.

Em watches me carefully, so I try not to let my eyes linger. "Honestly, I didn't think you were coming here. Aiden was pissed when he showed up, so I figured you turned him down or something."

"Turned him down?" I guess she doesn't know how many times he's been the one to leave me wanting more.

"Listen," Em says, "I don't know much because—well, because it's Aiden we're talking about—but I can see that he's different with you. I think he likes you. I've known Sam for forever, but I don't think they were right together."

"You don't?"

Em shakes her head. "Don't get me wrong, I thought they'd make it while they were together. But then they broke up, and even though they both say it was amicable, Aiden left. No one moves across the country after an amicable breakup, and if the breakup was bad enough to send him packing, there was probably something wrong with their relationship that the rest of us couldn't see. It took me a while to come to that conclusion," she says with a sad smile. "I was pretty hurt when he left us high and dry, but now that I've had time to think about it, I'm sure he did the best he could given the circumstances—whatever they may be."

"Yeah," I say as I consider her words. My breakup with Garret comes to mind, and how wrong I was about him from the start. I knew he had flaws, but everyone has flaws. It wasn't until after we broke up that I could see the paper-thin foundation our relationship was built on. "I can relate."

"Exactly." She pours a mimosa from the pitcher on the table and hands it to me. "Cheers to ending things with the wrong people."

Clinking glasses with her, I take a sip and feel better

about the whole situation. I'm still smiling until I look over at Aiden again and see him laughing at something Sam must have said, and it sends the sip of mimosa to my stomach with the weight of a rock.

57

Aiden

I don't know how long Sam and I have been talking, but even though she hasn't said anything outright, I'm starting to get the feeling that she'd be open to getting to know each other again.

Or maybe she's just naturally a flirt without meaning to be.

Either way, I notice when her hand touches my arm, her freshly manicured nails looking out of place against my tattoo. Moving my arm out of her reach, I run a hand through my hair and say, "I should get back."

Her face falls slightly, but I try not to read into it. She was probably hoping I'd invite her back with me.

But, like I said, I'm not reading into it.

"Oh, okay," she says quietly. "Will I see you before you leave?"

"I don't think so." It doesn't take me long to answer, and she nods in a sort of resignation. She knows it's done between us. There's no going back—there can't be. We had a good time together, and I loved her—god, did I fucking love her—but that part of my life is in the past, and that's where it'll stay.

"Well, if you change your mind—"

With a shake of my head, I cut her off. "Sam, I won't."

She nods, finally taking the hint. "It was good seeing you," she offers with a small smile.

"You too." It comes out sounding like a goodbye, but I'm surprised that I mean it. Seeing her wasn't terrible. It wasn't as painful as I thought it would be, and there's a sort of liberation that comes with that.

She goes back to her table, and I look up at mine to see Claire sitting with everyone.

Shit.

She's animated as she talks to Em about who knows what, and my heart swells at the sight of her. I love seeing her like this—all tanned and glowing. She looks happy, and she looks like she's having fun.

Locking eyes with Ethan, I mouth *"How long has she been here?"*

He mouths back, *"A while,"* and he might as well have slapped me with the look he gives me.

Claire catches him and turns her head my way. When our eyes meet, I get the sinking feeling that I've disappointed her. She still smiles at me, but she doesn't look as animated and carefree as she did a moment ago, and knowing I'm the cause of it makes me feel guilty as shit.

Once I get to the table, I don't bother taking a seat. "Hey, when did you get here?"

Claire looks up at me, and her face reveals nothing. "A little bit ago." She takes a sip of her drink and there's another empty glass next to her.

She's already on her second drink.

I'm an asshole.

"You should have texted me. I had no idea."

Placing her glass down, Claire gives a small shrug of her shoulders. "I did."

"You wha—" I pull my phone out of my pocket to check. I'm an *asshole.*

Clear as day there's a message from her telling me she's about to leave and asking if we're still here.

She sent it almost an hour ago.

I can't believe she texted me an hour ago. *What the hell is wrong with me?*

"I'm sorry. I guess I didn't look at my phone."

"It's okay," she says as she draws circles on the bottom of her glass with her straw. "You were busy."

I wasn't busy. I was stupid.

Em widens her eyes at me while Claire isn't looking, but I have no idea what she's trying to tell me. She's probably telling me that I'm stupid, but I already know that, Em. Thanks for nothing.

My brows furrow at her as I try to figure out what the hell she means, but then Claire looks up at me again, so I rein it in. "I wasn't busy. I didn't think—Can we go for a walk?"

Why can I not talk right now?

Claire gets to her feet but shakes her head. "It's okay. I should probably get going anyway. I have some things I need to do."

That's bullshit. She's in fucking Florida with nothing to do except run like she always does.

Chad reaches for my arm. "I'll go for a walk with you," he says sarcastically, and the rest of the table laughs.

Flipping him my middle finger, I don't take my eyes off Claire. "Let me walk you out."

She opens her mouth, looking like she's about to reject my offer but then seems to remember we're not alone and changes gears. Tucking a stray hair behind her ear, she mutters, "Sure. Okay," as she grabs her bag.

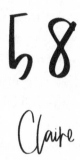

58

Claire

I wave a quick goodbye to everyone at the table and set down enough cash to cover my part of the mimosas. Em says, "You should come over later if you're free. We'll just be hanging out."

"Thanks, I'll text you." I'm not sure how much I believe the words coming out of my mouth. I *would* plan on going to their house later, but now that I've spent the past twenty minutes watching Aiden having a great time with his ex, I feel weird.

Weird.

Not heartbroken.

Not angry.

Just *weird.*

Like I've just eaten at a new restaurant that I thought

would be great, but now my meal sloshes around in my stomach. Too soon to know if the feeling will pass, or if I'll end up getting food poisoning.

Aiden and Sam's relationship feels like a puzzle to me. Everyone loved them together, but now that they've broken up, they all seem to agree it was for the best. His friends are still friends with her, so clearly no one had to pick sides. They say it was amicable, but Aiden moved back to New York. And perhaps most importantly, I seemed to have completely slipped his mind while he was with her.

Which is fine. I mean, they dated for almost two years…and I only reconnected with Aiden three days ago. It makes sense that she'd be his priority.

The logical half of me knows this.

It's the other half—the emotional half—that feels…

Weird.

Aiden follows me, but I don't slow my pace or wait for him as I make my exit. Walking under the wood archway of the patio, I'm about to keep going when his hand grabs my arm.

"What?" I ask, turning to face him.

He pauses, taking me in. "You're upset."

"No, I'm not." I notice my arms cross as I say it, and I drop them.

"Then why are you acting like this?" Those blue eyes that see right through me search for an answer.

Adjusting my bag on my shoulder, I say, "I'm not acting

like anything." It isn't true, but denial is my strongest line of defense right now.

"You are," he says, a twinge of his frustration bubbling to the surface. "And instead of saying what's on your mind, you're running again."

This makes me roll my eyes. "Aiden," I groan. "I'm not running!" Looking past him, I spot a secluded area of beach with only a few people sitting on towels. "Look," I say as I walk over to the edge of the pier and point. "See that spot over there? I'm going to sit there and finish reading my book, okay? I'm not running. I'll literally be right there."

He closes in behind me as he says, "Claire," in a low voice that sends goosebumps down my arms, and I freeze. "As much as I appreciate the update on your future whereabouts, that's not what I mean by running." He steps away from me, and I turn to face him. Rubbing the back of his neck, he says, "I should have texted you back." He glances at the restaurant behind us. "I should have been at the table with everyone when you got here." When I don't say anything he adds, "I'm sorry. You have every right to be pissed at me, but if you are, we should talk about it. Because trying to avoid whatever it is you're feeling right now? *That's* running."

Having always been an *actions speak louder than words* type of person, I'm not sure what to make of his apology. He looks sincere, but trusting people hasn't worked out well for me recently. I know I should tell him what I'm feeling, but something inside me shuts down, and instead, I hear myself say,

"Nothing's bothering me."

Unimpressed by my answer, Aiden's face hardens. "Really?" His jaw ticks once the word is out.

I look off to the side at a few people passing by because it feels easier than lying to him directly. "Yes, really."

"Huh." With a nod, he turns and walks away from me, and the same sense of panic I felt the other night grips me. The familiar feeling of an hourglass running out of sand fills me with each step he takes.

"Wait! Where are you going?" I ask as I start after him.

Aiden doesn't stop. Instead, he points to the same area I had pointed to earlier and says, "I'm going to sit over there with you until you're done reading your book or whatever, and then we're going to talk."

Hurrying to catch up, I reach out to try to stop him. "You can't just watch me read, Aiden."

He somehow manages to catch my hand in his, interlacing our fingers. "And you can't strip down to your underwear in front of me and then act like you want nothing to do with me." He looks over his shoulder with challenge brewing in those eyes. "You know, since nothing's wrong."

"Aiden!" I try to wiggle my hand free, but he only grips tighter. Bringing the back of my hand to his lips, he says, "If you're going to keep breaking my rule, I'm going to break yours." Kissing the back of my hand, he adds, "So fucking hard."

And the way he says it makes my stomach do an uneasy

flip. Forced to swallow before I speak next, I manage to get out, "That's really not necessary."

Looking back at me again, he gives me a smile that's bound to make any girl melt. "But it'll be fun."

I've never seen this side of him.

He doesn't let go of my hand until we reach the part of the beach I had pointed to from the pier. "Go ahead. Read your book."

I let out a huff and try to ignore the fact that my hand feels empty without the warmth of his. "I'm not going to read while you sit here doing nothing."

"Who said I'd be doing nothing?" he asks as he takes his shirt off and sits on the soft sand with his legs out in front of him. Staring out at the ocean, he says, "I'm on a beach in Florida. I'll be just fine."

My eyes rake down his body, taking in every muscle and every inch of his golden skin.

I shouldn't stare at him.

But I can't seem to tear my eyes away.

I never thought Aiden Lewis would be the type of guy to work out, but I'm starting to think he's definitely doing *something*. "Do you work out?" I ask without thinking.

The corner of Aiden's mouth twitches, and he squints up at me. "Are you checking me out?"

My face turns hot. "What? No. I didn't mean—I was just assuming." Taking a hard seat next to him, I add, "Forget it," and hate how pathetic I sound.

A low laugh escapes him. "Read your book, Claire."

"I will," I snap back. "That's what I came here to do." Shifting myself away from him so that he's out of my line of sight, I open my book where I left off.

He doesn't say anything else.

I don't say anything either, but even though I can't see him, I can still *feel* him when he's this close to me. There's no way I can focus on the book like this. We both sit in silence for just about as long as I can handle, him staring at the ocean and me staring down at the page.

Finally, he asks, "How's the book?"

"Good." I clear my throat. "It's really good."

"Really?" he says in a way that lets me know he doesn't believe me.

I glance up at him. "Yeah."

He moves next to me, leaning back on his elbows, and I hear him mutter, "Hm."

My sense of resolve snaps, and I ask, "What?" finally turning to look at him.

Breaking his gaze away from the ocean, he says, "Nothing." I don't know what he's playing at, so I look back down at the page, but then he adds, "You just haven't turned the page. I never had you pegged for such a slow reader."

59

Aiden

Claire slams her book shut and stuffs it back into her bag. "I'm not slow. I just can't think right now."

She's cute when she's flustered.

"Want to talk about it?" I ask, already knowing the answer.

"Ugh." She pushes up from the sand and gets to her feet. "No," she says as she walks toward the ocean.

I don't follow her.

Instead, I sit back and watch her as she gets her toes wet. She's still wearing a pair of cut-off denim shorts that make it impossible not to look at her ass, and I can't help imagining that white t-shirt getting wet. I watch as she bends over and washes the sand off her hands in the water.

If there's one thing I know for sure, it's that Claire Ackerman is gorgeous.

"Stop looking at me!" she yells as she dries her hands on the sides of her shorts.

"I'm just enjoying the view," I call back to her. "The ocean is beautiful, you know!"

She shakes her head, but then she pushes her hair back with one hand to keep the wind from blowing it in her face as she looks out at the water. I wish I could take a picture of her like this without her noticing, but she'd probably march over here and rip me a new one.

The thought of her reaction tempts me, but instead, I get to my feet and join her. She glances at me when she sees me approach, but then quickly fixes her eyes back on the water. Walking past her, deeper into the ocean, I say, "Why don't you put your clothes over there and swim with me?"

She shakes her head.

Letting out a sigh, I obligatorily ask, "Why?"

Crossing her arms, she says, "You said you'll break my rule. You'll probably say something crude about how I look in a bikini."

"Oh, so now you're shy?" I ask with a raise of my eyebrow.

She seems to think about it for a moment, biting her thumbnail. "Fine," she mutters before she turns and marches back to where we were sitting. "But don't say anything about how I look!"

"No promises," I call back to her from the water. "You've made it clear we're done with the rules!"

She flips me off before unbuttoning her shorts, and it's probably the greatest thing I've ever seen. Claire Ackerman flipping me the bird might have just made me fall harder than I've ever fallen.

I'm screwed.

The bikini she's wearing is light pink and makes her new Florida tan that I love so much stand out even more. It takes everything in me not to bite my lip as she walks toward me again. When she gets back to the water, she gives me a skeptical glance. "Why are you being so quiet?"

"Because you told me not to say anything."

She crinkles her nose. "Yeah, but this is weird, too."

Backing further into the ocean, I lift both arms in a shrug. "I don't know what you want from me, Claire. I can only be so many things." Turning around, I plunge into the water. I needed someone to slap some sense into me and the ocean is the only thing here that can do it.

60

Claire

When Aiden comes back to the surface, I can't help watching as he pushes his hair back. He's always been good-looking, but right now he's shirtless on a Florida beach, and that sheds new light on things—literal sunlight on the guy I've found attractive since I was sixteen.

He looks up and catches me staring at him, so I quickly ask, "Aren't you worried about what's in the water?" to deflect.

His lips quirk in amusement. "Are you?"

"I don't know…" I say as I look down at the not-so-crystal blue waves. "I can't see the bottom."

He follows my lead and looks down at the water himself. "You're right. We should probably stick together."

My head snaps up, and I glare at him. "That's not funny."

"Who's laughing?" he says seriously. "I'm just trying to help you out."

"Sure," I mutter as I stare down at the water and take a few more steps further into the ocean. When I look up again, he's biting back a smile. "Don't make fun of me," I snap.

He treads water a few feet away, and his smile only grows. "Of all the things I'd like to do to you, that's not one of them."

My eyes widen, but I ignore his comment. "I won't be able to reach the ground over there, you know."

"I'll come over to you if you talk." His eyes sparkle like he knows he has me beat.

Crossing my arms, I say, "We're already talking."

Aiden shakes his head, his wet waves dripping water as he does. "Not good enough." When I don't say anything right away, he says, "Tell you what, either you come over here and tread water, or I come to you, and you tell me what's going on in that head of yours."

I stay where I am, the water just hitting my hips. "What's going on in my head isn't very entertaining."

It's silly and immature.

And sort of embarrassing.

And makes me look insecure.

"Do we have a deal or not?" he asks.

He's infuriating. "I have questions," I finally say.

"So do I," he fires back.

I have nothing against treading water, but if I can ask

Aiden about his past without him being closed off to it, I guess I'm willing to play. "Okay," I finally say, "a question for a question."

"Alright." He makes his way over to me, and when we're both close enough to touch, he adds, "Ladies first."

"So chivalrous," I say dryly.

He cracks a smile, but he looks a little on edge—not unlike how I'm feeling. "Let's hear it, then. What does Claire Ackerman want to know?"

I bite the inside of my cheek as I consider my first question. "Why did you tell me to hook up with Chad?"

Aiden rubs a palm against his chest like I've punched him. "Jesus, Claire, no warmup? You just go straight for the kill?"

Trying to hide my smile, I watch my hand as I touch the surface of the water. "This *is* your warmup." Glancing up at him, I can't fight my smile. The dumbfounded look on his face brings it out of me.

"Shit," he says as he runs both hands over his wet hair. He seems to consider his answer for a moment before he takes a step toward me. "The truth?"

"That's the point of the game, isn't it?"

He takes a deep breath before beginning. "Okay. I'm good at not feeling things, and I didn't want to feel anything with you. You had your rule about no flirting, so I figured you didn't want that from me anyway." He stops to make sure I'm following, so I give him a nod. "Chad is the king of casual hookups, and I thought that might be what you needed...to help you get over your ex."

I study him carefully. "But then you got mad at me for kissing him."

"Yeah, well," he says as he rubs the back of his neck. "I didn't think seeing you kiss him would piss me off as much as it did."

The summer heat threatens to burn my shoulders, so I kneel in the water to cool off. "Okay, your turn."

Aiden kneels with me, the waves making us sway back and forth. "Why were you in such a hurry to leave The Patch?"

Chewing on my bottom lip, I find it easier to look just about anywhere else as I answer. "You looked like you were having fun with Sam. You didn't check your phone to see if I had texted you...I don't know." Finally bringing my eyes to meet his, I add, "It just seemed like you might still have feelings for her."

Shaking his head, Aiden says, "I don't," and I want to believe him.

"Why did you guys break up?"

His face hardens. "Is that your next question?"

I nod.

When he starts talking, he almost sounds monotone like he's removed himself from the story as much as possible. "I met her in the city. We dated for a little while back home, but she was coming to Florida for school, so I came with her. It was one of the easiest decisions I've ever made. I don't even think I really thought about it. She knew Em from when they were little, and Em's boyfriend needed another roommate. That's how I moved in with Ethan and Chad, and things were good." He pauses, and I let him collect his thoughts. "I wasn't a student, and even though she said she didn't care about me not going to school, I could tell it bothered her. One day I got off work early and went to campus to surprise her with lunch. I figured it would be good for her to see that I could still be a part of that half of her life. But as soon as I walked up to her building, I saw her sitting outside at a table with some guy in her class. They were holding hands and having what looked like a serious conversation. Then, when they got up to leave, she kissed him, and I knew it was over."

My mouth drops open. "And did you confront her?"

Looking almost offended by my response, he says, "Of course, I did. She said she had accidentally hooked up with him at a party and that he liked her. It was a party she had invited me to, but I couldn't go because I was working. She wanted to see where it would go with him, so I left."

My words tumble out of my mouth slowly. "So, the kiss wasn't even the worst of it."

"Nope."

The pit of my stomach warms with anger, but it's quickly replaced by sadness. "And they're all still friends with her because they have no idea what she did."

Aiden shrugs. "She asked me not to say anything. She

was worried about what they'd think of her. She's known Em for most of her life, and Em loves me. I think she just didn't want to lose her friend."

My eyebrows pinch as I piece it all together. "So, you just bottled everything up, said goodbye to your life here, and moved back home…and she got to go on like nothing ever happened?"

Moving closer to me, Aiden smooths his thumb over my wrinkled brow. Letting out a low laugh, he says, "It's nothing to get worked up over. It happened over a year ago."

"She's selfish," I mutter, still glaring out at the water. If Garret had asked me to do the same, I probably would have laughed in his face.

And then kicked him in the shin.

61

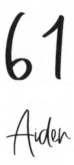

Aiden

"Yes, I can see that now." I can't help smiling at her as I say it. She's fired up about this, and the only other person who's gotten mad at Sam on my behalf is Mike.

Finally looking at me, she says, "You didn't deserve what she did to you, Aiden." She doesn't let me say anything before she adds, "I wish I knew about this before I saw her. I would have…told her or given her a look—I would have given her a look that let her know that I *know*." She gives her best resting bitch face to what I'm assuming is an invisible Sam.

"Claire."

"What is wrong with people?" she goes on. "Don't they ever consider someone else's feelings before they do some-thing?"

"Claire."

"Like how hard is it? If you don't want to be with some-one anymore, don't be with them! It's not like anyone is forc-ing you—"

That's when I kiss her. I kiss this feisty, sweet, bird-flip-ping girl, and when I pull away, she's staring at me with wide eyes.

"Claire," I say again, and this time she doesn't talk over me.

Still looking a little dazed, she goes, "Hm?"

"It's my turn to ask a question."

62

Claire

That kiss made me almost forget about the game entirely. A kiss from Aiden is bound to make me forget most things actually, because once he kisses me, all I can think about is him doing it again.

Letting out a small sigh, I say, "Okay, fine. What's your next question?"

Aiden's blue eyes turn dark as he looks at me. We're still so close, and all I can think about is his mouth on mine.

In a low voice, he finally says, "What do you want from me?"

I don't answer right away. The question alone is enough to make my heart race, but I also can't think straight.

Tucking a loose strand of hair behind my ear, he says, "Just tell me what you want." His fingers trace behind my ear and down my neck, leaving a trail of goosebumps in their wake. "Do you want me to be a distraction?" His hand dips under the water as he slowly teases the length of my spine. My back arches at his touch, bringing us closer, and a familiar heaviness settles between my thighs. His blue eyes stay locked on mine as he quietly says, "Want to use me to forget?" Gripping my hip, he slides his thumb under the hem of my swimsuit bottoms, and my heart jumps to my throat.

Swallowing, my voice comes out barely above a whisper. "I thought you didn't want to be my rebound."

Cupping my thighs, he pulls my legs around him. I can feel him getting hard against me, and it only makes it more difficult to focus. "I don't," he says, his nose skimming mine. "But seeing her today gave me some clarity. I was wrong about her—about what I thought we had. It made me realize that with you…" His voice trails off, but his eyes stay glued to mine, making it impossible for me to look away.

"What?" I ask, barely breathing. I know by *her*, he means Sam, but I have no idea how his last sentence will end, and it's killing me.

He lets out a breath of laughter. "With you, I'll take whatever I can get."

Wrapping my arms around his neck, I tighten my legs around him. There's so much going through my head right now, but I seem to have forgotten how words work. I can't help rocking my hips against him, my body knowing how it wants to respond before my brain has caught up.

Aiden sucks in a breath, and his hands grip me harder,

blocking my movement. "Don't do that." But the way he says it makes me only want to do it more. He seems to read my mind, and prompts, "Answer the question."

My words come out sounding breathless. "I don't know."

His eyes pierce into me. "That's a copout."

I can't help looking down at his mouth.

I know that I want to bite his bottom lip. I know that kissing him makes me feel more alive than I thought a kiss could make me feel. I know that when I saw him talking to his ex, I was jealous.

And I know that I want to be with him.

The realization makes my eyes snap back up to meet his, and I find his pupils blown, the black swallowing nearly all of the blue. "Okay," I somehow manage to say, "I know what I want."

His jaw ticks slightly like he's nervous. "And?"

"And I want to hear you say it first." My gaze quickly dips to his mouth again before registering the slight lift of his eyebrow.

"You already know what I want." He kisses me just under my ear, and my breath catches. "I want you." He kisses my neck, the feeling of his lips hot and heavy in light of the cool ocean breeze. "All of you." Moving his lips to the other side of my neck, he kisses me again, sending another wave of electricity down my spine. "And I don't want to share you with anybody else." He waits a moment before pulling away to look at me, but by the time he does, I'm already nodding.

"Okay."

Placing a hand on my cheek, he smiles at me, and it's a genuine smile that makes those dark blue eyes almost sparkle. "Okay?"

Instead of answering him, I take his bottom lip between mine. The sound he makes into my mouth sends my hips gently rocking again, and this time, instead of telling me to stop, he parts my lips further with his tongue. He tastes like day drinking and summer, and it's my new favorite combination. His palm cups my breast under the water, and even though I still have my bathing suit on, my entire body tingles at his touch.

"You are so beautiful," he practically groans, and if I didn't feel like a such ball of electricity, those words probably would have made me melt.

My hands grip his hair as I kiss him deeper. It's like every inch of my body craves to be touched by him, and every touch I get only leaves me wanting more.

I might as well be an addict.

So when his hand moves away from my breast and slides into the front of my bathing suit bottoms, I'm done for. His fingers know exactly what they're doing as he brings me closer and closer to the edge. My body matches his movements, wanting more. I've never been so removed from my thoughts, but right now I'm not even sure that I'm thinking anything. My body takes full control, and all it cares about is feeding this new, growing hunger.

His fingers slip inside of me, making me gasp. Aiden breaks our kiss, suddenly seeming to remember where we are. "Shit. We can't do this here."

Panting, I manage to get out, "There's barely anyone here, and we're practically underwater."

For a moment, it looks like he's considering what I've said, but then he shakes his head. "No, we need to go. I want to make you come, and I'm not doing it in the middle of a public beach."

My entire body runs hot at the sound of his words, and I can't help moving more against his hand. As much as I want to protest, I know we can't stay here. This doesn't stop the groan that comes from me as I drag my teeth over his bottom lip, letting go as slowly as I can.

"*Fuck*." The word drags out of him like I'm physically torturing him, and my legs instinctively tighten around him at the sound of it.

"Yeah, we should go," I manage to say against his lips, but my body contradicts every one of those words.

"We need to," he says between heated breaths as his hand slips out of my bathing suit. "Now."

I'm left frustrated, desperate for him to finish what he started, so when he grabs my hand and leads me out of the water, I don't waste time.

The following moments are a blur.

We grab our clothes and my bag and practically run back to my Airbnb. I've never been more glad to be staying so close to the beach. Aiden's hand grips tightly around mine as he leads the way, practically dodging traffic to get us there in a matter of minutes.

Once we're at the door, he kisses the back of my neck as I try to punch in the code on the padlock. When I get it wrong the first two tries, he says in a low voice, "Unless you want to give the neighbors a show, I suggest you get that door open."

His breath against my ear makes my spine prickle. "I'm trying," I hiss as I twist away from him. When the little light turns green, I turn to look at him with a triumphant grin only to be met with his lips on mine, his body pressing me into the door. He reaches behind me to push down on the handle and walks me into the house backward, his mouth never leaving mine.

We somehow make it to the same bedroom he left me in earlier, and he doesn't waste any time. Within seconds, I'm on the bed and he's holding his body over me the same way he did this morning. His still damp hair leaves droplets of water on my stomach. My skin cools with each one, but then quickly warms with his large hands claiming every inch of my exposed skin.

I didn't think it was possible, but I want him more now than I did a few hours ago.

He's already shirtless from the beach, so I run my hands down his bare chest until I can slip my hand into his shorts. I nearly gasp at his size as I wrap my fingers around him. His eyes flutter shut and he sucks in a breath as I pump my hand.

"Fuck, Claire," he breathes as he drops his head.

I need more, but when I remove my hand to try to pull him toward me, he holds himself steady, staying just out of reach. "Please," I practically whimper, reaching for him again.

Aiden's eyes darken. "Don't beg," he says roughly. "If you start begging me, this won't last as long as I want it to."

His words alone are enough to make a moan escape me, and his mouth twitches in response. There's a wicked glint in his eyes as he slowly lowers his mouth to my stomach. The kiss is warm and tender, and his eyes never leave mine. He moves his mouth lower, kissing me again.

And lower.

Until his face is between my legs, his eyes still locked on mine as he kisses my skin and slowly pulls my bathing suit bottoms off.

Having his eyes glued to me is getting to be too much, so I look up at the ceiling just as his mouth presses into me. As soon as his tongue slowly slides over my skin, parting me, my back arches in response. It feels like he's teasing me with his slow gentle strokes, and my hips roll, meeting his movements. The heavy heat inside me builds more quickly than I ever thought possible. Aiden slips one finger into me, then two, and I grab hold of the sheets. His fingers pump in and out of me steadily, matching the strokes of his tongue, and I can't take it anymore. My hips rock, chasing the orgasm. Daring to look down at him, I utter, "please," again, and his eyes darken.

His voice is rough when he says, "What did I say about begging?"

My hands move from the sheets to his hair, desperate for him to give me what I need. As soon as my fingers tighten on his locks, a moan escapes him, his voice vibrating against me. He stops his slow teasing movements, and I'm no longer gripping his hair to try and drive him further, but now I'm gripping it for fear of losing control. Between his fingers and tongue, my body doesn't take long to shatter into a million pieces under his touch. He stays there until the last wave washes over me like the aftershock of an earthquake.

Slowly pulling away, he holds himself over me again.

Pushing my hair away from my face, I stare up at him, stunned. "Wow."

Aiden tilts his head, a crooked smile playing at the corner of his mouth. "Wow?"

"*Wow,*" I say again, laughing. Pointing to the nightstand next to the bed, I add, "I bought condoms."

A low chuckle escapes him. "In a hurry?"

"Yes," I say with a nod.

Too slowly, he leans over me to reach for a condom. His chest is above me, and I can't help letting my fingers run over his muscular stomach.

Before I know it, his mouth is on mine again, this time with a hunger I've never seen from him. He claims my mouth, my neck, my collarbone, my shoulder, and everywhere his lips touch adds fuel to the fire burning inside of me.

He points to my bathing suit top. "Off."

It doesn't sound like a question, but I quickly nod anyway. Within a matter of seconds, my top is on the floor.

Sucking in a breath, he groans. "Fucking hell, Claire."

I'm not used to anyone looking at me the way he is. Like he wants to possess me but feels like he's at my mercy. But I love it.

Pulling at the ties of his boardshorts, I say, "Off," as he stares down at me. His mouth quirks and he obliges.

Tearing the condom wrapper with his teeth, he easily rolls it on, but before he presses into me, he kisses me again. "You're beautiful."

I wrap my legs around him, and he takes the hint. Slowly, he pushes into me, his lips swearing against my skin as he does. Once he's fully inside me, I can't hold back the sound that escapes my throat. Burying his face in my neck, he starts to move, his teeth biting down on my shoulder as he does.

Then he stops.

"Aiden?"

"Just give me a second," he breathes. Looking at me, his blue eyes almost completely swallowed by black, he says, "There are a lot of things I'd like to do to you." He starts to move in and out of me, and the feeling is enough to make my head fall back, a moan escaping me. "And I wasn't expecting you to feel this fucking good."

And I get it.

Because I wasn't expecting him to feel this good either.

63

Aiden

Incessant buzzing pulls me from my sleep. Taking my free hand, I rub my eyes and glance around the room. My other arm lies stuck under Claire. The phone that woke me buzzes again in the other room, and I close my eyes, willing it to stop.

I had her in every room of this Airbnb.

And I'm exhausted.

I don't know how long we've been here, but we're on the living room floor, Claire's arms wrapped around me. I lost track of how many rounds we went, but it was enough to make us both crash. She's still asleep. Her breathing slow, and her body heavy against mine.

This past year, I've been gambling with a string of one-night stands and casual hookups, and now, because of sheer, dumb luck, I feel like I've won the jackpot. With Claire, it's more than just physical—and the physical is still mind-blowing. I want to cherish this girl. She has me thinking about stupid, sappy shit.

Like how I want to hold her hand.

And take her on dates.

That being said, she's also the best sex I've had.

Holy fucking shit is she the best sex I've had.

I thought Sam and I had a good sex life, but with her, it was more like a game of cat and mouse. We were always trying to one-up each other, making it more like a competition than anything. Jasmine and I even had a good thing going for a while, but it was more comfortable than anything else.

Claire isn't afraid to openly react to things, and just thinking about those reactions makes me want to wake her up and go again.

Brushing back a strand of her hair, I kiss her forehead to push my luck. She murmurs something I don't understand and wraps her arm tighter around me. More heavy breathing follows, and I know she's out again.

It was worth a shot.

The vibrating phone starts again.

I let it ring.

The room falls quiet, but only for a moment before I hear it again.

I try to ignore it.

The last thing I want to do is move from this spot, but when the damn phone starts going off again, I carefully move out from under Claire, doing my best not to wake her. It turns out that not waking her isn't difficult. This girl is passed the fuck out.

This better be important.

Once I'm up, I make my way to the bedroom where it all started and find my shorts. Pulling my phone out of the pocket, I check the screen.

Nothing.

No missed calls or texts. No notifications.

The buzzing starts again, so I pull my shorts on and follow the sound. Claire's phone lights up in her beach bag. Part of me feels like I shouldn't look, but whoever it is has called her at least three times now. I know she doesn't have the best relationship with her parents, but what if it's someone important?

I reach for the phone and immediately want to throw it when I see who's calling her.

Who's *been* calling her.

Garret's fucking name lights up in big letters with a picture of the two of them together looking like the happiest of couples.

Well, she looks happy.

He looks like a fucking prick who wears pastel-colored polo shirts and too much hair gel. Claire holds the camera out with both hands, an adorable grin on her face, while he casually has his arm thrown around her shoulder. He looks like he's more in love with himself than he is with her, and I can't help wondering what she ever saw in him.

I stare at the phone until it stops ringing, and the missed call notification pops up on the home screen.

There's a slew of text notifications, too.

And Claire's settings aren't private. I can only see part of the messages, but that's more than enough.

Garret: Baby, I want you to feel…

Garret: You won't regret this

Garret: I can't wait to see you on…

Garret: I'm hard just thinking about…

My hand tightens around the phone, and for a second, I consider actually throwing it. I don't know her passcode, but if I did, I'm not sure I'd be able to resist checking how that last message ends.

And what the hell does Garret want her to feel?

My mind comes up with plenty of answers, and I hate every single one of them. How could I have been so stupid? I let myself fall into the same trap that I swore I'd never fall into again.

I'm pissed.

Pissed at myself.

Pissed at Claire.

Pissed at fucking Garret.

This is why I'm better off alone.

This is why I stopped trying.

This bullshit feeling in my chest is why I don't get involved with people.

Dropping the phone back in the bag, I grab my stuff. I can't talk to her—not when I'm feeling like this. I need to cool down.

Before opening the door, I turn back and look at Claire still wrapped in a throw blanket and sleeping on the living room floor. As angry as I am, I hate leaving her like this. Her back is exposed, the blanket only covering her lower half, and she looks almost angelic as she lies on her stomach, her hair splayed out around her as she rests her head on her folded arms. As I stare at her, my sharp anger turns into a gut-wrenching ache that's somehow more painful.

She was supposed to be different.

64

Claire

It's dark when I wake up, and for a moment, I'm lost. That's probably a normal reaction when you wake up on the floor. Wrapping the throw blanket around me, I get to my feet and look around the Airbnb.

"Aiden?"

Flashbacks of us naked throughout this entire place flood to the forefront of my mind, making me blush even though there's no one around.

Why is no one around?

Aiden should be here, right? Maybe he went to the bathroom? I take a few steps in that direction, but the door is open. I check both bedrooms, and then I just stand in the front entryway, looking around at the mess we made. The open concept doesn't exactly leave many places for him to hide, and considering all his stuff is gone, it's fair to assume he left.

Disappointment weighs heavily in my stomach at the re-alization. Scanning the kitchen counter for a note of some sort seems to be a waste of time, too.

There's no sign of him anywhere.

Still holding the blanket around my shoulders, I head into the bedroom and grab my phone out of the beach bag. There are a ton of notifications from Garret that make me roll my eyes, but none from Aiden. Scrolling past the Garret spam, I click on Aiden's thread and type a message.

Me: I can't believe I fell asleep. All okay?

My eyes stay locked on the screen in hopes that those three dots will appear, but after a minute I give up and set my phone down on the bed. The clock on the nightstand lets me know that it's only 8 pm. So at least I haven't slept too late.

Just late enough to leave me starving.

I take a shower, put on my ugly Florida t-shirt, and clean up the Airbnb. By the time I'm done, it's almost been an hour, and still no word from him.

I can't explain it, but I have a bad feeling in the pit of my stomach. Why would he just leave? I thought we had gotten past any weird back and forth between us, and this feels wrong.

Grabbing my phone, I pull up Em's contact info.

Me: Hey, is Aiden over at your place?

Thankfully, the three dots appear right away.

Em: Yes, and he's as grumpy as ever. You should probably get over here.

Her message confuses me. The last time I saw Aiden, he was in a great mood.

A *really* great mood.

I ask Em for the address, which she sends right away. It looks like they're in Grand Central too and only about a ten-minute walk from here, so I don't bother waiting for an Uber. I change back into the shorts and shirt I wore earlier and head out the door.

The night air feels cool on my skin after getting too much sun this afternoon. When I left to go to The Patch, I wasn't expecting to end up on the beach with Aiden for most of the day. My cheeks and shoulders have turned pink, and I almost wish I had a light sweater to fight the constant chill.

I wasn't expecting a lot of what happened today.

The butterflies in my stomach go wild at the thought of seeing him again. And it suddenly occurs to me that I don't know how I should act around him in front of his friends. Has he even *told* his friends? Em didn't seem to give any hint that she knew what happened between us when I texted her, but then again, it was a short conversation. *Would she have said anything if she knew?*

My spiraling thoughts continue until I'm led to the address Em sent. I can hear music playing from inside. It isn't as loud as it would be for a party, but it's probably louder than most people listen to music on a Sunday night.

Ethan answers when I knock, and my already uneasy stomach isn't settled by the look he gives me. He tilts his head for a moment before opening and shutting his mouth like he doesn't know what to say.

After a moment of awkward silence, I mutter, "Uh, Em said Aiden's here?"

That seems to snap him back to the present. "Right, sorry. Come in," he says just as Em comes rushing around the corner.

"Claire!" she half exclaims, half whispers. "Come with me." She grabs my arm and leads me down a hallway to the left of the front door. "Do you know what's wrong with him? I thought maybe you two fought with the way he's been acting."

My eyebrows crease together. "Not at all."

Em frowns and glances at Ethan who's still standing at the end of the hall waiting for us. He lifts both hands in a sort of shrug and walks further into the house. Turning back to me, she says, "Sam showed up a few minutes ago."

The butterflies in my stomach feel like they've all just turned into bees. "Oh?" I ask, not sure how I should react.

Giving me a sympathetic smile that makes me want to turn around and go home, she nods. "He came here in a bad mood, but I didn't know he invited her here. I would have told you."

The more I talk to Em, the more I want to find Aiden and figure out what's going on. "I'm sure everything is fine," I say, and I don't know who I'm trying to convince more, her or me.

"Yeah," she says as she turns to lead the way, but she doesn't sound convinced. "He's right over here," she offers as she walks me through the apartment.

Speaking of the apartment, the Natty Shack is...wow. There are large road signs up on the walls saying things like "Right Turn Only" and "No Outlet." The other wall décor consists of a large banner for an energy drink that you might see at some sort of sponsored sports event and a neon Heineken sign. The kitchen sits to the left of the living space with the famous Natty backsplash. It's made up of empty cardboard beer cases that have been flattened and somehow stuck to the wall like a Natty collage. Beyond the kitchen lies the family room, which would look normal if it weren't for the stacked couches.

Yes, *stacked* couches.

There's one couch on the floor, and behind it sits a second couch on top of some type of wood platform like a makeshift movie theater.

Em seems to read my mind because she says, "Yeah, I haven't had the chance to redecorate since the guys lived here without me."

I suddenly feel bad. I wasn't trying to look down on her place. There's just *so much* to look at. "If anything, it's impressive," I say honestly.

Em laughs nervously. "At least it's clean now."

I'm about to laugh with her but then my eyes land on

Aiden, and her comment doesn't seem as funny as it did a moment ago.

He's on the couch with a drink in one hand, the other draped over Sam's shoulders as she snuggles up to him. I don't know if the similarities to how I found out Garret was cheating on me come into play, but the sight alone might as well have knocked the wind out of me.

"Claire!" Chad yells from the far end of a beer-pong table. He waves his arms with more enthusiasm than I can handle. "Team with me!"

The best I can offer him is a weak smile. "Maybe a little later," I manage to say.

Aiden takes a sip from a red Solo cup, his eyes momentarily locking on mine as he does. That look says that I shouldn't have come here—that much I know for sure.

Ethan and Chad continue their game of beer-pong, so I walk up to Aiden and Sam, my feet getting heavier with each step. By the time I reach them, I don't even know what to say.

Luckily, I don't have to come up with anything. Sam addresses me before I have time to think.

"Hi!" she says, beaming at me. "I'm Sam. Are you friends with Em or something?"

She stares up at me with her twinkling blue eyes that are nothing like Aiden's. His eyes are deep and dark like the ocean, whereas hers are almost clear like ice. The combination with her brunette hair makes her striking to look at.

"It's nice to meet you," I say to avoid being rude. My eyes

flicker to Aiden before adding, "No, I'm sort of friends with Aiden."

Aiden raises an unconcerned brow at me before taking another sip, and it takes everything in me to not sound angry when I ask, "Can we go somewhere and talk?"

65

Aiden

Claire's trying to act like everything is fine in front of every-
one, but I can tell the red in her cheeks isn't only from the sun.
She's pissed, and she's trying to hide it. I guess I'd be pissed if
I was caught in a lie, too. I should have known she'd be fake.
That's how she fooled me in the first place.

Even with no makeup on and pissed off at me, she's still
fucking beautiful. Her hair is up in a bun on her head with
stray pieces falling all over the place, and all I can think about
is how many times I had my hands knotted tightly in her hair
today as I made her come over and over again. The memory
is enough to make me clench my hand into a fist over Sam's
shoulder. I don't even know why I invited Sam here. She's not
who I want, but after how many drinks I've had, she makes
me feel less pathetic.

When I left Claire's Airbnb, I knew I needed to cool

down. The first few drinks did that, but then I kept drinking. And the more I drank, the more I realized what happened today.

I got played.

Claire fucking used me even when I told her she *could* use me. I could have just fucked her. I didn't have to get my feelings involved, but she lied.

She's a liar.

Turning to Sam, I grumble something that sounds like, "I'll be right back," and I'm starting to think maybe I've tossed back too many. I'm used to having a few beers when I'm out with friends, but I've been drinking straight whisky since I left Claire's place, and I haven't exactly been drinking it slowly.

Sam looks back and forth between Claire and me, and I know she's dying to know what's going on between us.

Not because she cares about me.

But because she's always putting her fucking nose in everything.

Eying me suspiciously, she eventually says, "Okay…I'll be here when you get back."

I nod, or at least I think I do. Getting up from the couch, I lead the way and walk out onto the balcony without bothering to turn on the outdoor light. The last thing I need is all these nosy fuckers watching us hash things out.

I don't look back at her, but I know she's following me. It's like her body being close to mine is enough to set my nerves on high alert. Part of me expects her to reach out and touch me, and when she doesn't, it leaves me aching for her.

Who am I kidding, I've been aching for her all night.

Flopping into the hammock, I put a hand behind my head, passively staring at her as I wait for the storm.

She's flushed from her day in the sun, and it looks like she took a shower recently. I can tell from here that she smells amazing, and it makes me grateful for the distance between us. Any closer and I'd probably press her up against that wall just to feel the euphoria of being close to her one more time.

She crosses her arms, and even though her eyes look wounded, there's a fire behind them. "Do you mind filling me in?"

Even through the darkness, I can see a vein pulse in her neck. Earlier today I had my hand wrapped around that neck as I buried myself inside of her and told her how fucking perfect she was.

"Fill you in on what?" I ask, trying to get my thoughts back on track.

She lets out an exasperated sigh, and I'm glad she's pissed at me. Let her feel some of what I feel. "This!" She gestures to me in my hammock like it's a bad thing.

Lifting my head to look at her, I ask, "Oh, you don't like that I'm lying here? Minding my own fucking business?" I get to my feet, relieved that I'm not stumbling drunk yet. That's the last way to look convincing during an argument. I march up to her until her back is against the wall. She smells like coconut and SPF, and it takes every ounce of my diminished, drunk self-control not to see if she tastes like it, too. "Is this what you want? Is this better?"

Her mouth falls open as she stares at me, and it takes everything in me not to bite that bottom lip.

"N—no," she stammers, her voice wavering.

"You got what you wanted. Check it off your fucking list and move on." I take a step away from her because being this close to her isn't good for me.

Or maybe it's just too good for me to resist.

The flash of hurt that crosses her face makes me feel like an ass, and I have to remind myself that she's getting back with her ex. She's going to run back into Garret's arms, and he can't wait for her to feel his pencil dick.

Her eyes are practically slits when she asks, "Why is Sam here?"

"Because," I say, lowering my voice to drive the point home, "I want her here." Something inside her dims, but I pretend not to notice as I add, "Which is more than I can say for you." My eyes narrow, and our noses are nearly touching when I say, "Go home, Claire."

She sucks in her bottom lip and bites down on it as she glares at me. "So that's it then? You used me and I shouldn't have come here?"

What a fucking joke. I scoff and say, "Yeah, Claire, I used you. That's what happened."

Turning to step away, she pauses, looking back at me with what I can only describe as disgust. "You know, we all have shit from our past, Aiden, but that's not an excuse to be an asshole." She walks away, and without turning back, she mutters, "Enjoy the rest of your night."

"I plan on it!" I call after her as she slams the door.

And then I'm alone.

Even with the sound of the music inside, it's too quiet out here. Or maybe my thoughts are just too fucking loud.

Doesn't matter, I guess. Both are better than going inside with everyone right now. Walking back to the hammock, I plop down and try to pretend this day never happened.

Who the hell does Claire think she is? She's the one who obviously plans on getting back with fucking Garret, and she's going to walk in here like *I'm* the bad guy? The night I saw her in the bar, I should have minded my own business. I should have let her walk out that door and not gone after her. I should have let her ride the train to fucking Florida, alone.

My solitude doesn't last long before the sliding doors open again. I look up, half hoping for it to be Claire, but it's Sam who's decided to join me.

"So," she says slowly. "Do you want to tell me what that was about?"

"No," I answer without looking at her.

She sits with her back against the wall even though I'm still in the hammock. "Well, it didn't seem like nothing. She looked pretty upset."

I don't say anything.

Out of the corner of my eye, I can see Sam nodding. "Em

says you like her."

"Em needs to keep her mouth shut," I snap.

A light laugh escapes her. "Yeah, well, that's not exactly how she does things." After a moment, she says, "Aiden, come sit with me."

Turning to look at her, I rub a hand over my face before getting out of the hammock. I don't know why I listen to her. I guess some habits die hard.

Looking up at me, she asks, "Did she hurt you?"

I scoff. "It's nothing I can't handle."

She nods, knowing she's put me through worse. "Why did you tell me to come here tonight?"

"I—I don't know," I say in defeat as I rub the back of my neck. "I guess I just needed to." I slide down to the floor until I'm next to her with my back against the wall. "I thought it would help." My head falls in my hands as I rake my fingers through my hair.

"Hey." Sam's voice is gentle as she turns to kneel in front of me. "You're one of the best people I know. I feel so stupid sometimes." I lift my head, to see what she means, and she adds, "For messing up what we had."

I force out a laugh. There was a long time that I would have given anything to hear those words, but now that she's saying them, I feel nothing. She's not the cause of my pain anymore. I need to shut down my feelings for Claire. I only reconnected with her a few days ago. She shouldn't have this much power over me.

But then again, Claire has always had too much power over me. That's why I avoided her when I was seventeen, and that's why I should have avoided her again when she walked into that bar.

"It doesn't matter," I say when I realize I still haven't answered Sam.

She holds my face in her hands, and I'm too drained to pull away from her. "It *does* matter," she says. "I was so terrible to you, and you didn't even tell anyone. You didn't have to do that. I owe you, and I want to help you."

Looking into her eyes, I'm hit with a strange feeling. She's so familiar to me but so foreign at the same time. Her hands are uncomfortable on my face, and I don't want her this close to me. I'd rather have this conversation with Em. I'd rather have Claire come back here and make me feel like shit some more. Hell, I'd rather Chad be the one talking to me on this balcony, but too much has happened today, and there's nothing left in me to let me care.

So when she presses her lips against mine, I don't bother telling her to stop.

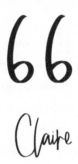

66

Claire

I held back the tears until I left, but my entire walk home was wet with them. My stomach rumbles with hunger, but at the same time, I have no appetite. As I sit on the couch of the Airbnb, I don't have much motivation for anything. The TV isn't even on. I'm just sitting in silence with dried tears and my lingering, throbbing anger.

He called *Sam?*

My chest tightens as I picture the two of them still at the party together. How is it possible that I wasted years on Garret, but Aiden Lewis feels like my biggest mistake yet?

I have terrible taste in men.

Violet has texted me a few times asking how things went with Aiden earlier, but I can't bring myself to answer her. I still haven't opened Garret's string of texts from earlier, but he's the last person I want to give my energy to right now, so

I leave them unread.

Tucking my legs to my chest, I lean my head on the tops of my knees and stare out the dark window. I can't see anything outside, but my reflection in the glass looks pitiful. A wave of fresh tears burn my eyes, and I swipe my phone open to check the train running times for tomorrow.

Luckily, it looks like there's a train going back to New York tomorrow morning, which is perfect because I haven't extended my stay at the Airbnb yet. I had planned on doing that earlier today, but then Aiden and I got...distracted.

Blocking the memories from this afternoon, I purchase my ticket home and start to get the Airbnb ready for checkout.

△   △   △

The morning sun shines through the windows with a stunning golden glow, and I almost forget about the chaos of yesterday.

As soon as the memories hit me, I get out of bed and gather my things. I don't want to be here any longer than I have to. The long afternoon nap and my argument with Aiden made it impossible for me to get much sleep last night. Once I got back here all I did was cry, pack, and cry some more.

My sundress is the only thing clean, so even though I'm starting to hate the sight of it, I put it on and do my best to hide the fact that I was crying most of the night. My eyes are puffy, and there's only so much mascara can do. Taking a long look at myself in the mirror, I finally resign, accepting that this is what I look like today.

Most of the packing and cleaning was taken care of last night. I needed something to distract myself from thinking about what Aiden and Sam would end up doing together. Considering I was up most of the night, this place might be cleaner now than it was before I started staying here.

My eyes do one last sweep to make sure I've gotten everything I need before locking up and walking out into the town of St. Pete.

I love it here.

As much as I hate what happened yesterday, it won't tarnish my view of this cute town. I hope one day I can come back here and make better memories. Part of me wonders if I should stay longer and try to make better memories now, but I'm too raw from everything that's happened. One day I'll come back here with a fresh mind and a full heart.

Settling down at the beachfront diner, I order a breakfast that I would usually never be able to finish and a coffee. Having not eaten anything since yesterday afternoon, my stomach feels empty, and the fact that my heart has taken so many blows, leaves the rest of me feeling just as hollow.

"Is someone meeting you?" The server asks with a friendly smile. He's blonde, tan, and has perfectly white teeth. Actually, he reminds me a little of Chad.

"No," I answer with a polite smile. "It's just me this morning."

"I like a girl who can eat." He winks before walking away to put in my order.

If yesterday had ended differently, I'd probably be getting breakfast with Aiden instead of sitting here alone.

He probably would have spent the night.

And I probably would have woken up to that incredible smile.

Feeling safe.

And cared for.

And seen.

But it all would have been a lie.

My chest tightens when I realize Sam is the one waking up next to him instead, but I try not to let myself feel down about it for too long. Like Garret, Aiden just isn't the person I thought he was. I don't want anything to do with the Aiden I saw last night. He was cruel in a way I didn't know possible.

I guess, no matter how much you think you know the facts, there's always that chance that none of it is real.

There's always that chance that it's fiction.

67

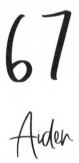

Aiden

Squinting my eyes against the glare of the morning sun, I try to see which asshole is in the kitchen this early, slamming cabinets and clanking who knows what like a fucking ape.

I only feel a little bad when it turns out to be Em.

Groaning, I shield my eyes from the incoming light. "Go back to bed, you're worse than a damn rooster."

"I'm going to assume that's a yes for coffee, then?" she asks, unphased.

I give another groan in response.

"Yeah, I thought so," I hear her mutter under her breath.

I lie awake on the couch, glaring at the ceiling as I listen to her move around the kitchen like it's the middle of the fucking day. I don't know what left me feeling more hungover, the whisky I drank last night or my fight with Claire.

Or the kiss with Sam.

Sitting up, I let my face fall into my hands as I'm forced to relive glimpses of the night before. Thank god I shut it down before it went any further, but I should have never let it get that far. Being comforted by her felt wrong, and we both knew it. She took advantage of the situation because it was in her favor. That's what Sam does. I was drunk, and she saw it as a way to crack open the door I had nailed shut. She must be lonely and bored—why else would she want me back in her life? Sam may do things that I don't expect, but if there's one thing I've learned, it's that she'll always do whatever's best for Sam.

For some reason, guilt weighs heavily on my chest when I think about the fact that I kissed her back. Dread boils in my stomach at the thought of telling Claire until I remember that I don't have to tell Claire anything because Claire and I aren't speaking.

Em sets a hot cup of coffee on the counter. "Coffee's up." She steps back and leans against the cabinet as she sips her own.

Her eyes stay glued to me as I get up from the couch and sit at one of the kitchen barstools. Taking a sip, I sigh. "Thanks." Bringing the cup to my lips again, I notice she's still watching me. "What do you want?"

Raising an eyebrow at me, she lies, "I don't want any-thing."

I give her a pointed stare. "Em, you're in the kitchen at the ass-crack of dawn, making enough noise to wake the entire apartment, all to offer me hot coffee. So either you want something from me that I need to be awake for, or you want me gone. Either way, you want something."

She seems to consider this for a moment, before saying, "Okay, fine. Walking over, she sets her cup down next to mine as she stands across from me. "First of all, kissing Sam last night was stupid."

"She kissed me," I answer without looking at her even though I know she's right. Her judging eyes narrow, and I raise a hand. "I'm not trying to defend myself. It was stupid."

This seems to make her feel better. Her shoulders drop as she says, "Will you please tell me what happened with Claire?"

Hearing Em say her name makes my fist clench under the countertop. "She lied to me."

Her eyebrows shoot up. "She did?"

"She might as well have." I shrug. "Turns out she's been talking to her ex again, and it sounds like they're getting back together."

A frown pulls at the corner of Em's mouth as she considers what I've said. I don't know what there is to think about. It all seems straightforward, but when she finally locks her gaze on mine, it's with a furrowed brow. "Are you sure? That doesn't seem right."

"Yeah," I mutter as I bring my palm to my forehead like I can buff out this fucking headache. "I saw the texts." At the mention of those messages, a fresh wave of heat runs through me. Claire put up a good act—I'll give her that much.

She gapes at me. "You did not go through her phone!"

By her reaction, you'd think I just said I dumped her on the side of the road and kept driving. "No." Crossing my arms on the kitchen counter in front of me, I say, "She was asleep, and her phone kept going off. I could only see the beginning of his messages, but that was enough."

She gasps like any good audience member. "What did she say?"

"What do you mean?"

Em stares at me expectantly. "When you asked her about it!"

Taking a sip of my coffee, I shrug. "I didn't."

Setting down her coffee cup mid-sip, she says, "I'm sorry. What?"

"I didn't ask her about it."

"Aiden!" She reaches over and smacks my arm. "You can't do that!"

Rubbing the part of my arm that she hit, I don't say anything. I don't understand why she's freaking out. Did she miss the part where I saw everything I needed to see?

She hasn't shut her mouth, still looking at me like I'm a psycho. "Aiden, you need to call her and sort this out. Right now."

She doesn't get it. "Em, I saw the texts. They're definitely getting back together. He was hard and wanted her to feel

something—I'm going to take a wild guess and say it's probably his cock."

She frowns for a moment before she shakes her head.
"Gross. But yes, you need to call her because the last time I
talked to her, she was telling me a very different story."

"Wait," I say, perking up. "What did she say to you?"
Nothing Em says will erase what I saw, but I'm still desperate
to know.

I'm pathetic.

"Not a lot," she answers casually. "She said something
about meeting up with him once she got back, but she wasn't
looking forward to it and definitely did not plan on *feeling* anything of his—if you catch my drift."

"When did she say this?"

"At The Patch," Em says as she walks to the coffee maker
and tops off her cup. "You were busy talking to Sam, I think."

Of course, I was. "Shit."

"Yeah, exactly." She brings her eyes level with mine.
"*Call her.*"

"Fuck, fine." I grab my phone out of my pocket and click
on Claire's name. Part of me hopes Em is right, but another
part of me doesn't want that at all.

Because if Em is right, I royally fucked up.

68

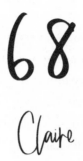

Claire

I've nearly eaten myself into a food coma. Skipping dinner last night with a splash of emotional eating has left the three plates it took to bring out my breakfast almost completely empty.

How could Aiden hate a place with such good breakfast food? In New York, my breakfast is always something I eat on the go. I need to be able to hold it in one hand so I can get to where I'm going with the other, and I need to be able to eat it fast.

I'm not sure if taking time to sit down and overindulge in a southern-style breakfast is just a Florida thing, but after everything that has happened recently, it's the highlight of my trip. I'm sure if Aiden had eaten with me this morning, this breakfast would have been enough to shift his views on the Sunshine State.

The thought of him brings back that creeping tightness

in my chest, and I do my best to shut it down.

Do not think about Aiden Lewis.

Do not think about Aiden Lewis.

Do not think about Aiden Lewis.

My mantra doesn't work—probably because his name is in it.

Refocusing my thoughts, I try to plan out everything I'll need to do as soon as I get home. I'll miss my classes today and likely part of the day tomorrow, so there's no doubt that I'll have some catching up to do.

My phone buzzes on the table next to me, and my mouth goes dry at the sight of the name.

Aiden Lewis

"No," I say out loud. Declining the call, I mutter, "Screw you, Aiden."

"Ouch," someone says above me, and I look up to find my server grimacing. "You didn't even let it ring."

I try to laugh off my embarrassment. "Yeah."

The phone immediately buzzes again showing Aiden's name, and the server raises his eyebrows to see how I'll react.

I decline the call again and give him a tight smile. "He'll get it eventually."

He laughs. "I'd hate to be on your bad side. Here's the check, but no rush."

"Thank you," I say as I get money out of my bag.

By the time I'm left alone, he's already calling again.

I don't answer.

69

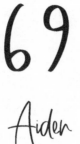

Aiden

I slam my phone down on the kitchen counter. "She's ignoring me." I open a text message to her and start typing.

Me: Claire, answer your fucking phone.

Em comes to look at what I'm typing before I send it. "Ah, the angry asshole route. Good strategy."

I glance at her before looking at my phone again. She's right, but that doesn't stop me from scoffing as I delete the message. Getting to my feet, I put my phone in my pocket.

"Where are you going?" Em asks as she steps out of my way.

I don't bother looking at her as I answer. "To talk to her." As I walk to the front door, I add over my shoulder, "Thanks for the coffee."

Claire's Airbnb is about a ten-minute walk from here, which is probably a good thing. I could use some time to figure out what the fuck I'm going to say. I still think she lied. What else would Garret be so excited for her to feel once they see each other again?

But if there's even a small chance this isn't her fault, I need to know.

Because if this isn't her fault, she's worth doing whatever it takes to fix this.

70

Claire

The sun beats down on me as I wait outside the diner for my Uber to take me back to the train station. Aiden hasn't called again, which I keep telling myself is a good thing.

Even if it doesn't feel like a good thing.

He was probably just calling to pour salt on an open wound and tell me how great his night was with Sam. I grip the straps of my beach bag a little tighter at the thought.

I can't believe I slept with him.

Up until now, I had only ever slept with Garret.

The way Aiden pulled out all the stops just to walk away at the end has me feeling used. Sometimes relationships don't work out. You give it your best shot, and things fizzle. Or you think you'll be together for a long time, but you learn that it's not a good fit. If Aiden and I didn't work out under normal circumstances, I would have been okay with it—the same way

I'm okay that Garret and I broke up. But it was all a trick to get me to sleep with him, and I'll probably never know the reason behind it. A tear threatens to fall, but I quickly wipe it away.

I figured after what happened between him and Sam, that he would have understood better than anyone what it's like to feel used.

What it's like to feel betrayed.

Unless he lied about his breakup with her, too. Maybe Aiden was the one who cheated, and Sam was the innocent one.

I guess I'll never know.

When I first found out that Garret had cheated on me, I felt so dumb—like I should have seen all the signs but didn't. With Aiden, I'm surprised that I *don't* feel dumb. He played his game too well for me to see any red flags, that much I'm sure of.

Or at least telling myself that makes it less mortifying.

I'd like to think that anyone would have fallen for the same trick because he's *that* good.

My mind replays footage of the past few days with Aiden on repeat, and I almost don't realize my car has arrived next to me on the curb until the driver rolls down the window and says my name. I give him an apologetic wave before quickly taking one last look around the adorable beach town and getting in the back seat. There's so much I still want to see here—so much I'd still like to do, but I wouldn't enjoy any of it like this. As much as I'm not ready to say goodbye to St. Petersburg, Florida, I'm more than ready to go home.

71

Aiden

Heart pounding, I jog up the front steps to the Airbnb and knock on the door. The walk over here gave me plenty of time to think and plenty of time to hope.

I hope I'm wrong about everything.

I hope it's all a misunderstanding.

I hope Claire is the person I thought she was.

And if she is, I hope she'll forgive me.

She still hasn't opened the door, but I didn't expect anything different. I bang my fist against the rustic wood again. "Claire, we need to talk about this."

No answer.

My fist pounds harder. "I know you're pissed. I'm fucking pissed, too. Just hear me out." After another moment of silence, I lean my head against the door and add, "Please."

The door swings open, and I scramble to stand up

straight, but it's not Claire who opens it. A short man, probably in his fifties, stands in the doorway with an eyebrow raised. Taking a step back, I look at the house thinking maybe I knocked on the wrong door, but this is it.

"Uh," I mutter as I try to look around the man blocking my view.

"I'm going to go ahead and assume that the young lady you're looking for was my last renter."

Pure panic floods me. "She checked out?"

The man nods, leaning against the doorframe with his arms crossed. "Left the place pretty damn clean, too."

"Fuck," I say as I run both hands through my hair. "When?"

Looking me up and down, he takes his sweet time trying to decide if I can be trusted with such information.

"When?" I ask again with a little more urgency.

Letting out a sigh, he says, "Checkout isn't until 11, but she sent me a message around 8:30 this morning letting me know she locked up."

I'm already halfway down the steps when I say, "Thanks." It's only just after ten, but Claire could be anywhere by now. The good thing is, I know where she'll end up if she isn't there already. Opening my phone, I call Ethan and ask for a ride to the train station.

12

Claire

Seeing the platform again brings a swarm of mixed feelings along with it. When we first arrived in Florida, I was broken but new at the same time. Now, I'm just broken. Like a station wagon with too many miles under its hood.

The boots are back. My sandals were easier to fit in my bag, and the less I have to carry, the better. I may be in the same outfit I arrived in, but I look different—even to me. My skin has tanned, and my hair has lightened from the sun. Those changes I like, but I'm also a little more withdrawn, a little less hopeful, and I have this crushing feeling that I'm not going to be as happy as I felt yesterday with Aiden for a very long time.

Which I know is ridiculous.

But it's there. The sinking feeling in the pit of my stomach that knows how badly I wanted things to work out differently.

My phone vibrates in my bag, and my heart leaps. I know I shouldn't feel a rush of excitement when he calls, but I do.

Maybe he at least feels some remorse.

Not that it matters.

Just because I want an apology from Aiden Lewis does *not* mean I have any intentions of forgiving him. I guess it's just nice to know that he's reaching out.

I pull out my phone, but it's not Aiden's name on the screen.

It's Garret's.

After a moment of internal debate, I sigh and swipe to answer.

"Hello?"

"Hey," he says in a rough voice like he just woke up. "Are you okay? You never answered me yesterday."

I smooth down the material of my sundress. It's funny how just a few days ago, I wanted to wear this because I knew Garret loved it. Now I can't wait to retire it in the back of my closet and never look at it again. "I know. Sorry about that. I've just been…busy." Flashbacks of yesterday rush through my mind, and it's enough to make me shift in my seat and cross my legs.

"Oh." He pauses, and then adds, "I was worried maybe my texts scared you off."

I probably should have read them. "No, not at all. I just haven't had a lot of time."

He's quiet for a moment, and I know he wants to ask

what I've been doing, but he also knows that he's lost that right. "So, you're doing okay?" he asks instead as a workaround.

"Yeah," I lie.

"Good."

We're both quiet for a moment.

There's only so much you can say to your ex over the phone when you're a thousand miles away and just made the colossal mistake of hooking up with the only guy who made a lasting impression on you in high school.

Eventually, he asks, "I'll see you Wednesday then?"

I look up at the clear, blue Florida sky and take a deep breath. "Yeah, I can meet with you between my afternoon classes, but, like I said, you have to come to the city."

"I'll be there," he answers quickly. During the past year, Garret has taken the trip to see me *once*, and it was after he first dropped out and needed to get the rest of his stuff. Every other time we've seen each other, it's been because I did the two-hour train ride to see him. I'm not making things easy for him this time. If he wants to see me so badly, he can make the effort. "And Claire?" he says after a moment. "I can't wait to see you."

It's strange how a phrase I've heard countless times suddenly makes me feel trapped. I bite my lip, not sure how to answer. I may slip out the occasional lie, but there's no way I can say that I'm looking forward to seeing him. Considering I'm feeling the exact opposite, there isn't even a grey area to play around with. I *don't* want to see Garret, but I agreed to it because we were together for a long time, and it feels like the right thing to do.

Glancing around the platform, I quickly say, "Hey, it looks like my train is here. I have to run. Bye, Garret," and hang up the phone before he can say anything else.

Setting my phone down on my lap with trembling hands, I steady my nerves and try to enjoy the still quiet platform with no train in sight.

13

Aiden

Ethan drives like a grandma.

"Can you not go any faster?" I ask impatiently.

He laughs. "Has your year back in New York made you forget that 99% of the drivers here are senior citizens?"

My head falls back against the headrest. "Fucking old people."

Ethan laughs as he gets in the left lane to pass a crawling Cadillac. "You think she's worth all this?"

"Ye—no. I don't know," I say too quickly. I'm agitated, and I hate that I don't know if this is a huge waste of time. Things would have been so much easier if she had just stayed at her Airbnb until checkout. She said she's not a morning person.

Unless she couldn't sleep because of the shit I said to her.

I picture Claire tossing and turning all night alone until

she gives up on sleep entirely, and it makes my stomach heavy even though I haven't eaten anything today. I'm an idiot for thinking she'd still be there. Morning person or not, if there's one thing I know about Claire, it's that she's a flight risk.

He nods, taking in my answer. "For the record, I thought she was pretty cool, and Em likes her a lot. So does Chad."

I scoff. "Yeah, that much is obvious."

"Oh, come on." He rolls his eyes. "Chad's like that with *everyone* at first. I'm pretty sure he tried getting with Em before I started dating her. He's a good guy, though, and he's rooting for you."

This gets a laugh out of me. "Yeah, Chad told me he hit on Em, and she shot him down. Said she doesn't date white guys."

Ethan grins. "That sounds about right."

We finally turn into the parking lot of the train station. There's no train. The empty platform sends a jolt of hope into my throat. Turning to Ethan, I say, "Thanks," and I hope he knows how much I mean it.

"Go," he says. "I'll be here if you need me."

I know he means if I need a ride back to his place because she's already gone. Giving him a nod, I step out of the car and don't waste time.

When I get to the platform stairs, I take them two at a time. There aren't many people around, so it's easy to scan for her once I reach the top.

My eyes scan the area, and then I look again.

And again.

I keep checking, hoping I overlooked something.

But she's not fucking here.

Walking up to the ticket booth, I ask the question I already know the answer to. "Was there a train to New York this morning?"

"Let me check," the middle-aged woman says as she glances at her computer. "There certainly was. Looks like you've just missed it, honey. Left about five minutes ago."

Five minutes.

I missed her by *five minutes*.

"We do run that line tomorrow, too. Do you want to purchase a ticket?"

"Yeah," I mutter. "What time?"

She glances at the screen again. "Tomorrow's train will be here at the same time, 10:20."

She hands me the ticket, and I mutter, "Thanks."

My walk is a lot slower as I go down the platform stairs and back to Ethan's car which still sits in the parking lot. He knows how things went as soon as he sees me, so he doesn't bother asking stupid questions—another reason I like him.

Instead, he asks, "What time do you need to be here tomorrow?"

Staring out the window, I say, "Five minutes earlier than we got here today."

74

Claire

This train ride feels so much longer than the one going to Florida.

People have gotten on and off. Sometimes I sit alone, other times I have someone next to me, but no one breaks the silence.

I have no one.

I did text Violet to tell her I'm coming home, but I'd rather wait to fill her in on everything that's happened—in case I break down. It's easier to keep myself together when no one asks me if I'm okay.

Because I am definitely not okay, but I'll pretend for as long as I can.

Aiden creeps into my mind uninvited, and I have to continuously give him the boot. He's called me once in the past twenty hours I've been sitting here, but I didn't answer.

Looking down at my phone, I check the time.

6:34 a.m.

Most of the night I've been able to fall in and out of sleep, but I'm tired and knowing I still have eight hours left only makes me feel more drained.

75

Aiden

This morning, I'm up before Em.

When she finally rolls into the kitchen at 7:30, I've already made coffee and poured her a cup.

"Well, good morning," she says, taking the mug from my hands. "You're much more alert this morning."

"Funny what not being hungover can do for you." I hold up my coffee. "And I've already finished one of these."

She takes a seat on one of the kitchen barstools. "So what's your plan?"

I've had all night to think about this, but when she asks me, I still shrug. "Go home and try to find her."

"In New York City," she says flatly. "Yeah, that shouldn't be a problem."

I stare down at the cup in my hands. "I have to try." Ever

since talking to Em yesterday morning, I've had a twisting feeling in my gut. She's better at reading people than I am, and the more I think about what happened with Claire, the more I think that I'm the one who fucked up.

So as much as I hate New York City, and getting back on that damn train, I have to.

I have to try.

Em's quiet for a moment, but I can feel her watching me. Her eyes might as well hold the heat of the Florida sun. I feel like an ant and she's the one holding the magnifying glass.

"You *like* her," she finally says with a sense of wonder in her voice, like the thought had never occurred to her.

Lifting my gaze, I say, "I thought we already established that."

"No," she says shaking her head. "I mean, you *really* like her."

Still not sure why this is such a shock, I can't help when my voice comes out sounding more like a question. "Yeah?"

She sets her cup down excitedly. "Like you're willing to wander around NYC—which let's be real, is not your favorite place—for who knows how long, trying to find this girl." When I don't say anything, she adds, "With no plan."

Taking another sip, I say, "I'd do a lot more than that if it means she'll talk to me."

Em is trying her best to control herself, but she's practically giddy as she holds her mug up to her lips in a terrible attempt at hiding her grin. "You *love* her."

"Em," I say in my best disapproving tone, but her accusation still makes my neck hot. "I've basically known her for less than a week."

"Not true!" she exclaims, setting down her coffee cup a little too hard. "You guys went to high school together, right?"

I nod because this conversation is making me too uncomfortable to speak.

"See, you guys go way back. Much longer than a week." Her head tilts as she remembers something. "You know," she says, training her stare back on me. "I'm pretty sure I knew I loved Ethan after like three days."

"Good for you?"

She rolls her eyes. "I'm just saying it's possible!" Both of her hands smack down on the kitchen counter. "Okay. So, what do we know? Where can we start?"

I sigh as I think of all the things I know about Claire.

She drinks sangria when she's happy and gin when she's not.

Her nose crinkles when I try to compliment her like she doesn't believe me.

And when she smiles, the concrete inside me seems to chip away.

I let my head fall in my hands as I stare down at the kitchen counter because none of those things will help me find her.

Finally, my head snaps up. "I know she lives with this girl Violet we went to high school with."

"And?"

I think for a moment. "And that she's studying education at Steinhardt."

She nods. "I'd start there."

Downing the last of my coffee, I say, "Yeah, I guess I should." I set the cup in the sink. "Where's your guy? Getting his beauty sleep?"

She taps her fingertips against the ceramic mug in her hands. "He's in the shower. He should be out soon."

I can tell she's thinking about something as she stares down at her coffee, so I ask, "Em, what is it?"

She lifts her gaze, meeting my stare. "I just hope I'm right. I don't know Claire well, but I don't think she'd go back to her ex. Everything she said about the guy was negative. It just doesn't make sense."

All I can do is nod to that because I hope she's right, too.

76

Claire

I'm finally in the kitchen of our Bay Ridge apartment as I watch Violet organize her new rolls of colored duct tape. I've pretty much given her the run-down at this point.

Florida–good.

Aiden–bad.

"I can't believe him," she says as she tears off a piece of blue tape with her teeth and sticks it on the board. "He was so set on it *not* being a casual hook-up, and then he dips as soon as you guys actually hook up?" She tears off another piece with her teeth before spitting, "Asshole."

I didn't bother telling her about my plans to meet up with Garret tomorrow. It'll only get her more worked up. Aiden could have tied me to the train tracks like an old movie villain, and she'd still hate Garret more. Garret is, as she puts it, *a preppy, entitled, sissy-boy,* or just *Sissy-Boy* for short.

Violet looks over her shoulder at me. "But the sex was good?"

"Vi!" I force out a breath of laughter. "Seriously?"

She casually waves the roll of orange duct tape in her hand. "What?" When I don't say anything she turns to face me. "Oh, come on. I've kept you in the loop on all the guys I've sampled."

Grimacing, I mutter, "I wouldn't say that I sampled him."

She huffs out a breath, briefly sending her black bangs flying into the air. "It's not a bad thing, Claire. How else are we supposed to know what works and what doesn't?"

I raise my eyebrows as I stare down at the pink roll of duct tape I'm turning in circles on the counter.

"Well?"

I was hoping she had gone back to work. "What?"

An exasperated sigh leaves her lips. "Did he *work* for you?"

I stare at her with furrowed brows. "You are being so weird about this."

Seeming to give up on me, she walks over to what looks like a recently opened Amazon box with more tape in it. "No, you are!" She rummages around for whatever color she's looking for. "I've been waiting years for this moment, Claire." She gives me a pointed stare. "Years!" Going back to looking through the box, she adds, "Talking about this stuff has always been a one-way street because I've been the only one getting any, and it's not like we were going to talk about being with Garret—because gross." Holding out a roll of yellow in an accusatory way, she goes on to say, "And now you have dirt, so spill!"

I plop down on the barstool next to me. "Fine. It was great."

"Great?"

"*Great,*" I say, and it's almost painful to admit.

Violet's eyes narrow. "What an *asshole.*"

77

Aiden

I'm on the damn train, and nobody smells like cat piss.

18

Claire

As happy as I am to have my entire closet full of clothes to choose from, I'm in no mood to dress up. I opt for jeans and an Imagine Dragons concert t-shirt from freshman year. As I'm walking toward the door, I throw my hair up in a messy bun. Violet has taken over our entire apartment with her duct tape and supplies, so I almost miss her sitting cross-legged in our family room as she compares color pallets.

"I'll see you tonight!" I call out to her. Before closing the door, I catch her throwing a thumbs-up in the air.

Our apartment isn't as close to campus as we'd like, but it's what we could afford with our scrappy combined income. Grants, tutoring sessions, and Violet's sporadic art sales have gotten us through the past three years. It hasn't always been easy, but we've made it this far.

Pushing aside thoughts of my current financial situation,

I take in my familiar scenery. It's beautiful outside, and the temperature feels like a reward after being in the Florida heat for the past few days. I try to take the great weather as a sign that I'm exactly where I should be. Here, in New York, focusing on school.

Not Aiden Lewis.

School.

79

Aiden

Fuck this fucking train to fuck.

80

Claire

Being back in the classroom is exactly what I need. Taking diligent notes is a great way to not think about the things I shouldn't be thinking about, and being around so many people serves as a good distraction, too.

My second class of the day has just ended, and I'm happy to report that during the past two lectures I had very few thoughts about Aiden.

"Claire!"

I turn around to find a girl from my class, Maddie, waving to me. "We're heading to the library to work on our papers. Want to come?"

I'd love to go with her. I have a lot to make up after missing the past two days, and getting a head start on the next paper would be a great way to take something off my plate. "I can't," I say with a sigh. "I'm meeting someone during my break, but if you guys go later this week, let me know?"

"You got it," she says with a smile before catching up to the others.

Gathering the rest of my things, I swing my bag over my shoulder and head out to the busy streets of New York City to a nearby coffee shop. I told Garret that I have an hour between classes, so he should meet me any minute now.

The walk only takes a few minutes, and before I know it, I'm sitting at an outside table, and my nerves are getting the best of me. I ordered a coffee and a pastry, but now that I think about it, I probably should have skipped the coffee. My anxiety is through the roof as it is, the last thing I need is to add caffeine to the mix.

Nervously picking at the pastry in front of me, I can't help glancing around the busy streets for any sight of him. The sooner we get this meeting over with, the sooner I can get on with my life.

It takes a few minutes, but as soon as I catch a glimpse of him walking this way, I drop my gaze and practically hold my breath until he's at the table and says, "Hey."

My eyes snap up to meet his.

"Wow," he says with a sense of surprise. "You look different."

"So do you," I blurt with a weak smile. I don't know why I said that. He looks exactly the same.

He's extremely put together, and for half a second, I let myself wish I had spent a little more time in front of the mirror this morning. My messy bun has gotten gradually messier throughout the day, and the concert tee is so old that the neck is misshapen and stretched out.

Compared to his freshly pressed khakis and blue button-down, I probably look like I've been hit by a bus.

But I'm not here to impress Garret.

Giving me an amused raise of his eyebrow, he takes a seat across from me. "It's great to see you."

Running into the issue of not wanting to lie to him for the sake of his feelings, I deflect by saying, "You're right on time," and as much as I try to make it sound natural, it sounds like I'm just stating random facts about our encounter for the sake of having something to say.

He takes a seat across from me. "Of course, sweetheart. This is important."

My gut tightens at the pet name. How can a name that used to seem endearing suddenly feel so condescending? How did I never notice how it sounded?

Once he sits, he immediately grabs hold of my hands, and my natural response is to cringe away from his touch. I fight the urge, but can't help staring down at our hands that suddenly look so wrong together. I wonder if he notices how sweaty mine are, but he doesn't say anything about it. Instead, he dives right into an apology. "I'm *so* sorry, Claire. I don't know what I was thinking."

Pulling my hands away from him, I try to discreetly wipe them on my pants before resting them on my lap. "Yeah," I say, sounding breathless. "I don't know either." I glance around at the other coffee shop goers, already looking for an escape. His eyes are too focused on me, and all it's doing is making me think of the intensity I feel when Aiden looks at me.

Or how he used to look at me.

When my eyes rest on Garret again, I can't help wondering why I dated him for so long. I feel turned off looking at him now, and I'm not sure how I never felt this before. Staring at him with newfound clarity, I feel more like Violet than I do myself.

Because he does sort of look preppy and entitled. He looks like the type of guy who would never show his raw emotion, or open up about his mistakes. And if he's not willing to do either of those things, I have to wonder what we're both doing here. When he called me before I walked into The Patch, I was so set on finding Aiden that I didn't even ask Garret why he wanted to meet up. He just kept insisting that he needed to see me, and I eventually gave in for the sake of getting off the phone with him.

"Baby, please don't throw away the past two years because I was stupid. You know I've been going through a lot. Ever since moving in with my dad, I've been lost. He's never there because of work, and you're always here. I haven't really—"

"You could have stayed," I say flatly.

"What?"

My shoulders lift in a small shrug, regaining my bearings. "You didn't have to leave when you dropped out. You could have kept living in your apartment here instead of canceling your lease early. You could have stayed with me."

He frowns and shakes his head. "Do you know the kind of stress I've been under? That internship last year nearly killed me. I couldn't stay here."

I take a deep breath before answering. "I thought maybe you needed some time off and would come back, but for the past year I've been the only one making an effort."

His eyebrows furrow. "I've made an effort."

"By sleeping with Shelly?" I give him a pointed stare. He still refuses to admit what he did, and my patience is wearing thin.

"Seriously?" He rubs his hands over his face in frustration. "I'm trying to move past this. Why would you bring that up? And I never even said I slept with her."

I gape at him. "Why would I bring up you sleeping with someone else? I don't know, Garret. It kind of feels like a big deal." I don't bother hiding the shock on my face when I say, "Wait, did you come here thinking we would get back together? Because there's nothing for us to move past."

He leans back to look at me. "You knew that's why we were meeting here."

Forcing a laugh, I sputter, "N-no I didn't."

"Seriously? What about everything I said to you in my texts?" Crossing his arms, he leans back, staring at me with expectations that I have no intention of meeting.

"What texts?"

He gapes at me. "I drunk texted you after we talked, and you were on board with everything!"

Reaching for my bag, I get my phone and open the thread with Garret's name. I've been avoiding looking at my phone lately. The last thing I need is to compulsively check if Aiden has called every twenty minutes. I didn't even realize that I had still left the texts from Garret unopened. Everything that happened in Florida apparently occupied every ounce of my brain power—even if it was the last thing I wanted to think about.

Opening the messages, the heat of embarrassment raises my body temperature as I read.

Garret: Baby, I want you to feel how genuine I am. I won't mess this up this time.

Garret: You won't regret this

Garret: I can't wait to see you on Wednesday

Garret: I'm hard just thinking about being inside you again. Wednesday night I'm going to rock your world.

Oh, this is not good.

Long after I'm done reading, I still stare down at the screen, unable to bring myself to look at the guy sitting across from me who wants to *rock my world.* Finally, when I can't fake slow reading anymore, I dare to lift my gaze. "I never read these," I say quietly.

His eyebrows furrow. "What do you mean? Yesterday you said my texts didn't scare you away."

"I had no idea…" My voice trails off as I look down at my phone again. I had no interest in reading these because I figured they weren't important. I've been so consumed with all things Aiden, that I didn't even remember that I had unopened messages on my phone, and any time I *did* remember, checking them felt like too much of a burden. "Garret," I say softly. "We're not getting back together."

He moves forward, his voice dropping into the familiar harsh whisper he likes to use when he'd rather be yelling. "Why the hell did I just come out here then?"

I just shake my head, bewildered. "You practically begged me to meet with you, so that's what I'm doing."

"Yeah, so we could talk about getting back together!" He does a worse job of keeping his voice low this time, and when I don't answer, he mutters, "What a waste of my time," as he gets up from his seat.

Something ignites inside me. "What a waste of *your* time?" I stand up from the table so we're on the same level. "Was it fair for me to be the only one making the two-hour trip for the past year? Was it fair for me to make the two-hour trip just to find you with another girl? Don't talk to me about what's been a waste of fucking time, Garret."

"I told you, she's just a friend!" He's yelling now.

Crossing my arms, I make sure to keep my voice even as I say, "I know you're lying. Did you honestly think I'd believe you? That I'd come crawling back to you? Look at yourself, Garret! I'd have to be out of my mind to ever date you again."

He seems to go through a series of thoughts, his face reddening with each one, before he blurts out, "Fine! I slept with her, is that what you want to hear?"

Even though I knew this, his confession still shocks me, and it takes me a moment to recover.

When I don't say anything right away, Garret reads my expression with a smirk. "What do you look so surprised for? I thought you knew, right? You're always the one who knows everything?"

"I did know," I try to say, but my voice is small, and he continues to talk over me.

"You probably already know that *she* was the one who came onto me." His voice rises, and if we weren't in New York City of all places, people would probably notice. "And I'm sure you know that she couldn't keep her hands off me the night we met." He shrugs. "I tried to resist at first. I tried to think about you, but…" he looks me up and down, shaking his head.

"But what? I slipped your mind?" I ask knowingly, but as soon as the words leave my lips I picture Aiden talking to Sam at the patch, and a fresh wave of pain knocks me in the chest.

Garret scoffs. "But you're no Shelly Velasco."

"Fuck you, Garret," I hiss as I start to gather my things, ready to walk away from him. I'd give anything to disappear right now. My entire body feels like it's shaking as my heart pounds in my chest.

Garret beats me to it, leaving me alone sitting at the table. As he walks past me, he mutters, "Yeah, this isn't going to work."

"You think?" I ask as he marches down the busy street. Refusing to give him the satisfaction of looking over my shoulder, I sit back down at the table and try to breathe.

It's like every cell in my body tingles from the fire scorching through my veins, but at the same time, I don't feel anything. I'm numb as I stare down at my half-eaten pastry.

I've changed.

I don't know how, or why, but I know that if this argument had happened before Florida, I wouldn't have stood up for myself. There's certainly no way I would have cursed at him. That sort of fight has never been in me, but now it is. Maybe something good did come from my time in Florida— my time with Aiden. Because now that Garret has walked away, I only allow myself to focus on the sense of relief that fills me with each of his fading footsteps.

81

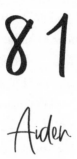

Aiden

I've never liked the city, but after almost thirty hours on that damn train, I can safely say I hate it.

I hate New York City.

As I walk to Claire's fancy-ass college *again*, I start to deflate. There's no way I'll find her. I've already aimlessly wondered around the campus and neighboring blocks. Even narrowing down the search to Steinhardt, there are still way too many people to comb through. I'm coming up on the crossroad I'll have to turn at, and I'm considering giving up. I'm exhausted, and the longer I'm here, the more this feels like a fool's errand.

But then I stop in my tracks.

Some asshole yells at a girl in front of a coffee shop, and I'm not the only one who sees. A few stragglers have stopped to watch this guy tower over his girlfriend like a narcissistic dick.

It isn't until Claire gets to her feet to defend herself that I realize it's her. Her back is to me, but after this weekend, I'd know that girl anywhere. Her shoulders tense as I assume she stares Garret down with a look that could kill.

My eyes move back to her ex, and I'm surprised I didn't recognize him from the picture on her phone because he looks exactly the same—not a hair out of place. The only difference is that instead of wearing a fucking polo shirt, he's gone full dress shirt for this occasion. He looks like a tool. He was probably one of those jocks in high school that got more attention than he deserved, and now he'll validate the rest of his life based on those four years.

Prick.

The sight of the two of them at the table brings flashbacks of when I caught Sam with that asshole from her class, but if one thing is clear, these two don't look like they're about to get back together.

They don't even look like they like each other.

When he walks away from the table and heads toward me, there are a lot of things I could say to him. But I don't even look at him. Instead, I watch Claire carefully, and even though her back is to me, she looks defeated as she collapses back into her seat. Not necessarily in a way that makes me think the love of her life just walked away from her, but the way her shoulders slump makes me think she's sick of the bull-shit. She folds her arms and puts her head down on the table.

All I want to do is make her happy again because, as much as Garret is a walking department store ad from hell, I know I'm responsible for part of her pain, too.

And whether intentional or not, she's responsible for part of mine.

Maybe they had plans of getting back together, but when he got here, she realized she couldn't forgive him.

Or maybe he said the wrong thing, and she changed her mind.

Maybe she thought she could be happy with him, but after seeing him show up dressed like a fucking dad at a dance recital, she knew it wouldn't work.

Just because whatever happened at this coffee shop didn't go well, doesn't mean shit. She could have still wanted him.

There's only one way to fucking find out.

82

Claire

"Claire."

I know that voice.

As much as I feel a groan building inside me, the butterflies in my stomach flutter back to life at the sound. I'm not
sure if butterfly traps are a thing, but if they are, I'd like to
eradicate the pests in my stomach as soon as possible. Zero
part of me should feel anything fluttering for Aiden.

Zero.

After a deep breath, I lift my head from the table and
stare up at him. He's wearing jeans and a t-shirt, his brown
jacket in hand, like the night I saw him in the bar—before I
knew he'd break me. Even after everything, I can't fight how
attracted I am to him. His dark, blue eyes still make me feel
like he can see everything beneath the surface, and I'm forced
to swallow the lump in my throat that forms at the sight of

him. Glancing around at the bustling street, I try to steady my nerves before looking up at him again. "What are you doing here?"

He's calm, but there's still a fire burning inside me, and the last thing I need right now is for Aiden to make me feel worse than I'm already feeling.

"We need to talk," he says without taking a seat.

I get to my feet because no guy is going to tower over me as he *talks* to me. "No, we don't." I start to collect my things, throwing them into my bag with a little too much force.

He sighs. "Would you just listen to me?"

"No, Aiden. You made me think you wanted more, you made *me* want more, then what do you do? You fuck me, drop me, and run back to your ex. So, no. I don't think I need to listen to anything you have to say." I'm practically panting by the time I'm done, but I do my best to hide it. He visibly winces when I curse, and I take a small amount of pride in it.

"I didn't—I thought you were—"

Throwing my bag over my shoulder, I ask, "What did you do with Sam?"

His face falls, but he says nothing.

"What did you do with her?" I ask again.

Running a hand through his hair, he says, "We kissed, but it wasn't—"

"I have to go to class," I say as I turn to leave. That's all I needed to hear.

"Claire!"

There's a desperation in his voice that's hard for me to ignore, but I don't turn around. Keeping my head down, I walk as fast as I can, weaving through the sea of people that suddenly feel like my greatest defense.

83

Aiden

"Claire, would you just talk to me?" I call after her as she zig-zags through the masses.

Damn, this girl is quick.

When we hit the crosswalk, it's green and she picks up her pace to a jog.

So do I.

I'm not losing her. Not when I'm this close to finding out what happened. "Claire!"

She's almost to the entrance of the school when she glances over her shoulder at the sound of her name. For a second, I think she may take off sprinting, but her shoulders sag as she stops and turns.

When I catch up to her, she's staring at me with uncertainty behind those eyes. "Aiden, we have nothing to talk about."

"But—"

"No." She shakes her head firmly. "I have to go to class. I *want* to go to class. I need some normalcy today, and I don't want to be distracted right now, okay?"

I want to blurt out all the things I'm dying to say, but all I hear come out of my mouth is, "Okay."

She falters slightly like she was expecting to argue with me more, but then she just says, "Thank you," and turns and walks away.

I stare after her like I'm standing in wet cement. Unable to tear my eyes away from her, I watch as she makes her way into the building and out of sight.

She doesn't look back.

She doesn't even pause.

She seems more upset now than the last time I saw her. The space between us has given me time to calm down, but it seems to have had the opposite effect on her.

Just my fucking luck.

Well, I'm not going home—not after how hard I've worked to get here. This is the closest I'll ever be to her, so if I don't talk to her now, it'll never happen. She can go to class and do whatever she needs to do, but I'm not giving up.

I walk to the front entrance of the Steinhardt building and take a seat.

The only thing left to do is wait her out.

84

Claire

Class drags.

This morning, I wanted nothing more than to get back into a good headspace and focus on my studies again, but after talking to both Aiden and Garret, I just want to go home. I want to eat tacos with Violet surrounded by colorful duct tape and get on with my life. Class is about to end, and all I can think about is getting to the subway station as quickly as possible to do exactly that.

But when I get out of class, I find Aiden sitting outside the entrance.

It's been almost an hour and a half since I walked away from him.

He's been sitting here for *an hour and a half.*

Something softens inside me, but I'm determined to hold onto my anger. I don't stop to talk to him. I keep walking, but he scrambles to his feet and hurries after me.

"Claire, please." He catches up to me within a few strides.

Without looking at him and without slowing my pace, I say, "How stupid would I look if I forgave you? I already feel dumb for trusting Garret, and now it's worse because I was dumb enough to trust you, too."

"And how stupid would I look if I messed everything up over a misunderstanding?" he asks as he walks with me—uninvited.

I glance at him out of the corner of my eye because I have no idea what he's talking about.

He sees that he's caught my interest and starts talking faster. "There were texts on your phone that made me think—"

The blood drains from my face, and I stop in my tracks. "Texts?" If Aiden read about Garret wanting to rock my world, I'll never recover. Then a second thought occurs to me, and I glare at him. "You went through my *phone?*"

"No!" He looks flustered. I don't think I've ever seen Aiden Lewis flustered. Running a hand over his face, he says, "Listen, you were asleep, and your phone kept going off. I only saw what was on the home screen, but…"

"But what?" I demand.

"But that was enough to make me think you were planning on getting back together with him."

Part of me wants to explain, but then I remember every-thing he did. He could have talked to me. All he had to do was ask me about the texts, and I would have told him the truth. But instead, he probably hooked up with his ex-girlfriend.

I want her here…which is more than I can say for you.

That memory alone brings my guard up again. Rolling my eyes, I start walking, but he cuts me off.

Shoving his hands in his pockets, he says, "I might have been wrong, but that's what it looked like."

Sidestepping around him, I head toward the subway sta-tion. "You couldn't have been more wrong."

85

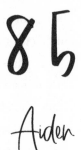

Aiden

Jesus, this girl will not give me a break.

I follow her into the subway, and we both swipe our cards and walk through the turnstiles. Once we're on the platform, I grab her hand and pull her toward me. She tries to wiggle her hand out of mine, but I tighten my grip. The feel of her skin sends a pulse of electricity through me, and I almost lose my train of thought.

"Did you talk to Garret about getting back together?"

She glares at me. "No."

My eyebrows pull together. "I don't see how I could have misunderstood the messages I saw."

"Well, you did." She gives her hand another jerk to try and pull away from me, and this time I let her.

"I'm sorry."

Her eyes finally meet mine, and there's a fucking storm

brewing in them. I take advantage of the fact that she's giving me her attention and add, "For the record, I didn't fuck you and drop you. I was pissed, and I lashed out, and if those texts didn't mean what I thought they meant, you didn't deserve it." It's a contingent apology, but without knowing what happened between her and Garret, it's the best I can offer.

Her eyes are glossy, and I know she's fighting back tears. I hate myself for making her cry. I reach out to touch her cheek, but I wish I hadn't. She steps away from me, and I'm not sure what else I can say.

"It doesn't matter," she says as she hastily wipes a runaway tear from her cheek. "You crossed the line, Aiden."

I've never been on this end of things. I've never had to regret my actions. Even when I've had my heart ripped out, I always had a clear conscience.

This is so much fucking worse.

The subway arrives, and the doors slide open. I half expect Claire to get pissed at me for getting on the train, but she doesn't say anything when I follow her. She sits in one of the empty seats while I stand a safe distance away clutching the handrail.

I can't help watching her as she looks down and smooths her hands over the bag in her lap. She's avoiding my stare, but the lack of eye contact allows me to finally take her in. Her knee bounces as she stares down at the floor of the subway, her chest rising and falling in shallow breaths. The bun on her head leaves loose strands around her face, and the concert t-shirt she's wearing could probably swallow her whole, but it doesn't matter.

Claire Ackerman is beautiful.

86

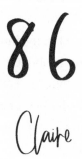

Claire

I can feel him watching me, and it's getting harder not to look at him. He's so calm, and even though I'm still angry, I find it refreshing. Like he's the cool ocean waves wrapping around my sunburned skin—it feels nice to have him here until I remember he comes with rip-currents and sharp rocks.

Slowly, I dare to steal a glance his way, but he isn't looking at me like I thought he'd be. His eyes are downcast, and seeing him this way leaves a pang in my gut. I know I shouldn't consider anything he's said, but I can't help mulling over his words.

He saw the drunk texts from Garret—the texts that talked about us getting back together and having crazy makeup sex.

But he was so cruel.

None of it feels justified.

The longer I stare at him, the more I'm convinced that he resembles a reflection of myself. Both of us are broken and full of regret. His remorse practically drips off of him as he stares down, seemingly consumed by his thoughts.

Then he lifts his gaze, and as much as I want to, I can't tear my eyes away. Those blue eyes pin me in place the same way they always have, and I'm too intrigued to know what lies behind them to do anything about it. Locking eyes with him steals the breath from my lungs and makes my heart race. The longer he looks at me, the harder it beats in my chest. My lips part, looking for words that won't come, and when he mouths, "Can I sit?" all I can do is nod.

His body carefully moves into the seat next to me, and I try not to notice the home-like feeling of familiarity that washes over me as it does.

"I didn't answer your calls," I say quietly.

"Yeah," he scratches the side of his head. "I noticed."

Tilting my head to look at him, I add, "But you came all the way here anyway."

He shifts his weight uncomfortably but says nothing.

Doing the math in my head, I ask, "Did you fly back?"

His face falls. "No, but I fucking should have."

My lips twitch, but it's short-lived. Feeling somber again, I ask, "Aiden, why are you here?"

Resting his elbows on his knees, he looks down for a moment before answering. "If you didn't lie to me, I don't want to be the reason this doesn't work."

"I didn't lie to you." Letting out a sigh, I pull my phone out of my bag, "I know the texts you're talking about. Garret was drunk—and apparently delusional."

Aiden bounces his heel against the ground as he stares at the phone in my hand. "Can I see?"

I open my mouth to make a comment about him not trusting me, but when I look into his eyes, I can see what he's feeling so clearly.

He doesn't trust me.

Because he doesn't trust anyone.

When Sam deceived him, she didn't only break his trust in her, she broke his trust in people. The realization squeezes around my heart. Garret broke my trust in him, but I still give people the benefit of the doubt. Aiden keeps his heart guarded, and he doesn't want to take my word for this.

I hand my phone to him without saying anything and watch as he reads over the messages.

"Huh," he finally says, his foot no longer bouncing.

"What?"

He hands my phone back to me. "Believe it or not, those messages are more PG than I thought they'd be."

I glance down at the messages again before locking eyes with him. "How so?"

He nods toward my phone. "I could only see part of the text, but I assumed he 'couldn't wait to see you' naked on the kitchen floor and 'wanted you to feel' his—"

"Please don't." I grimace just thinking about where he

was going with that.

And then I laugh.

I don't know what comes over me, but I laugh, and it feels ridiculous. Eventually, I'm able to get out, "The kitchen floor?"

He shrugs. "I liked seeing you there."

That shuts me up.

I swallow the lump in my throat and try to get back on track. "So, you thought I was making sexy plans with my ex, and that's why you got so mad?"

His mouth twitches at *sexy plans* but turns serious again to answer my question. "I should have just asked you about it, but I was too pissed. I hate being lied to, and I thought you were the last person who'd do it."

"But I didn't—"

He holds up a hand to stop me. "I know. That's why I'm here. If anything, I owe you an apology."

"Because you kissed Sam," I mutter.

He shakes his head. "She kissed me. I kissed her back at first, but I stopped it."

I know why he kissed her. It's the same reason why I kissed Chad. What I don't know, is if I should trust him.

Before I can think of anything to say, he adds, "I shouldn't have talked to you the way I did either. I was mad and drunk, and..." He rubs his hands over his face before shaking his head. "There's no excuse."

"Yeah," I say quietly as I stare down at my hands.

That much I can agree with.

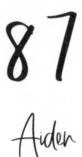

87

Aiden

The silence between us gnaws at me. Claire hasn't said anything for a while. I'm assuming she's pissed that I kissed Sam, and it doesn't matter that I stopped it.

I still did it.

I still broke what little trust she had in me, and acted like a complete asshole to her when she didn't deserve it.

There are a million things I want to say right now. I want to ask her what she's thinking. I want to know if she'll at least call me when she decides what to do about us—if she hasn't written me off already.

I want to tell her how badly I want this.

But instead of saying any of those things, I sit here with my elbows on my knees and try to respect the fact that she needs time to think.

A few more minutes of silence go by, and the only solace

is the fact that she's here with me. Occasionally our arms brush with the subway's movements, and all I want to do is reach for her hand. It's probably a good thing that mine are laced together in my lap. I'm like a kid who wants to touch a pretty object but knows there's a good chance he'll break it—and the last thing I want to do is break her more than I already have.

Claire

My brain feels like it's at maximum compacity with all the thoughts violently buzzing inside my head. I keep playing the weekend on repeat in my mind, trying to see through any cracks in Aiden's story. When Garret and I broke up, I swore I'd never trust my judgment when it came to men, and after Aiden left me the other night, those feelings solidified.

So, as much as I want to trust him, I'm not sure that I should.

Because I'm not sure that I can trust myself to make that call.

He hasn't said anything for a while now, and I can't help wondering what he's thinking. Is he not talking because he's having second thoughts? Does he wish he wouldn't have come here? Is he waiting for me to say something? The questions overwhelm me. I know I should use this time to talk to him—

to figure out if we can move on from this. My commute only lasts so long, and with each passing stop, I feel that pesky hour-glass in the back of my mind.

He wrings his fingers in his lap anxiously, and part of me wants to reach out and take his hand.

But I don't.

As much as I want to ease the tension between us, I can't bring myself to do it. Gripping my bag tighter like a make-shift stress ball, I try to take a controlled breath to clear my head.

It doesn't work.

I'm counting down the stops until we reach Brooklyn, and the closer we get to my apartment, the more I feel like it's too late to start this conversation with him. My commute has dwindled down to mere minutes, and I can't unpack every-thing I'm feeling that quickly. I need to collect my thoughts, but then again, I've had the past half hour to do that, and I've failed miserably.

89

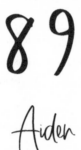

Aiden

"This is my stop," she finally says as the subway starts to slow.

Not exactly the words I was hoping to hear.

I nod without looking up at her. I think I've made myself look like enough of a jackass for one day, but my mind still races, trying to figure out how to fix this. I have no idea what I have to do to make sure I don't lose her. She may not want to be around me right now, but there's nowhere else I'd rather be.

The subway comes to a stop, and Claire gets to her feet. She swings her bag over her shoulder and stands near the doors, waiting for them to open.

My heart pounds as I try to think of any last-minute thing I can say to change her mind, but there's no point. I messed this up, and now I have to live with it.

The blood in my ears drowns everything out, and I almost don't hear her when she says, "Aren't you coming?"

My head snaps up just as the doors open. She's looking back at me with an unreadable expression, but the fact that she's looking at me at all fills the deflated balloon in my chest. I don't waste time getting to my feet, scrambling to follow her off the subway.

We don't say anything until we're out of the station and walking the streets of Brooklyn. I can tell she's anxious by the way she grips her bag and occasionally chews on her thumbnail, but she's not giving any hint as to what she might be thinking.

I wish I knew what was going on in that head of hers.

We walk for about five minutes in silence before she says, "You should know, my roommate has been trained to hate you."

I force out a laugh, relieved that she's said something. "Violet, right?"

She looks over at me like she's surprised I remember and nods. "Yeah."

"Is that what you're worried about?" The sudden conversation after so much silence makes my heart race in my chest.

Claire tucks a loose strand behind her ear. "Yeah—I don't know. I'm worried about a lot of things, I guess."

"Like?" I dare to ask.

She sighs. "Trusting you mostly."

349

Her words come out sounding tired, like even the thought of doing such a thing wears her down. It feels like a punch to the gut, but I know I deserve it. "I'm sorry."

She looks at me again, and there's so much sincerity behind those brown eyes when she says, "I know." After a pause, she adds, "It's okay," and I want to believe her. Then she reaches for my hand, and it feels like a piece of me clicks back into place. I don't understand why she's reaching out to me, but I don't question it. Taking her hand in mine, I give her fingers a squeeze. Claire and I may be nothing alike, but at the root of it, we're the same. We both grew up with parents that didn't love us as much as they should have, and have been burned trusting the wrong people as adults.

She's too good for me. Anyone can see that, but I'll learn to be better.

I'll stop running from her.

It took me a while to realize it, but I've been guilty of breaking my rule long before she has. I ran from her in high school because I was scared, and as soon as I saw those texts from Garret, I ran again.

My fingers wrap around hers a little tighter, like I'm afraid she might float away. If Claire ever wants me to go, I'll go, but I'm done running from what this could be. I'm done not trying for fear of failing. She deserves someone who will stay and fight for her, and that's who I want to be.

We climb the steps to her apartment, but before she puts the key in the door, she looks back at me. "Fair warning, there will be tape."

My eyebrow lifts. "Tape?"

She nods but doesn't explain further—she doesn't have to. As soon as the door opens, I see what she means. There are stacks of different colored duct tape everywhere.

Like if someone was trying to build a fucking fort out of duct tape.

Suddenly, a girl with black hair pops up from behind a literal wall of the stuff. We can only see her from the stomach up, but she immediately points an accusatory finger in my direction and says, "Why is he here?"

I raise an eyebrow before looking at Claire, who doesn't seem nearly as phased as I thought she'd be. Instead, she just answers, "I'll explain everything later."

Putting my hands in my pockets, I lean against the entryway and say, "Hey, Violet." I don't remember her from high school other than vaguely being able to picture her with Claire. If I had passed her on the street, I doubt I would have recognized her.

Ignoring me completely, Violet looks back at Claire. "Do we approve?"

Even though the question isn't directed toward me, a weight lands in my chest at the sound of it because I'm dying to know the answer. I watch carefully as Claire sets her stuff down, the familiar drumming in my chest picking up its pace.

Her eyes flicker to me before saying, "I think so," and that might as well be the greatest compliment she's ever given me.

"I see," Violet says. She then turns to me and points two threatening fingers to let me know she'll be watching, so I give her a nod in return.

She's fucking weird.

Claire brushes her hand against mine to get my attention. "My room is this way."

"Don't give me a reason to use this tape!" Violet calls after me.

Not sure what she means, I just say "I wouldn't dream of it." Once Claire and I round the corner, I lean in toward her and ask, "Did she just threaten to take me hostage?"

"I wouldn't put it past her," Claire says with a breath of laughter as she looks over her shoulder at me, a small smile tugging at the corners of her lips.

She laughed.

She might not know if she can trust me, but she laughed.

And I'll take it.

The walls of her bedroom are white, the bed yellow, and everything in between follows the same trend.

I'm about to say something about all the yellow, but she turns on me as soon as we're alone. "So, let me make sure I understand this." Her eyes narrow as she stares at me for confirmation, so I nod. "You thought I was making plans to get back with Garret at the same time we were…getting to know each other. You assumed I was lying to you, left to go hang out with your friends, got drunk, and told your ex-girlfriend to come over?"

Her lips pinch together as she leans toward me, waiting for me to acknowledge what she's said. I'm not sure where this is going, so I keep my mouth shut and nod again.

"Then I showed up and confronted you, and after I left, you kissed your ex, but you stopped it?"

I could say that technically Sam kissed me, but I'm not that much of a dumbass, so I nod again.

"Then you realized you may have been wrong about the texts and wanted to ask me about it, but I didn't answer your calls."

Another nod.

She takes a deep breath. "So you traveled up the entire east coast and came to the city just to see if we could try..." she gestures back and forth between us, "whatever this is?"

I take a step toward her. "I want 'whatever this is' more than fucking anything."

She stares at me for what feels like forever before taking a step closer. I don't dare move, not wanting to mess up whatever's happening to make her possibly give me another chance. Claire studies me as she says, "You hurt me," and takes another step.

"I know," is all I can think to say. I can barely breathe with her scrutinizing me, and the less space left between us, the more my words seem to get caught in my throat. When she keeps staring at me, my heart falters. I can't lose her before I have her. "I'm sorry," I blurt out. "I jumped to conclusions.

I'll do whatever it takes to make it up to you." My words feel like a desperate attempt, but they won't stop. "We can take things slow—we can go back to being friends—just don't shut me out." Sighing out a breath, I add, "Please let me prove to you how much I mean it."

Her eyes stay locked on me as she takes one final step, closing the space between us completely. My nerves ignite with her this close, and when she presses her lips against mine, the kiss breathes new life into me.

I suddenly don't feel like I was on a train for 30 hours.

I don't even feel like I was in the damn city all afternoon.

This makes every second I spent in that hellhole worth it.

90

Claire

It may be a small kiss, but I know Aiden understands what's behind it. It tells him that there's hope for us. When I got out of class today and saw him sitting at the entrance, I felt hope. I may not have wanted to feel it, but it was there like a trick candle that can't be completely put out.

My lips are still close to his when I say, "Haven't you heard? I could never shut you out."

He lets out a breath of laughter, but a frown quickly follows in its wake. "I've heard that you should." Running a hand through his hair, he steps around me and sits on the edge of my bed. "I want to do this right for you." He glances up at me, and adds, "For us."

He's still looking at me with so much vulnerability, and I know I have to forgive him. I have to give us a chance—because even after all the pain he's caused, I want him here.

And I don't want to be his friend.

"We'll have to figure out how to see each other," I point out. I still have a year of school left, and that's if I don't go to grad school. A spark ignites in those blue eyes at the sound of my words, and any remaining ice inside of me immediately thaws.

He's serious as he says, "I'll visit whenever you want."

He answered so quickly, that it catches me by surprise. "You will?" I'm not used to anyone being so willing to go the extra mile.

He gives me an incredulous look. "Claire," he says as his lips quirk into a smile. "I've already gone to fucking Florida for you, and that was before you knocked me on my ass." Dropping his gaze, he goes on to say, "Now that I've fallen, I think it's safe to say two hours on a train won't be an issue."

At the word *fallen* my skin runs hot, and I walk over and climb on top of him, my legs falling to either side of him as I straddle him on my bed. He lifts his eyes to meet mine, surprise clearly written in them before he seems to breathe out a sigh of relief and wrap his arms around me.

"Tell me more about this *falling,*" I tease, even though my heart is practically stuck in my throat.

His head falls forward, but he can't hide his smile. Running his hands from my hips, up the length of my torso, and then back down again, he finally lifts his gaze to meet mine. His words come out breathless as he says, "To be fair, I didn't stand a chance."

"No?" I ask as I adjust my arms, resting them on his shoulders. I'm trying hard not to look like a bundle of nerves, but I know my cheeks are flushed.

Aiden shakes his head, his blue eyes sparkling. "When you flipped me off on that beach, I was done for."

My head falls back as I laugh, my body relaxing, and it's such a great feeling. Then I bring my gaze back to his and the way he's looking at me somehow beats it. His tight-lipped smile only makes my own spread across my face. "I should have known that would be the way to your heart."

He smiles, a flash of white teeth and dimples, before saying, "So it's settled then. I'll visit you, you'll visit me, and we'll both hope to god that Mike doesn't make this fucking awkward."

I raise an eyebrow. "Mike?"

"Yeah."

My mind reels, but there's only one Mike that comes to mind. "As in Mike Murphy from high school?"

"The one and only," He says with a single nod of his head. "He's my roommate, and he's going to be all over this."

Part of me wants to groan. Mike was always loud, crude, and never as funny as he thought he was, but maybe he's changed. I know I have. "As long as he doesn't threaten to take me hostage, we should be fine," I eventually say.

Aiden laughs, and it's my new favorite sound. "Don't worry. He's no Violet," he says as his hand slides under my t-shirt and grabs my bare waist. "Think I should be afraid of her?"

"Absolutely," I deadpan. "I have no idea what she's capable of."

His smile grows as his fingertips burn into my skin. It's getting harder for me to think straight. "So we're doing this?" he says, and despite everything, there's still a level of vulnerability behind those blue eyes.

Even though I know my answer, I still say, "I want to hear you say it first."

Aiden locks eyes with me, his fingers tracing circles on my lower back. "Claire, haven't you heard?" He kisses me softly, his lips teasing mine. "You're my next great adventure."

Then I kiss him.

His lips are soft and warm, and he easily flips us so that he's hovering over me. What we have is undeniable. My body craves more of him with every touch, and I realize that the reason I can get out of my head with him is because, despite everything, I *do* trust him.

He makes me feel safe, and cared for, and seen, and that's enough for me to dive in head first. He saw me for who I was back in high school and sees me for who I am now. The only difference is, now that we've found each other again, we're not letting go as easily.

When it comes to Aiden Lewis, I'm all in.

And I don't want to share him with anybody else.

Epilogue

A lot can change in three years.

It's easy to feel a false sense of permanence in our everyday lives. Even when you know things won't last, you still go to bed most nights assuming tomorrow will resemble today.

Three years ago, Aiden couldn't picture a day that he would no longer live with Mike.

Claire couldn't picture a day when she would no longer live in the city.

Chad still can't cope with the fact that the Natty Shack's days are numbered.

And yet, as different as their lives have become, three years later they're together. Ethan, Em, and Chad have flown to New York to visit Aiden and Claire. Even Mike and Violet join everyone at the local brewery to see, *the Florida friends,* as Violet insists on calling them even though she's met them countless times.

So many things are coming to an end, but they're celebrating.

The group lifts their glasses to the newly engaged couple, the clank followed by excited cheers and rushed voices wanting to know everything there is to know about the future wedding.

"Have you picked a date?"

"What do you want your dress to look like?"

"Open bar?"

Followed by a resounding chorus of, "Congrats!" and "We're so happy for you!"

Aiden can't take his eyes off Claire as she gushes over the rock on Em's hand. He's glad for Ethan and Em. They've always been two of his favorite people, and they deserve a lifetime of happiness together.

As he watches Claire, still holding Em's left hand in hers, his wheels turn.

To be fair, they've *been* turning.

They've been turning ever since he closed on the house that Claire loved in Beacon, promising to fix it up for her.

For *them.*

She moved in as soon as he got the keys, and every morning when he wakes up next to her, the thought is there. And every night when she falls asleep with her arms wrapped around him, the thought is there again—a persistent buzzing that makes his heart race and his hands sweat.

But in a good way.

In the *best* way.

Chad's familiar arm falls heavily over Aiden's shoulders. "So, you're next right?"

Snapping out of his daze, Aiden looks over at Chad. "What?"

Chad holds his hand up, wiggling his fingers to show an empty ring finger.

Trying to shrug off his arm, Aiden mutters, "For fuck's sake."

Chad's grip only squeezes tighter. "What? Didn't you already buy her a house?" Instead of waiting for Aiden to answer, Chad looks over at Claire and calls out, "Hey! He bought you a house, right?"

Claire's cheeks flush as she laughs. "He bought himself a house. I'm just the freeloading roommate." When Aiden shakes his head at her response with a smile pulling at the corner of his mouth, she playfully sticks her tongue out at him.

She's been dropping hints.

They're subtle and seldom—mostly just commenting on what she likes and doesn't like as it applies to jewelry.

But it's enough.

It's enough for Aiden to have a list on his phone of what to shop for when the time comes.

And enough to have Claire daydreaming about their life together.

"Aw, come on. Double wedding? Think about it!" Chad

exclaims loud enough for Claire to hear—for *everyone* to hear.

She shakes her head, but her cheeks burn brighter.

Finally succeeding at shaking him off, Aiden says, "Why don't you find someone to walk down the aisle with?"

Chad immediately turns to Violet, giving her a pointed stare, his hand outstretched to her like an invitation.

"Um, no," Violet says sternly.

Mike sighs with a shake of his head. "I've been barking up that tree for years with no luck, man."

Chad's shoulders slump, his face falling. "What's wrong, Vi? Don't want to give Mikey a chance?"

Her eyes narrow at him with his use of the nickname. She doesn't know him like that—she doesn't know him as anything more than a *Florida friend*. "Absolutely not."

"She won't let go of the guy I was back in high school," Mike says with a shrug.

Glaring at him, Violet says, "It's not like you've changed."

Blowing her a kiss, Mike just says, "One day, baby. You and me."

Rolling her eyes, Violet mutters, "My point exactly."

The group gets another round. They have a lot to catch up on. They'll probably be here all night. The more time passes, the more flushed Claire's cheeks get, and the less Aiden feels annoyed by Chad.

The more they drink, the more Claire tries to convince Em to give her a tattoo, and the less Aiden feels inclined to fight his smile when Chad tries his luck with Violet again.

And by the end of the night, Claire has picked her tattoo—even though Em still hasn't agreed to give her one—and Aiden can't seem to tear his eyes away from her. When she feels his eyes burning into her, she looks over at him and mouths, "What?" her grin growing.

And he mouths, "I love you." He's said those words to other people before, but they've never felt as natural as they do with Claire. He's never meant them as much as he does when he says them to her.

Playfully flipping him the bird, she mouths "I love you" back, and Aiden shakes his head, a low laugh escaping him.

She's his greatest adventure, and it's only just beginning.

The End

Newsletter

Scan the code for a steamy bonus chapter from Aiden's perspective!

Reviews and Other Books!

Check out Heather Garvin's other books, and while you're there, please consider leaving an honest review!

Acknowledgments

Before diving into all of the people who played a critical role in making this book what it is, I'd like to say thank you for reading it. Every time someone takes a chance on something I've written, I feel incredibly lucky. Without readers, books are just words on a page. Thank you for breathing this story to life.

If writing has taught me anything, it's that you can never have too many honest people in your corner who are willing to tell you when something isn't working. These are the people who, for whatever mystical reason, care about the story as much as I do and put the book's success over worrying about my ego. They're the ones who bring out the best in me by making me strive to do better.

Nothing I say in these next lines could ever convey how truly grateful I am for each of you, but I'll try my best.

To Corey Wys, the man of horror and gore, thank you for your unwavering excitement and ability to switch gears for this contemporary romance. Even though it's not a genre you typically read or write, you'd never know it based on the outpour of enthusiasm and support as you tore this book apart, chapter by chapter. I can't thank you enough for the level of care you put into this story!

And Katie Moye, the fantasy reader who, as it turns out, gives some damn good advice when it comes to romance! You always have a way of providing incredible feedback and making me laugh. Thank you for never holding back and always supporting this hobby of mine!

Catherine Broomell, my book swap reading buddy. As a fellow lover of contemporary romance books, I loved getting your take on Aiden and Claire's story. Thank you for pushing me out of my comfort zone and rereading chapters once changes were made. I can't tell you how much it means to me.

To Ava Rogers, the most polite constructive criticism! You are a pro at catching errors, and you are always right. Please never second-guess yourself because you are, without a doubt, smarter than me. As another valued friend who doesn't usually read romance, I can't thank you enough for your dedication to this story.

Gabby Spiller (@shegabsaboutbooks), I can't tell you how happy I am to have met you through our lovely little bookstagram corner of the internet. I've enjoyed sharing our love of books over the past few years and was thrilled when you agreed to read Aiden and Claire's story early. Thank you for your friendship and support!

And last but not least, I'd like to say thank you to Georgia Lomas. Your love for my first series spurred a beautiful friendship, and now I can't imagine my life without you! Thank you for always being my hype-woman when the imposter syndrome sets in. Your friendship is something I value most dearly.

Thank you. Thank you. Thank you.

About the Author

Heather Garvin works as a nationally certified sign language interpreter by day and writes a variety of romances in her spare time.

Aside from working and writing, she's also a wife, mom, and a fur mama to two dogs, two cats, and Tuskan: the horse who inspired the logo and name for her publishing company, Tuskan Publishhing LLC.

There's nothing Heather loves more than hearing from readers. Connect with her on Instagram!

heathergarvinbooks